Born of Empire

Sally Ann Melia

Dickson House

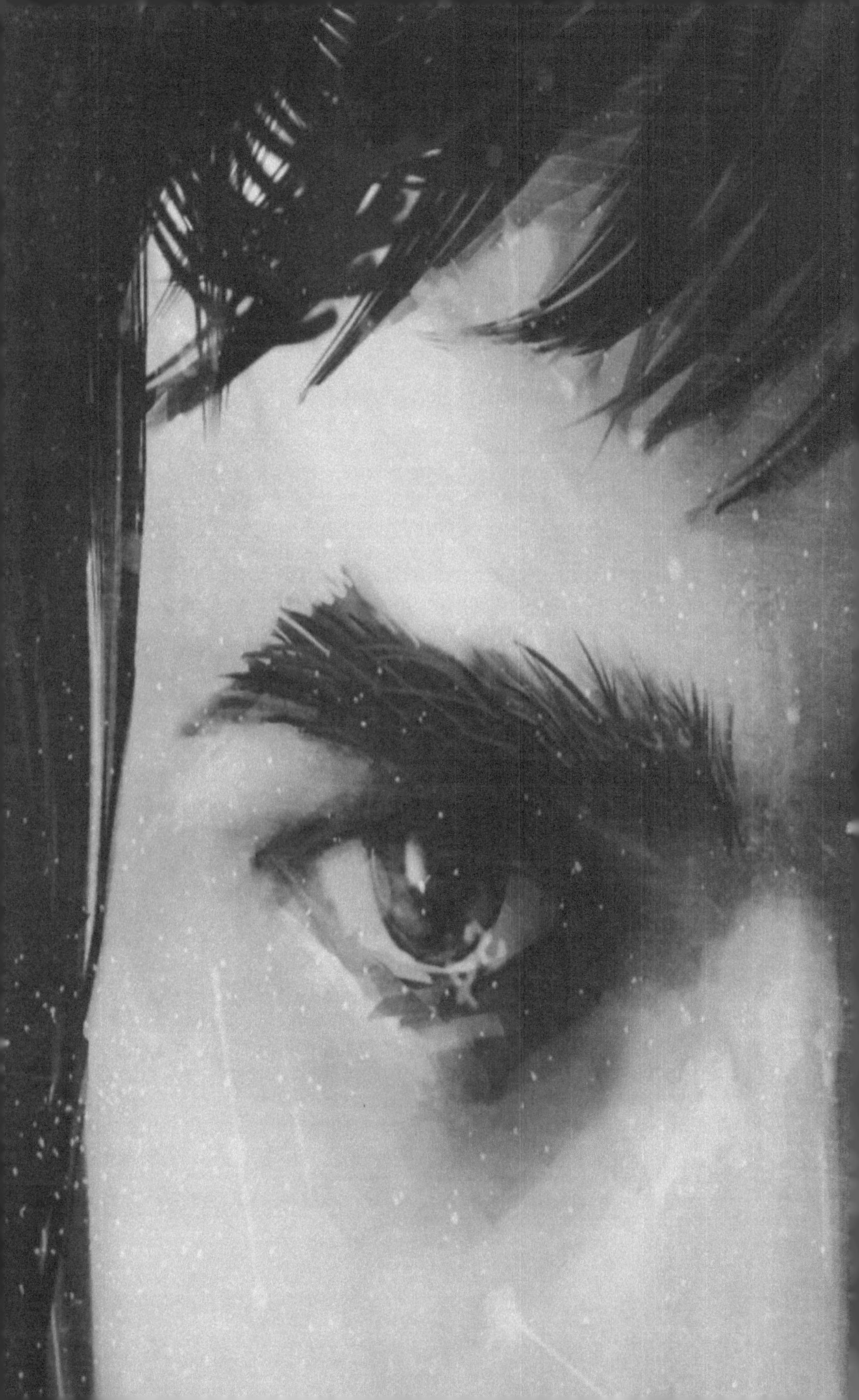

Book Cover and illustrations by Lazar Kacarevic,
planet.caravan@gmail.com, artstation.com/boink
2025 Covers by Damonza, New Zealand.

For David, Rose & Hazel.

*At the end of the game, the king and the pawn
are returned to the same box.*
Italian proverb

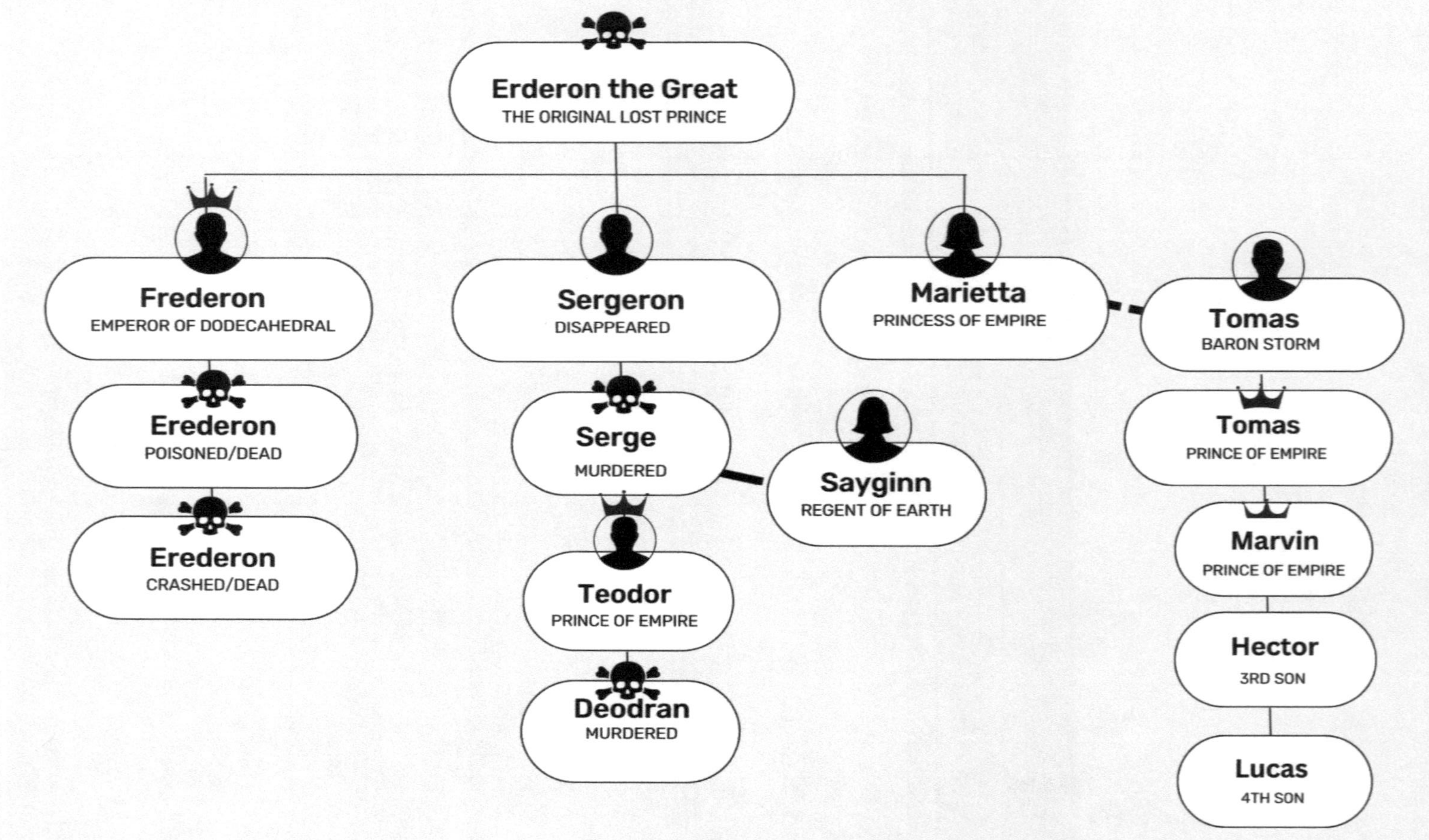

Erderon the Great
THE ORIGINAL LOST PRINCE
Frederon
EMPEROR OF DODECAHEDRAL
Sergeron
DISAPPEARED
Marietta
PRINCESS OF EMPIRE
Tomas
BARON STORM
Erederon
POISONED/DEAD
Serge
MURDERED
Sayginn
REGENT OF EARTH
Tomas
PRINCE OF EMPIRE
Erederon
CRASHED/DEAD
Teodor
PRINCE OF EMPIRE
Marvin
PRINCE OF EMPIRE
Deodran
MURDERED
Hector
3RD SON
Lucas
4TH SON

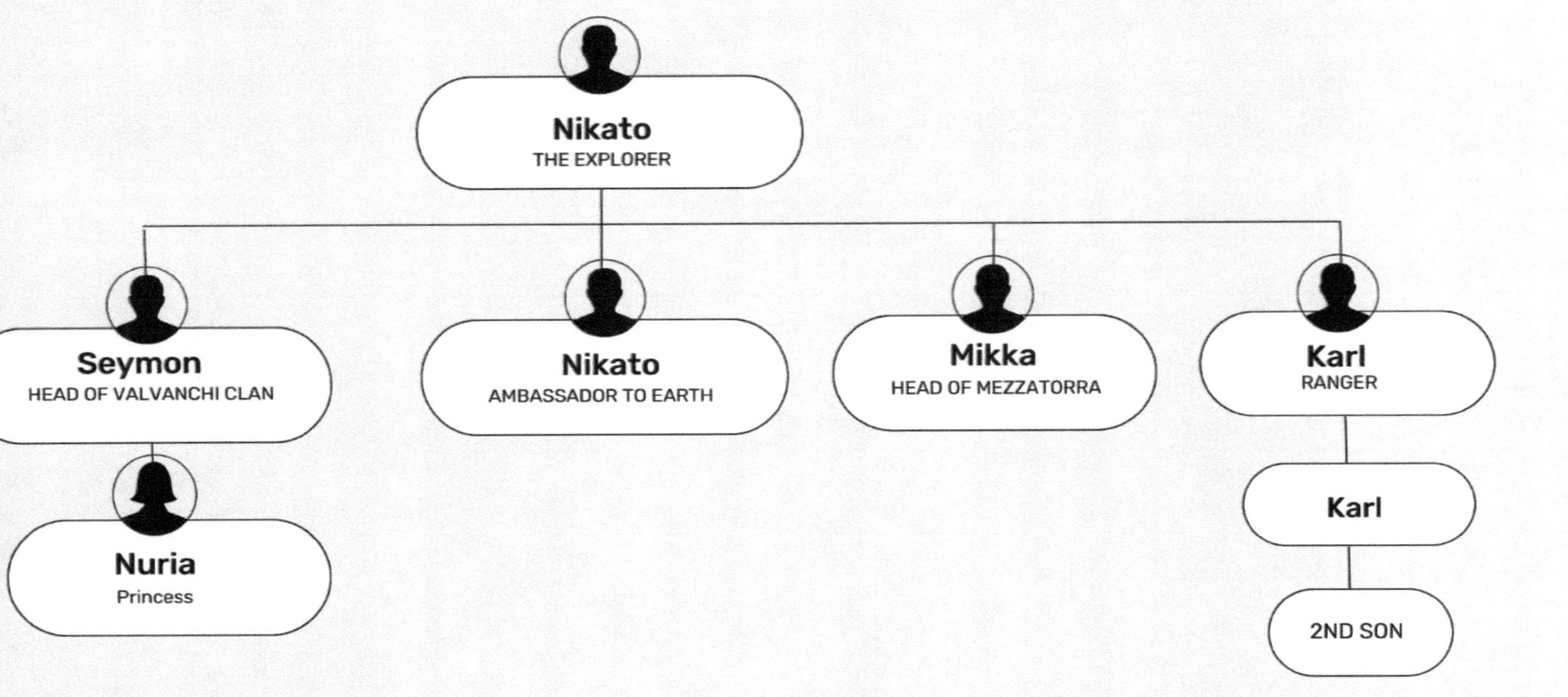

Nikato
THE EXPLORER
Seymon
HEAD OF VALVANCHI CLAN
Nikato
AMBASSADOR TO EARTH
Mikka
HEAD OF MEZZATORRA
Karl
RANGER
Nuria
Princess
Karl
2ND SON

Chapter 1

In the Light and Shadows of the Dome

With a whispered prayer, Guy Erma kissed his Dome medallion, slid it inside his shirt, and stepped up to the edge of the mat. In truth, he knew he needed no divine help today. No, all he needed to win this fight was to be ruthless and quick.

The bell had rung. To delay would mean disqualification.

Guy gripped the short fighting blades and somersaulted forward. He landed within easy reach of his opponent.

He twisted into a spinning high kick that smashed into the other's shoulder pad. He found his feet while the other was still off-balance, crouched and sliced his other leg in a circle close to the floor. In so doing, he swept his opponent's feet from under him. The other fell. Guy was quick to leap on top of him, riding astride his adversary's chest with two blades pressed to his neck.

"Yield?" Guy roared into his face. As he crouched over his opponent, Guy was imagining it was a great Scavengii pirate that he nailed to the floor. But when he blinked, he realised the boy was a Dome Militant Junior – aged sixteen like himself. *At least his opponent was Dome Militant*, Guy thought.

"I yield... I yield!" His opponent was so fearful he almost wept, and to see this sent a thrill through Guy – stronger than any other emotion. His heart beat fast. He rose panting, exhilarated and joyful. He had won!

No-one was watching. Why would they? Across the vast competition space, there were over two dozen blades-mats. Almost all played host to a fighting duo. As always, his gaze was drawn to where the gym opened onto the vast panes and verticals of the Dome. The light was bright, yet dark geometric shadows fell across the space. Guy loved this gym. He always fought better here, in the light and shadows of the Dome.

> In the light and the shadows of the Dome, so help me God.
> I learnt my skill; I learned my craft.
> For my life will be among the stars.
> I will shield my homelands, the protector of its mothers and children.
> I gift my life to this, so help me God. So, help me God.

It was a prayer of the Dome Militant.

One day, I will say those words, thought Guy. *And wear that uniform.* He heard a sharp ping and tapped his wrist communicator. Overnight, a quad of Scavengii pirates had slipped through the Star Gate and barreled down the orbital accelerator, positioning themselves over the 14th North Latitude—possibly scoping Nigeria's oil fields. But the Dome Militant had been ready. The first combat footage had just been uploaded, and he selected the captain's visor cam to follow the action.

The captain moved with lethal grace, his sharp blade flashing under the visor's night-vision overlay. Despite their alien ferocity, the Scavengii pirates fell swiftly to the Dome Militant's blades and long swords, their dark blood staining the cruiser's deck. Guy nodded in approval. The lead ship, a S-class jet cruiser, was still intact. Another victory for the Dome Militant, and soon another asset for Earth's defense forces.

Across the gym, juniors trained in close combat, their blades clashing with a metallic rhythm. Only one in ten would be deemed worthy of joining the Dome Militant proper. *Was he good enough?*

Yes, the answer came, unbidden and fierce. He could almost smell the blood of the fallen Scavengii, feel the solid grip of the blade in his hand. He drew his practice sword and mimed a fierce thrust. *Straight to the heart. And twist. One day, very soon, alien invaders would meet the sharp edge of his blade. This was more than a dream—it was a premonition.* Guy thought with a sigh. *So, help me God.*

"Well done, Guy," Tilson, senior blades instructor and Commander of the Dome Militant bent to help him up.

"Sir! Thank you, sir."

"You do us all proud, you do." The man drew him over and patted the space on the bench beside him. Guy sat down. Together, they unbuckled his forearm braces — each with a line of three curved blades. Off came the calf greaves and the three blades along the back of his lower legs. They released the latches of the springing blades he wore beneath his feet. Soon, Guy had set aside all his fighting equipment, together with the two fighting daggers.

"I will be sixteen in time for the next intake, sir."

"You submitted your forms in time for the deadline?"

Guy nodded but winced. Meeting the deadline had been the least of his worries. His application to join the Dome Militant was flawed in another, more fundamental, way.

"You're not registered, are you?" Both Tilson and Guy knew that without his birth having been registered, Guy's application wouldn't be accepted. "Do you know who your parents are?"

Guy hesitated, his home in the attics of Old Fleet Street was not often discussed. While he was not alone to come from such a background, his situation was made worse by the fact that no-one, neither mother nor father had claimed him as their son. No one had given him a name—so he was "Erma" like all the other parentless orphans.

"Well, one of the models in my house always says I'm her son," he whispered—something he knew but could not prove. It felt like a betrayal to say it aloud, but Guy needed it to be true. "Loulou says I am her son."

Tilson stroked his chin. "Loulou, huh? I know Loulou. She's beautiful, but she has to think of her career – and if she were to register you. Well, the press— "He stopped, they both knew if it was revealed Loulou had a secret child, both she and said child would be hounded by the news reporters speculating on who Guy's father might be.

"Yes, I know it's a secret." Guy fidgeted, what could he do about his lack of parents?

"And you don't know your father." Guy knew Tilson wasn't expecting an answer, so he shook his head. Tilson sighed. "Thing is, Guy. I have lads who are registered – both mother and father – both of whom are pleading with me to take their sons. So, you see."

"But I'm the year's blades champion, and I was due to fight the prince."

"They said he had an injury."

Guy made a clucking sound. "Chicken, more like. My maths average is 97.4. Maths and blades. And I was born on Old Fleet Street." Guy stood so his face was opposite Tilson. "You need the best people for the Dome Militant! I am the best!" Too late, Guy bit his tongue. One never spoke to a senior officer in this way. However, Tilson was more amused than angry.

"Calm, Guy. Control." The man took his hand and patted it. "Calm, Guy. Control. You never know, maybe the fight with the prince will be reinstated."

Guy leapt to his feet and span his fighting blades across the palms of his hands. "Any place, any time, I'll be ready."

A communicator beeped a reminder. Tilson rose and placed a hand on his shoulder. "Keep training. Ask one of the older Militants to prep you. If you were to beat the prince, you'd be pretty much guaranteed a place in the Black and Gold." Tilson stood up – but, before he left, said. "Be ready, Guy. Be ready."

Be ready for what? Be ready to beat Prince Teodor at blades when the fight had been cancelled?

Practice over, Guy left the Dome and walked down the elegant tree-lined Old Fleet Street. House Jewel was the most ancient of the seven-story townhouses, with a spacious fashion boutique on the ground floor and an imposing, colonnaded entrance leading up to the VIP salons, for private clients, on the floor above. House Jewel was the oldest of the Earth fashion houses and it was Guy's home, but he never used the front entrance, instead he turned up a narrow alley to the back of the house.

Guy threaded his way through the crowds of factory workers who were heading into the tall, dark manufacturing units. The shifts changed at this time of day. The weariest of workers were those coming off the night shift, with dark shadows under their eyes, but these day workers were also pale and gaunt – even after a full night's sleep. Reaching the back door, Guy headed up the narrow, dark steps, and looked through the open doors. On the lower floors, the cleaners were in action. He tiptoed through the third and fourth floors, where the models still slept, and into the bright workshops; perfect natural light being deemed essential to fine fashion.

This was where the true craftsmen worked. Embroiderers, finishers and designers had been working through the night and were calling for fresh coffee and breakfast rolls. Guy smiled to see them, then ducked through the small cupboard door to a vertical ladder up to the highest loft in the house.

Guy crept up to where he had been born. Where he had lived his entire life, an unregistered Domeside orphan living in the attics of the fashion house, House Jewel, on Old Fleet Street.

He wasn't the only one. He counted forty-three half-brothers and sisters. Whether he was related to any of these children, he couldn't know. They were, however, the closest thing to family he had. They all shared one giant attic, fitted with a rudimentary communal bathroom, but only thirty bunks. So, a variety of cushions and mattresses were also strewn across the floor. Most of these children would end up working in the factory across the back alley, but not all of them. Old Fleet Street offered some opportunities for them as designers, artists, models – but for Guy one future beckoned: the black and gold uniform of the Dome Militant.

As Guy reached the top rung of the ladder, he expected to find the children sleeping. Instead, he found pandemonium. The orphans of Old Fleet Street were up and getting dressed, there were some tussles as they shared out the best clothes, and Guy parted two girls who were fighting over a hair-brush, pushing them to where thirteen-year-old Sara, the eldest girl, and designated mother of the attic, was swiftly combing tangled hair straight and expertly weaving plaits and tying ponytails.

"Sara, what's happening?" Guy said, pulling out his comb, to tidy up some of the boys.

"All the kids have to go to the cathedral, and we have to wear the new coats – lots of photographers are outside."

The orphans of Old Fleet Street were famous for their beautiful coats and the neat lines they formed to and from school, headed up by an exquisite model or handsome designer. Though excited, the children were well-drilled. As they marched down the main stairs, some were singing. Guy hung back watching.

"Sara?" Guy asked. He never trod the plush carpets of the main house.

"It's all right. We have permission. We'll see the new salon, too."

Guy peered down at the redesigned lounge. It was a minimalist, black and white combination – with one perfect, black Goran fur in front of a white geometric fireplace.

"What happened to the old fireplace?" Guy asked.

"They moved it."

"They moved the fireplace?" The main salon in House Jewel dated back three hundred years. It had been famous for a massive antique fireplace.

"Yes. The design team said it had to go, so they moved it to the Pink Salon on the second floor. But that new chimney is causing problems. Marline told me the fireplace was smoking last night. Let's hope they fix it. Oh, and happy birthday by the way."

"Thanks," he said.

"And say happy birthday to Marline too – tell her we have a surprise planned for later, after practice."

Guy nodded.

"For both of you. It's your birthday too."

From below, a designer called out. "Guy, if you're going out the front door, you need to wear a coat. If not, we'll throw you to the borgs."

Guy shook his head. He snapped his running blades to his feet.

"No thanks. I'll take the back stairs. It's quicker. I'm already late. I'll see you later."

"How much later?" Sara said. "Guy, you mustn't be late! They will throw you to the borgs!"

She was speaking to thin air. With his blades on his feet, Guy sped down the back stairs and out the fire exit.

Guy Erma left House Jewel and made his way across the Dome to the bistro. If House Jewel was the beating heart of Earth's legendary tailoring industry, the bistro in the Dome was its showcase. The walls displayed the latest fashions. The waiting staff were young models. Established 'faces' within the fashion business would often be lingering over coffee and chatting with customers and fans.

He was crossing the square when the Battle Borgs charged out from the military gym. All around, alarmed voices shouted then fell silent, punctuated by a few squeals. Women drew scarves over their heads or grabbed their infants to them, concealing young faces against their bodies. Children leapt back as they approached. Teens sprinted away to hide behind street furniture or alongside other Dome Militants.

The Battle Borgs of the Dodecahedron Dome were cyborgs – half-human, half-robot – but they were old. Some had a head of hair like a wig stuck to a robotic face, others had no hair, but had faces where the skin was mottled grey and black, with large cracks revealing the robotic mechanisms below. They had been so frequently modified – so extensively improved – that they retained little of their humanity.

"Throw him to the borgs!"

Guy knew not to run; he crouched down into a ball and covered his face with his hands. "Throw him to the borgs!" It was a constant threat made by his blade's instructors to lazy or distracted students. Guy had always thought it was a joke, although he had also heard rumours about youths being thrown into cages – given blunt blades to fight hardened Battle Borgs for their lives.

Fanning his fingers, Guy peered out as the last of the borgs passed. He steeled himself to look at their fearsome faces and forced himself to assess the strength of their metal hips and shoulders. *What moves would he use if he had to fight a Borg? Might he be one of the few who fought and survived?*

The Battle Borgs moved on, and the square returned to normal. A sigh of relief passed over the crowd. Guy straightened up, shook back his hair, and headed into Bistro Jewel. The place was crowded, he thought, and not with the usual crowd. These were off-planet visitors; strangers who had come from afar for Royal Ascot Weekend. He passed close to a table of Zaracans as they ordered a strawberry breakfast.

"Valvanski." Guy muttered, using the common slang name. One of the aliens glanced up at him. Guy glared back, thought up some crude images. *Serves her right*, he thought, seeing the startled look on the visitor's face. *Telepathic weirdo.*

Heading towards the back, Guy found them. Loulou and Marline were sitting together in a corner booth – one of the private ones, with curtains drawn back. Loulou was as beautiful as always, even this early, and with hardly any make-up. For over ten years, her slim, tall elegance – dark, geometric cut – pale skin, and eyes so brown they were black, had made her the undisputed face of House Jewel. She offered him a cheek as he arrived, and he kissed her.

"*Mother,*" he whispered.

"*Sssh*!" she replied. Nevertheless, she patted the chair next to her. Guy shrugged and sat down.

"Hi, Guy!"

Guy smiled at Marline. She had grown up as Guy had, in the attics of Old Fleet Street. Like him, she had no father and could only guess at her mother – but she had the jet-black curls, bright blue eyes, and smooth creamy skin characteristic of the all-important Domeside look. So, she no longer slept on lumpy, overcrowded bunk beds. She was one of the lucky ones. She had been offered a chance to escape a future in the dismal clothes factories. At sixteen, she was the youngest and newest House Jewel model, and Guy could not believe the transformation. He reached over to kiss her on the cheek, but she turned – and with more enthusiasm than he expected, she kissed him on the lips.

Guy pulled back and frowned.

Marline reached behind her and produced two sugar rolls topped with chocolate dodecahedrons. "Happy Birthday to Us, Happy Birthday to Us. Happy Birthday, Happy Birthday Happy Birthday to us!"

The people on nearby tables glanced over, even though Marline sang in little more than a whisper.

Guy felt self-conscious, because he didn't know who his parents were, he suspected everyone else was trying to guess his inheritance as well. He wondered what strangers saw when they looked at him and Marline. Two Domeside teens, identical as peas in a pod, same black hair, blue eyes, cream skin. Marline already a Domeside beauty, himself a scruffy, skinny boy with legs that looked like they had shot up overnight – and feet and hands too big for the rest of his body. Many would surmise they were twins, or at the very least brother and sister. *The agony of not knowing,* Guy thought. The one fact he knew for sure was they had been born on the same day in the attics of the great fashion House Jewel. Their births were unexpected, unwanted, and ultimately unregistered. By law, neither Guy nor Marline existed.

He sighed. *What would the future hold?*

Marline pushed a hand-wrapped present towards Guy. "Happy Sixteenth?" She smiled, but her eyes were sad.

"Happy sixteenth to you," then looked at the present. "I got no present for you."

"Well, you're not working, are you? You know I can afford it."

"Marline, the new face of House Jewel." He lifted a glass of juice in a small toast.

Loulou cut in and corrected him. "No. She's one of the Newcomers, not the face of House Jewel. She has a long way to go." She paused, seeing the look of despondency on Marline's face. "You were lucky to be selected Marline, but hurry and," she nodded to the rolls, "don't let any press catch you eating those." Then to Guy. "And hide that present, Guy. He'll be here soon."

Marline ripped a small section from the nearest sugar roll and popped it in her mouth, before anyone noticed. Guy hid the present under the table as he ripped open the paper. Inside were clothes – black socks and a fine t-shirt.

"I thought you could wear them under your uniform," Marline whispered, and looked over to a group of Dome Militant striding across the Plaza in their black with gold trim uniform.

Guy's mouth went dry and for a moment he could not even thank her. This small gift, it meant so much.

Someone else – at least one person – believed in his dream. "I will join the Dome Militant," he told Marline – taking her hand and squeezing it.

"I know you will." Marline replied. They laughed.

"I want to protect our people and our planet from off-world pirates and raiders. I want to fight the Valvanski on Sas Darona. I will be the greatest warrior the Dome Militant have ever known. And everyone will know my name."

"Shush." Loulou interrupted. "You still don't have your place - so don't brag."

Guy looked crestfallen.

Loulou looked past him "Oh, where is he?"

Guy and Marline peered about as well, munching their rolls.

"Do you see the Valvanski?" Guy murmured. "When I passed their tables, I made sure I was thinking of my bum."

"Oh, Guy, you shouldn't. Loulou says we must always think of our favourite dress when we see a Valvanski – no, not ski - Val-van-chi." Marline gave him a superior look as she continued. "The little princess was shopping on Old Fleet Street yesterday."

"Yeah, her father buys her whatever she wants," Guy replied with a sneer.

"But not in House Jewel," Marline said.

"Marline," warned Loulou, spinning back to them both.

"It was Guy!" Marline protested. "I know we're not supposed to talk about clients, but it's Guy!" She held up her finger and thumb pressed together tight in a mime that meant 'keep your mouth shut!'

He held up his hand, index and thumb pressed together, and nodded to both Loulou and Marline. This time, the finger mime meant 'I can keep a secret.'

Loulou rolled her eyes then looked at Marline. "Oh, what are we going to do with you?" Loulou scolded him, but she was smiling as she said it. "You have been offered a good contract by House Jewel - but still you want to join the Dome Militant."

"I won the championship. I'm good at maths. The Militant – it's meant for Domeside boys, like me. I don't wanna strut about in fancy clothes!"

"Being a model isn't about fancy clothes, and doing the catwalk is not about strutting," Marline interrupted. "You have to become someone's dream, as you walk, and pause, and yes, pose. You have to evoke passion and desire. And then off the catwalk, you have to know how to answer the press, how to make conversation with important people, how to behave when you're not working, how every day from the minute you wake is actually a workday. As a model everyone is constantly watching you. So, I don't know how you can think it's easy..." She paused as Guy took her hand.

"Marline, I know it ain't easy, but I have to join the Dome Militant."

Loulou opened her bag, "You need this." She nodded for Guy to look. He peered into the bag, then up at Loulou.

Guy whispered, "Is that a blood test? For me?"

Marline gasped; she had also seen. "That's illegal," she said.

"Sssh!" Loulou hushed her. She took a dual tipped white wand. Holding it under the table, she removed a cap off one end to reveal a sharp edge. This she pressed into the pad of her fourth finger, until her blood was soaked up a quarter of its length. Then she pushed the cap back in place and passed it to Guy. He glanced right and left, before repeating the process. Once his blood had soaked into the wand, he replaced the cap and handed it back to Loulou.

"Ok," Loulou said and concealed the wand in a side pocket. "I'll speak to Chartsie. I am sure that he will let you into the Dome Militant."

"Thank you, Loulou. I will run all your errands for a year." Guy replied. If Chart Segat, or as Domesiders called him Chartsie, took an interest, Guy was sure to get his place.

"Not if you're in the Militant you won't!" Loulou replied, and she laughed.

Marline pinched him on the arm hard and hissed. "You'll be on Sas Darona living in tents like the tribes — boiling your water to drink it, hunting for food, fighting Valvanski."

"Ow!" Guy looked at her in surprise. *Why had she pinched him?* And why was she glaring at him, and was she joking or was she being mean about his future life in the Dome Militant? Guy dreamt of seeing the tribes of Sas Darona one day, even if it meant digging his own latrines and boiling his own water.

"Marline, Guy's too young for that." Loulou ran her hand through his black hair and kissed him on his forehead, sighing. "So handsome."

For a moment, Guy thought she was speaking of someone else, and he felt a pang, because maybe she was thinking of his father. *Did she know? Should he ask? He checked her face for some clue whether she might finally tell him, but she was looking beyond him.*

"Oh, here he comes," she said, then added. "Stand up straight, Marline. And smile!"

Sure enough, Guy had turned to see Chart Segat arrive with the press in tow. He was the Administrator of the Dome, and Mayor of Domeside. He had once been a military commander, and while in recent years, he had gained a lot of bulk, Guy knew he was fit. *Didn't he train with his Militant every morning?* Guy liked how he wore his thick black hair worn in shaggy curls - not afraid to be a proper Domesider - he was both the face of Dodecahedron Dome and the leader of the Dome Militant.

"Segat! Segat! Segat!" The crowd chanted in unison, their clapping and stamping creating a syncopated rhythm that reverberated through the atrium. A half step on the *Seg*, a stamp on the *Gat*, and a sharp double clap that cracked like thunder. *Step Segat, stamp Segat, double clap.* The sound swelled, a pulsing wave of energy that echoed off the high ceilings and sent vibrations through the very floor beneath their feet.

Under a large banner reading *Five More Years*, Chart Segat paused, raising his hands to quiet the crowd. The noise subsided to a murmur, then fell into a reverent silence as he took a deep breath, surveying the sea of expectant faces.

"This night," he began, his voice clear and resonant, "the Dome Militant—our valiant Space Defense—protected Earth from pillage and murder." The crowd erupted in cheers, but Segat lifted his hand, and they quieted once more. "In a textbook attack, we also acquired four new spacecraft, including an S-Class jet cruiser."

Segat straightened, drawing himself up to his full height. His eyes shone with pride and determination as he proclaimed, "All hail the conquering Dome Militant, protectors of Earth and heroes of Empire!"

The atrium exploded with applause and chanting once more, the crowd's fervor matching the passion in Segat's voice. They were his people, and he was their leader, bound together by a shared vision of a powerful, unassailable Earth. He pointed up once more at the sign.

The Dome Debate
YES
Five More Years.

He stood and pointed, grinned and postured, groaned and laughed – all the time the photographers and their flying droids were taking pictures. Until, with an almost comic about-face, Chart Segat noticed Loulou. He shambled across the café towards her. The sheer size of the man made his progress through the crush of tables into a series of collisions and squeezes.

Chart Segat laughed this off with his usual loud bonhomie and self-ridiculing charm. Journalists loved him and kept sending in small camera droids to capture his every grin and grimace.

When Chart kissed Loulou, it was a photo frenzy. With the shouted encouragement of the newsmen, Chart kissed Loulou three times before the Dome Militant closed in. Chart Segat laughed to see one journalist struggling for one last photo while being blocked by a Dome guard twice his size.

"The only story this weekend is the Dome Debate."

Segat roared at the young man. "Five more years! Five more years of investment and progress. I don't care what Regent Sayginn says. Investment. That's what the Dome needs."

After the photographers had their shots, Chart Segat stepped up to the table. He took great care closing the curtains and batting any last camera droids away. Finally, the guards, the press, and everyone else were outside. Guy, Marline and Loulou were all alone with Chart Segat. A tray overflowing with fresh food and drinks arrived.

"Give us a hot cup, Loulou, darling. I'm parched. I am."

Loulou gave a small smile, picked up the pot to pour and murmured. "Chart, I need to talk to you."

Chart Segat gave a theatrical groan. "Please!"

Loulou handed him a full cup with a smile.

Chart Segat first sipped, then gulped the hot drink. "So, talk about what?"

"You remember Guy Erma, Chart. Well, he's sixteen today."

Guy looked gratefully at Loulou. Chartsie's reply was unexpected.

"Already! Sixteen already!" Chart Segat looked like he was about to say a lot more, except Loulou gave him a warning glance, so he concluded. "Funny to think he is the only one."

Guy had seen the looks passing between Chart Segat and Loulou. *So the grown-ups had secrets, so what? But what did Chart mean when he said, 'the only one'.*

"We can't throw this one to the borgs," Chart added with a laugh.

Loulou continued. "He wishes to join the Dome Militant."

Chart Segat turned to stare at her. "Do you not have a place for him at House Jewel?"

"Chart, well, of course, we're all working this weekend."

Guy sighed. Why had Loulou said that? She knew he hated all the fuss around the clothes, the sheer boredom of the modelling. *No wonder Marline only ever talked about the money.*

"I'm not interested in fashion," Guy shouted—louder than Loulou would ever have wanted him to. "I want to join the Dome Militant."

Loulou looked shocked, but Chart Segat cackled in a way that was anything but a laugh.

Loulou cut in. "Chartsie, House Jewel would love to have Guy Erma; of course, we would. But you need him more. He won the Dome blades competition, and he's good at maths. He is perfect for the Dome Militant."

"Sixteen already!" Chart Segat repeated then changing tack. "Good at blades, you say? Yes, that makes sense. How good?"

"My blades—any day, any time, any place," Guy roared.

Chart Segat drew back in mock fear, but his eyes were calculating.

"He won the Apprentice Blades," Loulou insisted. "He was going to beat Prince Teodor." She paused and reached inside her bag. "And there's this."

She passed something to Chart Segat, palm to palm – and he glanced down but then looked away even as he slipped it into his pocket.

But Guy saw. Loulou had handed his blood sample to Chart Segat. *That's it*, he thought—*she was giving him the proof that she is my mother. That means I'll be registered, and Tilson will have the proof to accept me.*

"Please don't use it unless you have to," Loulou said. "We both know Guy is good enough."

"Thank you," Chart Segat said and smiled at Loulou. "We sometimes make exceptions, even if there is no mother or father."

Why had he said that? Guy glanced at Loulou. She shook her head. He looked at Chart Segat who shared a look with Loulou. *They both know,* he thought. *Both Loulou and Chart Segat know who his mother was. Even without the blood test, so why were they persisting with this 'no mother, no father' line?* He needed to be registered at birth to enter the Dome Militant. With one word, Loulou could change his future. *Why? Why did Loulou not claim him, as her son? Why give Chart Segat the blood sample, but asked him not to use it?* She must know he needed a mother, and not just any mother, Guy wanted Loulou.

The irony was, if he had been born to a factory worker, his birth would have been registered – and his place in the Dome Militant apprentices almost certainly guaranteed. Instead, Guy was the son of a fashion model, his father unknown, his birth a secret. This put the Dome Militant beyond his grasp - unless Chart Segat made an exception.

Chart had helped other unregistered orphans... Would he do the same for Guy?

Their eyes met and Chart Segat reached to stroke his cheek. "Guy Erma, Domeside-unregistered orphan; I have a job for you."

Guy leapt to his feet. "My blades are sharp, and yours to command, sir."

Chart nodded but said nothing more. Instead, he reached into his pocket to pull out a huge roll of money.

He peeled off a large number of notes and gave them to Loulou – who checked them with a glance and relaxed a fraction.

"Have you everything you need?" Chart asked. Loulou nodded, and they kissed once more.

Guy had never seen so much money in his life. He tried not to stare but too late he realised Chart Segat had seen him. He rocked the hand with the money roll.

"Ah-ha! This interests you, don't it?" Chart Segat said, as he grinned and hid the money away. "What is it you really want, Guy Erma, money or power or something else?"

"I want to join the Dome Militant, sir."

"I thought so. Be good and you'll soon wear the black and gold." Chart Segat laid a hand on Guy's shoulder. "Be bad and I'll throw you to my borgs." He paused as if remembering, before adding. "No, I won't throw you to my borgs. Not you." He laughed, but his eyes drifted to some thought unseen.

Guy started to laugh. *Of course, they wouldn't throw him to the borgs; it was a Domeside joke. Wasn't it?* He stopped when he saw Loulou was not laughing. Nor was Chart Segat, but as he left, he repeated. "You're a good boy, Guy Erma."

Guy stood a moment – stunned. He turned to see Loulou. She gave no clue as to what she was thinking. Was she smiling... or sad? He couldn't tell. Still, he could not be late, so he said.

"I have to go—they're expecting me at the cathedral."

Chapter 2

The King of Earth

Teodor gazed out over London from a high turret where widows had once watched for lost ships.

Reckless, his mother would say, and she meant dangerously exposed.

"I don't care," Teodor said, but he knew he should, for his would-be assassins were many, and most were related to him by blood. "A few minutes more," he muttered.

The rising sun warmed the city, one district at a time. Greenwich, Isle of Dogs, Surrey Quays. Sunlight glittered across the wavelets of the Thames before reaching the city dome. When the light touched the first glass pentagon, so it lit up and bloomed. Reflected across its twelve panes, the dodecahedron shimmered gold. It was as if the sun itself had landed at the heart of the city. "Magnificent," he murmured and watched, as with a groan and a creak, the panels of the dome shifted, and the light dissipated. London shrank back into a grey dawn.

So quick, Teodor thought.

Too long, he heard his mother's rebuke. Because of her, Teodor was a direct descendant of the one-time Kings and Queens of England – declared Kings and Queens of Earth during the Great Reunification. And in two days' time, he would be sixteen – old enough to sit on the throne. But if he survived to eighteen, then he would come into his father's inheritance. Prince Teodor of Earth would be old enough to be the next emperor of the twelve planets of the Dodecahedral.

But only if he survived.

"I don't want to go," Teodor spoke his fear aloud. Some instinct was gnawing at him. *What, am I afraid? Afraid of the Dome?* The nightmare flashed before his eyes. It had been cold. It had been dark. He had been alone and afraid. *It had all felt so real. Why?* "Why do I have to go?"

He gripped hard onto the metal rail – so hard his knuckles shone white through his skin. Teodor had been at the opening of the Dome; not that he remembered it, but he had seen the recording. Just four years old, he had worn his uniform of Prince of Empire – alongside his father, King Serge of Earth. The first thousand Dome Militant had marched out, and his father had whispered, "'Salute them, Teo; you must salute them.'"

How many times had the news channels shown the footage? Every time Teodor winced to see how, aged four, he had screwed up his face and pulled himself up to his short, pudgy height. Clumsily, he had aligned his plump fingers to the brim of his cap. When his father saluted, the soldiers had responded as one – fists crossing their bodies to tap their hearts.

"Loyal to Empire!" they had cried. "Fear only God."

The sight and sound of it had been too much for his four-year-old self. Unexpectedly, he had fallen onto his backside. To Teodor's eternal shame, instead of letting him jump back to his feet, his father had bent down laughing to hoist him up onto his shoulder. The Dome Militant had cheered. "Forever Prince Teodor! Forever King Serge!"

Only, his father hadn't – hadn't lived forever. Just nine years later, he had been murdered. *Two years, one month, twelve days and* – Teodor sighed as he made the calculation – *twenty hours ago, the King had died. The Dome Militant should have protected their king that day. They should have, but they had failed.* In two days, Teodor would become King, for he alone had survived. And last night in his dream, he'd been terrified.

I'm not afraid of shadows of the night, Teodor squared his shoulders – but another thought intruded, unbidden. *I wish father were here.*

He heard footsteps on the spiral stairs and sighed. They would be sending him extra protection. And yet, whoever was coming was fleet of foot. He turned to look. A slim girl, in a white riding suit edged in turquoise, materialized on the small platform.

"Who sent you?" Teodor asked – then, before she could answer, "Tell them I will be there soon." And he turned his back on her.

But the girl remained. She came to stand alongside him, placing her hands on the rails, alongside his. "It's a wonderful view of the Dome, isn't it?"

So not a servant, Teodor thought, and he looked where she looked. Along the river, where the Strand became Fleet Street, the vast dome dipped one rim into the River Thames, then rose above the irregular roofs to its capped peak.

"Dodecahedron," he pronounced the syllables with relish.

The girl rose onto tiptoe and leant over the railings and pointed: "Is that Blackfriars Bridge?"

Without thinking Teodor reached to pull her back, only to have her stare at where his hand clasped her forearm. At once, he knew this was wrong, but he did not let go, just let his gaze drift to the long drop below.

"Yes, you're right," the girl replied and shivered.

Teodor nodded in approval, released her, then continued as if nothing had happened. "That's Tower Bridge. Blackfriars is near the entrance."

All right, so she's a visitor, Teodor thought, they were expecting quite a host of visitors this weekend.

"Tell me the names? My tutor told me they were pretty names, but I've forgotten them. How many of the old districts are under the Dome?" She hesitated. "I mean the Dodecahedron."

Tutor? He noted. *She must be someone of noble birth. They had told him the names of the guests and showed him photos, so who was she?*

"Well, from Blackfriars Bridge, it goes through Clerkenwell, past Old Street, then south around Spitalfields and through Whitechapel. The City of London is inside, as are the Barbican and St Paul's. Much of the old city was destroyed during the Chaos. The alien Zaracans built the Dodecahedron, you know?"

Teodor paused, remembering a Zaracan princess on the list. *What else had they told him about her?* He carried on talking as he tried to remember.

"My father planned the development inside. The skyscrapers, the sports stadiums, and there's a space shuttle port as well."

"Yes, all to hide his Dome Military," the girl replied.

An odd remark—but not if she was Zaracan. An alien might not know the names of London districts, but they would know of Earth's black and gold uniformed defenders. *Why could he not remember her photo?*

His communicator pinged. Teodor glanced at a few moments of news footage. It was remarkable—three squads of the Dome Militant had taken down a attacking quad – so four ships - of Sas Darona pirates, capturing an S-Class Jet Carrier in the process.

"Only two injured," he muttered, scanning through the details.

"How many Scavengii survived?" The girl leaned in, her eyes fixed on the screen.

"None." Teodor shrugged. "But the Dome Militant only fight with short hand blades and long swords, not guns or explosives."

"They wanted the Scavengii ship intact," she guessed, her voice edged with curiosity.

"Yes. And Chart Segat... well, he runs a tight ship."

"No prisoners. No quarter. Segat gave that order, didn't he?"

Teodor hesitated, then nodded. "I guess, but we have the right to defend Earth. The last time the Scavengii made landfall, they took a hundred women and girls prisoner. By the time the Dome Militant caught up with them, they'd already feasted on a third, and cut another thirty into meat. Of those who were rescued, so many didn't make it..." His voice trailed off, the memory clearly unsettling him. "Segat's methods might be brutal, but they work."

She studied him for a moment, her gaze unwavering. "Still..."

"I know what my mother says," he admitted, rubbing the back of his neck, "but all those rumors around his reputation—they're just that. Rumors. No one knows for sure." He looked back at the screen, where Chart Segat stood in the atrium of the Dome Militant, surrounded by chanting, stamping crowds. "It's going to be tough to find someone who can replace him."

"You have the protection of the Zaracan Democratic Union." As the girl spoke, she placed her slim hand on his arm. Her touch was reassuring. She could only be one person, Teodor realised. The reason they had not given him a photo of the Zaracan princess was that no human had ever seen her.

"Princess Nuria Valvanchi, I presume?" He bowed his head in greeting, then added. "You should not be up here, Princess. It's not safe."

"Yes, but you're here."

"At least stand behind me, so that a bullet has to pass through my body before it hits you."

"Which way?" she laughed. "Which direction will the bullets come from?"

"The street outside the palace," Teodor replied, as he tried to spread himself across the railing. How could she be so blind to the risk?

"And you would take a bullet for me?"

"Princess, your family, your father – they have control over all of Known Space."

"Not all." Nuria replied.

"But at least one thousand planets." Teodor said.

She peered at him, as if searching for some lie written across his face, "You know, no one has ever said that to me before."

"What?" Teodor glanced left and right – this high tower was extremely exposed and so stupidly dangerous. Why had he lingered so long?

"No one has ever said they would give their life so I might live."

"Princess, your family's protection extends to all twelve planets of the Dodecahedral. So if it's for my people, for my planets, of course, I would give my life for yours."

She stood still and solemn. "I believe you, Teodor," she replied. "Look, if you hold my hand, I can make us both invisible."

"You can do that?"

"It's one of the first powers. All Zaracan children want to learn it. Useful, you know? Until you realize all the adults connected with you can see right through it. But up here, there are no adults, so we'll be safe."

She held out her hand.

"Safer," Teodor cautioned her—then, with a shrug, he reached out and clasped her hand in his. His world shimmered grey and then returned to exactly as it was before. But when he moved, it was like his arms and legs were transparent – and you could see the balcony and the city through him.

"What other powers do you have?" Teodor hesitated, "Are you allowed to tell me, Princess?"

She gave a brief shake of her head but then added with an apologetic smile, "Please call me Nuria – almost everyone does."

"Then you must call me Teo, though nearly everyone else calls me Prince Teodor."

Her smile faltered and Teodor wondered why he had said that. Except, of course, it was true. Few people called him Teo these days.

"Prince Teodor! It's not safe!" A loud voice called from below.

Teodor recognised the voice. "We should go down," he said.

Hand in hand, they raced down the spiral stairs to the stables below. Patrice Macey, Prime Minister of Earth, was waiting.

"That tower is too exposed. How can any of us protect you if you take such foolish risks?" Then he saw the girl. "Princess Nuria!" The minister bowed, but before she could reply, he caught Teodor by the elbow and dragged him aside. "Teodor, a word."

"Our guest?" protested Teodor.

"Princess excuse us a moment." His prime minister bowed as he dragged Teodor aside. "Remember, the Zaracans are shape-shifters," he hissed. "They choose their appearance to please people."

"Really? I didn't know," Teodor replied, his voice thick with sarcasm.

"Sometimes they want to please just one person." The man nodded back to Nuria.

Teodor took another look. *Slim, blond and slight,* Teodor thought. *Riding clothes.* Slowly, it dawned on him. Her long hair was straw-like and untidy, like Lucy's. He scowled, so the princess had read the gossip about him and the stable girl. "Good luck, my prince. Be careful."

Teodor didn't hesitate. "Princess Nuria, welcome. I am honoured to host a guest who has travelled so far."

"Well, I'm sixteen this year as well," she replied, curtseying one more time – even more awkwardly than the first time. "I have nearly finished my junior education, but they give you a big project."

"You're doing a project?" Teodor asked.

"My science tutor said I could choose any subject I wanted. I found these images, and I fell in love. I mean, it's impossible not to fall in love with the cats, isn't it?"

Teodor looked a little startled. *Cats? Who called the giant, racing gorans 'cats'?*

"I have already been to Sas Darona to see giant cats in the wild," Nuria continued. "My uncle, Karl Valvanchi, took me to see a night camp. The male had such a fine mane. Savage, you know? When I heard that – on Earth – humans had tamed and raced them, I had to come and see for myself."

Teodor reviewed what she had just said. She had travelled from Zarac 1 to Sas Darona and on to Earth. The journey Nuria described was one only a handful of his people might complete in their lifetimes. She spoke as if this were a holiday. Why did the Valvanchi allow this girl so much freedom, not to mention the expense, to complete what was little more than school homework?

Don't be stupid, Teo! Whatever she might say, she's the heiress and hope of the Valvanchi and their one thousand planets, just as I am the last prince of Dodecahedral. Still... the planet Zarac 1 was many star gates away.

"Did you traverse the seven gates to reach here?" he asked.

"Yes." Her voice trembled as she spoke.

What was wrong? Was she lying? About what? Teodor listened carefully.

"My father said I could, and my uncle invited me to stay for Royal Ascot. Don't you think it's cruel to race wild animals?"

Her smile was fake. She was definitely lying... but about what? He wanted to go back and ask, but she had changed the subject. Teodor sighed; he knew all the arguments against racing wild gorans. He also knew the best response. With another bow of the head, he led her into the stable courtyard.

"Princess, welcome to the royal stables." Nuria looked around and her mouth fell open in wonder. The Royal Guards in their silver and red uniforms, patrolling, on the lookout for security breaches; the jockeys in their silk shirts and woollen leggings; the stable girls, each one eye-catching in her choice of coloured shirt and slim-fitting leggings; and being led out from their stalls into the dawn sunlight, the great two-metre-high racing gorans of Earth. Golden, tiger-striped, dark oak, black and snow-white: created in every hue of nature.

If there was one place in the empire Teodor loved above all others, it was right here, standing in the stables with his gorans.

"We try not to be cruel. Gorans are semi-nocturnal. They favour hunting at dawn. So, we train them at first light. Or did you think we were joking when we asked you to be here at this hour?"

"But it's not natural," Nuria persisted. "These cats no longer hunt."

"Oh, they would if they were hungry enough," Teodor replied with a laugh. "And they do not mind a bit of mauling if you upset them." He remembered a nasty injury he had witnessed just a month before, when an arm ripped from the body of an unwary guard. He turned to see the princess had stopped in her tracks. She looked like she had seen a ghost.

Not a ghost. She's reading my mind, Teodor thought.

"It was only a cyborg," he clarified. "We try to program them to be careful, but they have no sense around gorans. Now look."

From within a stable, a giant goran was being led out. So tall she appeared as a wall of fur – so close, Nuria only had to stretch out her arm to touch her.

"This is Blue Barbarina," Teodor murmured, reaching up to scratch the white, grey, and blue goran above the elbow.

Nuria was talking again. This time, Teodor felt sure she was trying to hide her fear because she was talking fast, reciting even.

"Her mother was an ice cat from Sas Darona. Yes, I know they are the largest of the goran cats. They live around the ice floes of the Southern Poles. They breed once every four years, and three cubs survive. A mother can bear five – but the two weakest are slaughtered." Her speech finished with an emotional sob.

"We all live in a harsh world, Nuria. Don't feel sorry for baby snow cats who are killed by their mother out of kindness – when the alternative is to starve, then freeze."

Teodor smiled sympathetically as she pulled herself together.

"Why Blue? I mean..."

"Obviously, she's not blue. Mostly white and grey, with flecks of blue. It acts as camouflage on the ice, but she is beautiful," Teodor said and smiled. "And Nuria, you must never approach a goran in the wild. But here, come. Stroke her like this."

"They explained about telepathic connection; how, if I connect with you, then I can ride as you ride."

"Well." Teodor hesitated. He didn't think a simple connection of minds could give the girl the physical aptitude to ride a goran.

"I dance," Nuria protested.

"They told me that ... to connect ... I will have to touch you."

An envoy from the Zaracan embassy had spent close on two hours explaining the etiquette to be followed around the Zaracan Princess. Teodor knew he had to follow all the protocols they had laboured to instil into him. Also, his people were watching. From the shadows and the sideline, the Royal Guards were on hand and attentive. From the stable offices, Prime Minister Macey watched. There was nothing for it. They all knew what he must do. There was no one else with the status to touch her. He reached around her shoulders and, winding his arm up her arm, he pressed the palm of his hand to the palm of her hand. He lifted her arm and reached out to speak to the goran with his mind.

Teodor waited. Nuria trembled against his shoulder. He wondered if this experiment was bound to fail. His father would have known how to do this. After all, his father had taught him to connect telepathically to the gorans. "A line of light," he had said. "Along which you can direct your thoughts and commands."

"Yes," Nuria agreed, and Teodor started – for he felt sure her mouth had not moved. The alien girl was speaking to him with her mind. "Show me the light, Teo."

Teodor closed his eyes and stretched his thoughts to merge with those of Blue Barbarina. Now, he saw what the goran saw, sensed what the creature smelt. Nuria's hair was perfumed with lavender and spices.

She's warm, soft, and smells good, Teodor thought.

"Now you're making me blush."

"Don't read my mind!" Teodor snapped back.

They fell apart.

"Maybe this isn't a good idea," Teodor muttered, even though he knew, without the telepathic connection, the princess would not be able to ride the snow goran.

'We cannot refuse the Valvanchis!' his mother had said. His ministers, his tutors, all echoed similar sentiments.

He looked at the princess again. Something had changed. Had she changed her hair? Her hair was no longer frizzy and blond, but long, smooth and silver. More than that, she had changed. Her blond, freckled skin had faded to a white shade of pearled turquoise that shimmered like starlight.

"We already have a connection," Nuria sent with a smile. "Now, you see me as I really am. I can no longer conceal myself now that our minds are connected. Even when I am invisible, you will be able to see me."

So that's what the alien Valvanchi looked like. There had been one or two photographs from when they had first landed on Earth over a hundred and fifty years before. Since those early days, they had been shape-shifting – taking on an appearance that was more acceptable to humans.

Teodor realised Nuria was listening - no, watching, all his thoughts. "I'm sorry. I didn't realise. This is an honour. I—"

"Well, if you are going to allow me to completely invade your mind, it has to be a two-way street. Now we are connected. I have lost the ability to conceal my true self. I too have given up my privacy."

"No one told me that."

"They probably don't know. Only a handful of humans have ever been connected to us. It's a rare thing – even amongst the Zaracan. Oh, everyone is connected to family and a few close friends – but little beyond that. That's why we call a telepathic connection a gift. And normally it's a gift of love."

"Yes, but you don't love me. All you want is to ride the gorans. Was that rude?"

Nuria was blushing. "Well," she said. "At least we are honest with each other."

"It's for the best. All right, so listen to me." Teodor reached out to stroke Blue Barbarina. "I am a friend – you are majestic and brave. You are beautiful and unique."

He turned to Nuria. "Now you try."

"You are beautiful," Nuria murmured. Blue Barbarina turned and bent down to Teodor and Nuria. She sniffed Teodor, then nuzzled Nuria's belly and chest. Without warning, the giant cat licked her face. Teodor laughed and rubbed the cat behind the ears. Nuria looked momentarily stunned – then did the same. Teodor left Nuria to enjoy the goran for a moment. He went to take the reins from the stable girl, who was waiting and watching.

"She's not even a real princess, you know."

"Lucy, shh," Teodor scolded her with good humour. Frizzy, untidy hair – he decided – looked better on Lucy. She looked like she had worked to achieve the look. And he knew she had been up at five prepping his riding gear. "She's our guest. Help her mount."

Lucy scrambled up onto the great snow cat and reached down to help Nuria up. She showed her how to take the front of two joined saddles.

"It's a training saddle."

"I know," Nuria replied.

"Thanks, Lu," Teodor called. "I'll mount now."

The girl jumped clear, and Teodor climbed a fine rope ladder until he was high enough to put his foot into the stirrup and swing up and over, into the saddle set across the goran's shoulders. He took his position behind Nuria.

"You need to rise in the saddle," he told her.

"Like this?" Nuria crouched atop the goran's shoulders; her body angled forward, head down, chin centred on the back of the goran's skull, eyes looking out along the line of the goran's muzzle to the path ahead.

Teodor shook his head in disbelief. Nuria was riding the goran as if she were him. He leant in beside her, checking how she was holding the reins. But her hands were perfectly placed.

"Okay, these are double reins. I'll let you take control for now." Teodor said. "You can ride her as fast as you wish, just shout if you want me to take over."

"It's just... I thought maybe..."

"This is how I learnt to ride with my father." Teodor interrupted her. "I know you want to ride your own goran, and maybe we can try that tomorrow. This is safer. Do you agree?"

Nuria smiled at him.

"Yes, safer is good. Only it does not look elegant."

"Huh!" Teodor snorted. "Who cares how it looks - this is goran riding – *the sport of princes, the death of mortal men*. Come, let's go!"

The goran was already moving at a trot, heading to the courtyard exit. Teodor looked back once. Through the central archway entrance to the stables, he saw the vast geometric shape of the dodecahedron dome. From this angle, it was a black outline in front of the sun – once again magnified in the bright dawn light, and undeniably menacing.

Not for the first time today, Teodor experienced a wave of fear – as if the Dome was some enormous beast he could not control.

"What!" Nuria exclaimed.

Teodor realised too late that he had transferred his fear to Nuria, and his goran felt it too.

Roar. The goran stood on her hind legs, her front claws raking the air in a show of defiance. While Teodor panicked and tried to regain his composure, to his amazement, Nuria clung effortlessly to the goran's shoulders and neck with her knees – sitting straight up and looking straight ahead.

As they watched the pentagons of the Dodecahedron adjust and the light dispelled, the dome seemingly shrank before their eyes, as it once more became transparent.

"Do not fear the Dome, Teodor King," Nuria said. "You are master here and all those men owe you their obedience."

"Yes, they do," Teodor added. "You're riding beautifully, Princess. I didn't think this would work. But you were right, and you're also right when you say I shouldn't fear the Dome!"

Even as he said this, he was at once assailed with fleeting images of his nightmare.

"What is that?" Nuria asked.

"Oh, never mind – it's just a bad dream."

"But are you going into the Dome today?"

"Yes, I have a charity event to help the orphan children of Old Fleet Street."

"Well, that's good, isn't it?"

"Probably," Teodor nodded, and he flicked the reins. "Shall we do this?"

Starting off at a fast trot, Nuria directed the goran across the garden and around the palace building. She rode as Teo, finishing the last ascent at a fast gallop before slowing, then pausing ahead of the long promenade of ancient trees. The straight avenue ran a full two kilometres back to the palace, designed for speed. "Designed to test your nerve, my boy," his father had said. "How fast dare you let your goran go before you rein her in? How fast, eh?"

"Shall I take this?" Teodor asked, taking the reins from her hands.

"Let's do it. You race her as fast as you can."

Teodor nodded as he focused. He needed speed. More than anything, he wanted to be fast. He pulled the princess to him as he lowered them both into the racing posture, where her chin brushed against the brow of the goran – and the cat's whiskers flecked his eyes. He called aloud to Blue Barbarina and off they raced. Two kilometres, it was short and fast, and finished with a brutal leaping hairpin turn. Inside his helmet, statistics flashed up across his visor. All the numbers were green. It was a new personal best.

Oh, if only his father could see this! But was it fast enough – if his father had been alive to coach him, would his goran-riding be faster and fiercer? Was he good? Or did they just say he was good? Would he make a good king—or was he simply the only choice? If only his father were alive. If only Erederon... Stop it. Stop it. They were dead. He was alive. He was the one. The only one. He sighed.

"Teodor, you are the finest prince of your generation." Teodor looked around. It was Nuria who was speaking to him. "And in two days you will be King."

"Well, not exactly the King," Teodor corrected her, he let the goran to choose her own pace as they headed back to the stables. "My mother rules. My mother is regent."

"That's good, isn't it, King Teodor? The title. But not the responsibility" Nuria used her telepathy to tease him.

"What is the point of a title without power?" came his immediate thought reply.

"Power?" Nuria asked. "What? Absolute power, like your uncle?"

"I want to reopen parliament, but my mother is too afraid. We still don't know who killed my father."

They had reached the stable block now, and Teodor kicked off from the high saddle and leapt clear to the ground. He ran to help the stable girls with a set of steps. He soothed and spoke to Blue Barbarina even as he helped Nuria to the ground.

"I could have jumped," Nuria complained.

"But you must be safe, Princess," Teodor replied. "A magnificent first ride." He stepped back and started to applaud her.

"Well done, Princess. It was a great honour to teach you."

Around them all the staff were applauding. A small turquoise and white pod arrived. Teodor led Nuria towards it and opened the door.

"Thank you, Teo. So will we ride again tomorrow?"

"I ride every day. And you would be most welcome." But he also knew it was unlikely to happen if it was not already scheduled.

"We'll meet at the Ascot Spring Ball," the princess replied.

"Ah yes, parties! All the fun of Ascot Weekend," he replied with a dismissive roll of his eyes.

"Well, I look forward to dancing with King Teodor," Nuria replied.

"As I said, not exactly the King," Teodor corrected her. Then he added telepathically: "In any case, call me Teo."

Teodor saw his footman looking meaningfully at a clock, so as the pod moved off, Teodor climbed back up onto Blue Barbarina. He was not going to miss this, his last short ride of the morning. Across the park, through the Buckingham Palace courtyard and around to the rear palace gardens and a small lawn where they had set up the blades mat under the balcony of his mother's bedroom suite. Teodor could not see her, and perhaps she was still inside – but whatever her state of dress or make-up, she would step out to watch him fight.

Teodor leapt clear of Blue Barbarina, to land lightly where two servants and another stable hand were waiting.

His communicator beeped. He looked down impatiently. What now?

Oh no! He was late. Three minutes late.

His mother would be furious.

42

Chapter 3

Mezzatorra

"Mezzatorra to Control. We are under attack, heavy attack. Requesting immediate assistance."

Karl drew a sharp breath in, but his reply was steady. "This is Captain Karl Valvanchi calling Mezzatorra."

"Karl. It's the SDLA. They're at full strength."

"We'll be there. Lock yourselves away."

Thirty-one years old, Karl Valvanchi was a Zaracan warrior. His skin was chalk-white, he stood just under two meters tall, with a slim military build. With his ice-white mane cropped to stubble, he appeared almost human; something he was not. He joined his men, and they pulled on their flying suits. As one, they leapt skywards and circled up. Karl glanced back. With its high perimeter wall and watchtowers, the centre was easy enough to secure. It was the remote units that faced the worst attacks.

Mezzatorra should be okay, Karl thought. The scientists had a secure vault. The so-called 'Sas Darona Liberation Army' were young hotheads and misguided malcontents from the local tribes. Some looting, some vandalism, after which the tribesmen and women would turn and run. If it came to it, they had no weapons of any real threat. Unless the Dome Militant reinforced them — unless they had help from the Dodecahedral.

Karl and his men soared towards their destination, arching over the wide grasslands of Sas Darona.

> Sas Darona, Sas Darona: Pearl of the galactic
> sea
> Sas Darona, Sas Darona, where forever my
> heart will be.

Sas Darona was a giant planet on the disputed border of the Zaracan Democratic Union and the expanding Dodecahedral Empire. The humans had tried to claim Sas Darona due to its vast reserves of monazite-9, a rare metal essential to the manufacture of space magnets. Too late. The Zaracans had filed exploration licenses with the United Races. Further disputes arose when the Zaracans discovered that Sas Darona was inhabited. Were the human tribes related to the humans of Earth?

Did it matter? The tribes discovered that Earth traders would pay real money for newly mined monazite-9. The attacks on their bases had multiplied.

"Captain, I can see a firewall," said his second, flying at Karl's right shoulder.

Karl stretched his sight to look. On the horizon, a white line of fire shot up from the ground. It was coming from the direction of Mezzatorra.

"Is that a shield test?" Karl asked, but the question was rhetorical. Something's not right, Karl thought, as he shouted. "Karl Valvanchi to Mezzatorra. Report please?"

No reply.

"Captain Karl Valvanchi to Mezzatorra. You requested assistance? Please respond."

One of the oldest bases on Sas Darona, Mezzatorra was a crashed shuttle wedged on a rocky outcrop. Too valuable to be abandoned, too remote to be useful, yet perfect for entomological studies.

"Karl Valvanchi to Mezzatorra, requesting clearance to land in one minute eighteen seconds."

Still no reply.

What was going on in Mezzatorra? All at once, there was a loud telepathic response.

"Negative, Captain Valvanchi, negative." It was a young female voice. "We have a grade one Cy-sect alert. We have initiated the protection shield."

"Cy-sect alert?" repeated Karl. His heart was in his throat. His next words were a strangled whisper. "Is it plague?"

"For God's sake, Karl, flee, fly, save yourself".

Karl and his six men were circling down to the base, with the team matching Karl's every move.

All at once, Karl shouted. "Abandon formation. Fly high, fly fast. Regroup further south. Retreat. Retreat."

As the squad split – twisting up and away, Karl looked down in horror, as he saw lines of white fire surround the base in its entirety. They reached up, then arched over. At their peak, the lines of light joined and started to spread like a vast spider's web. The branches and arms multiplied, until all Mezzatorra was encased in a dome of yellow light. On all sides, Karl's men dove and dipped between the lines of fire – before accelerating fast, up into the blue sky above. Karl rolled around a shining beam of fire, banked hard right to avoid another laser-fast connection, and then he was free and flying fast. He sent the new rendezvous coordinates to his men as he went.

What had gone wrong? Questions filled Karl's thoughts.

The shield had gone up! The final act of desperation of a community faced with Sas Darona plague. With a chill, Karl recalled the briefing by a white-coated entomologist. The plagues on Sas Darona were unparalleled in their ferocity. All animal species on Sas Darona were susceptible – and, once bitten, sixty per cent died. It was speculated that the peoples of Sas Darona remained primitive because the tribes were repeatedly destroyed by plague. Therefore, the Zaracans set themselves to studying the insects. Because of the dangers involved, the research was undertaken at the remote site of Mezzatorra.

What had the SDLA done?

Landing on the edge of the savannah, Karl and his men ducked into the forest. They stripped off their flight suits and shape-shifted their appearance as they ran. They started their run as slim, pale aliens. They regrouped around a vast evergreen, as a small troop of Sas Darona tribesmen. Wearing flat, supple leather lace-up boots, knee-length kilts of roughly woven linen, leather water bottles and meal packs strapped across their chests, they had as many as three pairs of matching fighting blades at their waists.

Karl split his men, sending two to Mezzatorra, while he headed off with the rest, following the heat signature of their fast-retreating enemy. Speeding through the woodland, the DNA traces of their enemies appeared before Karl's eyes like fading luminescent clues.

"They have a start on us," one of his men said.

"Not all of them," Karl replied. One set of traces shone brightly. "They have a laggard!"

It was not one tribesman, but two. Two young men, one bled copiously from a deep gash to his thigh – the other struggled to carry him through the forest. The Zaracans sprinted up behind them and leapt out on them from all sides. The two hesitated, fooled by their attackers' outward appearance; their fighting blades stayed at their belts. Their hesitation turned to fear, and even as Karl recognised the medallion, the stronger of the two shoved the metal disc into his mouth.

A Dome Militant medallion, even a glimpse was enough.

"Get them!"

Two of Karl's men took hold of the injured tribal warrior. From what looked like food pouches, they produced bandages – a small hand-held X-ray, and morphine capsules.

Karl himself grabbed the Dome Militant, disguised as a tribal boy of course, and unceremoniously pulled the metal disc from between his teeth. Too late! The young soldier had bitten hard into the dome-shaped poison crystal capsule at the heart of the medallion, and the poison was quick.

From a pocket at his belt, Karl pulled a syringe and speared it into the broken crystal, taking a sample of the poison. Within the syringe's chamber, intelligent chemicals turned dark red, as they worked to find an antidote. Karl had his arm around the young soldier's shoulder. His index and third finger were pressed to his jugular, feeling for a pulse. It was fading fast. Inside the syringe, the liquid changed from red to orange to green.

The Dome Militant soldier was no more than twenty years old; his skin was paler than those of the Sas Darona tribesmen. His body was heavier, with muscles toned from a gym, rather than outdoor living. Karl saw that they had tried to straighten his hair, and, at his temples, he could clearly see how the skin tint had been hastily applied. As the liquid in the syringe changed colour to green, Karl injected the contents into the soldier's neck and waited – pressing his fingers deeper. The pulse was still fading. Karl started on a second syringe.

Alongside him, Karl saw that his men had tended the other boy's wound. Karl could tell at a glance he was an actual tribesman, and under the effect of morphine, the injured youth was weeping and reaching to stroke his companion's hands, pleading with him to live.

Prayers would not save the Dome Militant soldier, Karl thought, as he glanced at the syringe in his hand. Still red, just a hint of orange. He waved to his men.

"You two, follow the trail – but do not engage."

They raced off along the forest path.

The antidote was ready; the syringe had changed from orange to green in his hand. Again, Karl stabbed into the jugular. Again, he probed with his fingers around the soldier's neck and the base of his skull. Nothing. He reached for a third syringe. His second placed a hand on his shoulder.

"He's dead, Karl."

Karl said nothing. He stretched the body out on the path, pulled the limbs straight into a pose of calm, closed the soldier's eyes and removed the Dome medallion and its chain from his neck. It fitted snugly into the palm of his hand – a ring of hard golden metal around a synthetic, purple-tinted crystal, shattered now, but previously it would have been shaped like a dodecahedron dome. Not just any dome. The large geodesic dome at the centre of London, the Dodecahedron-capped Dome, was the training base and military headquarters for the Dome Militant on Earth. The crystal had been filled to the brim with poison.

So, thought Karl, *the Dome Militant had finally devised a poison that worked faster than the best antidote. If experience were anything to go by, the poison would mutate to acid. He could bag up the body and take it back to camp but, within an hour, it would dissolve into dust. Karl shuddered. How many times had he seen this? A dozen, maybe twenty, fighters – some had been wounded, most had not. On capture, all had chosen suicide. No body, no evidence, no proof.*

He had one live prisoner, but the injured man was a tribesman. That was different. The United Races paid no heed to primitive tribesmen 'pointing bows and arrows' at Zaracan military units. He would be healed under the United Races charter and returned to his tribe. Again and again, the United Races had demanded proof of Dome Militant involvement. Karl looked again, as if to check the medallion clasped in his hand. This time, they had made a mistake. Or had they? As he watched, the poison ate into the metal.

"Ow!" Karl dropped the medallion as the acid burnt his palm. It fell from his hand down on top of the corpse. In a matter of moments, like paper on a flame, it had burned to ash and crumbled to dust. No proof.

And yet, something was not right. The tribesman's leg looked as if it had been ripped open by gunfire.

Karl spoke with sudden fear. "Can you manage him? I must go on to Mezzatorra."

Karl sped back through the forest, part sprinting, part flying. Within minutes, he was walking along the perimeter of the firewall. Mezzatorra itself was fifty meters away. The firewall was millimetres thick. It shimmered in the sunlight but was primarily an invisible yet deadly wall of heat. The same young admin assistant, who had radioed the warning, came towards him. Her name was Sonia, nineteen, newly arrived and lovely. At first glance, she appeared unharmed.

"They had explosives, Karl. They blew a hole through the vault walls. And then, they were inside. Oh, Karl, it was horrible. The lock-up is three rooms. We only had blunted blades. Well, we never thought. Three of us survived."

"So, they were armed? Guns? Lasers? Grenades?"

"No, just blades – hand blades. But they were fast. So fast, Karl. I knew the Dome Militant were the best blade fighters in Known Space, but." She started sobbing.

"You saw they were Dome Militant?"

"Yes, I mean no." She was panicky. Even in these circumstances, she hesitated to blame the Dome Militant.

Karl knew why. Relations with the nearby Dodecahedral Empire were bad enough without accusing them of terrorism.

"I don't know, Karl."

The firewall rippled like a veil on a breeze. In the distance, it disappeared into a haze. Bushes had been incinerated to ash along its perimeter. This black scar down the centre of the vegetation was the only visible sign of its presence. But it was there, if Sonia tried to walk towards him, she would be consumed by the flames.

"How many died?" Karl asked.

"Five of us, and we have found three of theirs too."

"What about the twins?" Karl asked but wished he hadn't. Gove and Jon were identical twins, brilliant geneticists and fun-loving party-boys, who enjoyed their notoriety in the tight circles of entomological research.

Sonia released a sob. "Gove was badly injured and bitten. Jon ended his brother's suffering," she choked, "and then took his own life."

Karl could not think of anything to say as he tried to imagine the laughing brothers reduced to fratricide followed by suicide.

"Oh Sonia, I'm sorry. Did you say bitten?"

"We've all been bitten. Look!"

She pushed her sleeve up high above her elbow and showed Karl the many bites down the white flesh of her inner arm. Already they were turning into giant pus-filled cocoons.

"Are those plague bites? Sonia!"

"We had to fight, Karl. They were stealing poison pills. That's how the main tank was smashed. It contained a swarm of over a hundred insects. We've all been bitten." She nodded to her colleagues who were lining up the bodies in the shade of a tall tree. "But we had to fight. You do understand?"

"They took poison pills?" Karl repeated, aghast.

"We think the tribesmen stole eight poison pills. If they had just wanted to take the monazite-9 or smash our equipment, we would have let them. But when they entered the vault, they only wanted one thing."

"And you are sure the tribes stole eight poison pills? Or was it Dome Militant?"

Sonia shrugged. "I saved one." It was a brick made of industrial glass and, within it, was a mini world of plants, soil, water and five or six insects. It might look like a miniature paradise, but there was also a small explosive mounted on the side.

The insects inside the poison pill were the jewel in the crown of the research undertaken at Mezzatorra. They were not Sas Darona plague insects; they were Cy-sects, cybernetic insects. Someone somewhere had decided Sas Darona plague could be used as a weapon. Karl mused. Someone else had speculated that instead of real flies, a weapon needed cybernetically and genetically enhanced insects. So Mezzatorra had delivered. Cy-sects (cybernetic genetically enhanced insects) possessed all the attributes of Sas Darona plague, but none of the drawbacks. Cy-sects did not require water to spawn. Their bites were one hundred per cent lethal, one hundred per cent of the time. They achieved Crystallescence in four hours or less, and they always spawned a further hundred thousand Cy-sects.

It was not that the Cy-sects were un-killable, fire destroyed them, but rather they were unstoppable, spawning a hundred thousand offspring every four hours. Such fast exponential growth meant these poison pills went beyond being deadly. They were planet-killers.

"Karl Valvanchi to control. They have eight poison pills. We have to lock it down. Nothing takes off. Nothing comes in. They have poison pills; they must not leave this planet."

He turned to speak to Sonia, only to see her crumble. At her back, the two others who had been carrying the dead now lay amongst them. Sonia was still alive, though. She moved her arms weakly, as if swimming against the ground and grass to find a more comfortable position.

The full horror of the attack threatened to overwhelm Karl, as he found himself counting, again and again, the number of the fallen. Eight of his people had died today, more than in all of the previous twelve months. Not only that, but the dead were not soldiers. They were eight leading specialists in a little-known field.

Karl had a choice: head off to chase and find the poison pills or stay here providing what comfort he could to this beautiful girl as she died. *Was it a choice?* Karl sank in the grass across from Sonia. She was within his reach, except the firewall was between them.

"It's not painful," she whispered, and closed her eyes.

As the Sas Darona plague made its progress through the flesh and bones of her body, her face remained recognisable – but she was the shape of Sonia, not Sonia herself. In the setting sun, her body shone – reflecting the light from a thousand different facets of the Cy-sect cocoons. The Crystallescence: a sight, Karl realised, which was hauntingly beautiful, but also...

Deadly. As the sun set, the cocoons split. For one moment, she was a quivering mass. Her body dissolved into a cloud of plague flies. They rose up from her corpse in a cyclone, leaving nothing behind. The Cy-sects seemed to smell Karl, and a large group swerved, spun and charged at the shield. Karl Valvanchi leapt back. Unnecessarily, the Cy-sect swarm fried and burned on the wall of fire.

Sonia had said one last thing to Karl. He felt sure it was the last thing she said when she was still truly human.

"Karl, Karl. Wait. I am starting to forget things. But this is important. We found this, Karl. We found this, and you need to have it."

She threw the metal disc and chain through the firewall.

Karl caught it one-handed. He did not have to look twice to know what it was. He stroked the medallion, polishing its surface with the oils of his palm. It was unmistakable. The large circular military ID tags moulded to resemble the Dodecahedron Dome were only worn by the Dome Militant military force who trained in London on Earth at the heart of the Dodecahedron Empire. On one side, there was the fighter's name, rank and serial number and, on the other, the motto of the Dome Militant. Karl ran his thumb over the circle of letters.

Loyal to Empire, Fear only God.

It's intact, thought Karl, *the proof he needed. Proof that the Dome Militant were at Mezzatorra*. He relaxed a fraction, enjoying this small moment of success.

Another thought occurred to him: *What did the Dome Militant of the Dodecahedron Empire want with poison pills?*

Chapter 4

Mother of Empire

"You're late," Regent Sayginn said, her voice clipped, but not without a flicker of tension as it travelled through the wrist communicator.

She stood at the high window, morning light warming her shoulders, gazing out over dew-wet gardens that stretched toward the distant stables. A delicate porcelain cup rested between her hands, untouched.

"Sorry, Mother," Teodor replied.

He didn't sound sorry. He never did.

Sayginn, Regent of Earth, might have appeared delicate—slim arms, narrow waist, small feet in velvet slippers—but her presence could still silence generals and senators alike.

She took a measured breath. "You have the best blades instructor in the city. And you're still late."

Below, the training mat gleamed—a pristine, cream-colored circle, ten meters wide, edged in thick black. Teodor's butler, who had once served his father, stood nearby. He was tall and silver-haired, with the composed stillness of someone who had seen too much to be surprised by anything.

The men from the Dome Militant stood at attention. Black and gold shimmered in the sun, their obsidian blades slung across their backs. Their expressions were carved from stone. Sayginn had once preferred gentler tutors for Teodor—men who bowed and murmured—but Serge had insisted.

The people of Earth sleep soundly in their beds because of the skill and bravery of the Dome Militant, Serge used to say. *One day Teodor will fight beside them. God willing, he will lead them.*

As usual, Serge had been right. These days, any ship that crossed into Dodecahedral space unannounced vanished—or returned repainted in black and gold, its crew replaced, and its flag torn down. Sayginn still found it ironic: *in the age of interstellar travel, warfare has returned to steel and blood—blades and flying daggers.*

"Teo," she said more gently. "You know better than to keep them waiting."

"Okay, okay," he muttered. He strapped on the leaping blades and reached for the leather gauntlets, their three curved knives catching the morning light.

His butler held out a tunic—an iridescent vest that shimmered like ice.

"What's that?" Teodor asked sharply.

"A diamond protection vest," Sayginn said. "A gift from the Emperor."

He hesitated, lips tight, the refusal almost forming. Sayginn stepped onto the balcony, silhouetted against the sun, her silence saying more than any rebuke. Teodor looked up. She nodded—first at the vest, then toward the press drones hovering nearby, their lenses blinking red.

"Go on, Teo. You must wear it."

He scowled but tugged it over his head.

"It's as light as silk," she said. "But no blade can pierce it. The ultimate protection."

"And it'll look good on the news," Teodor said dryly.

Sayginn flushed. He was right, of course. The vest would gleam on the morning feeds.

Now he was ready—leaping blades at his feet, curved knives along his limbs, the diamond shirt aglow, a dagger in each hand. He stepped onto the mat, a blur of polished steel and quiet defiance.

He twirled the daggers so they flashed in the light. "Let's begin," he said, voice flat but eyes burning.

Sayginn frowned.

Since when had he learned that trick?

Teodor noticed his mother watching but refused to let it distract him. Across from him, Dome Militant Commander Tilson stepped onto the blades mat with practiced calm.

"On guard."

The senior instructor spun toward Teodor. The prince blocked and deflected with ease—too much ease.

"You were late," Tilson snapped, launching a second attack. His blades spun in sharp, unpredictable arcs.

Teodor parried, more annoyed than threatened. "Blades isn't my only sport."

"There are a thousand boys down the river," Tilson replied, pressing in. "Not one ever keeps me waiting."

A pang of guilt hit Teodor, and his foot slipped slightly. Tilson surged forward, exploiting the opening.

Forced into a clumsy countermove, Teodor lashed out. "Goran riding is the sport of emperors," he said—and with sudden fire, launched into an aggressive counterattack, matching each blow to his words. He spun, struck, kicked. Momentum and anger carried him forward.

But then he disengaged, retreating to the edge of the mat, flushed and uncertain.

Was there ever a chance I could beat him?

"Ready," Tilson called.

This time, the commander didn't hold back. Teodor stumbled, struggling to find a rhythm.

"Calm, Teodor. Control."

He tried. For a few moments, he found it—until the final burst. The Dome medallion at Tilson's neck swung loose, spinning up toward Teodor's face. Reflexively, he flinched—and his heel crossed the black line.

The match ended.

"To step outside the blades ring is to die, my prince. Instant disqualification."

Teodor's shoulders slumped. "Your medallion..." he began, then stopped himself. A weak excuse. Everyone knew the rule.

"Unfair." He muttered, ripping off his gauntlets. The greaves followed, thudding to the mat. "This is only practice. Enough to beat some Domesider, anyway."

His eyes drifted to the golden gorans across the yard. He lifted a hand, summoning them with a focused thought. The creatures galloped toward him, curving their graceful bodies around his sides. Cameras clicked from the shadows. Let them see this: Teodor, flanked by gorans, every inch the prince. Even if he hadn't impressed his trainer.

"The Dome fight was cancelled."

"What?"

"I met with your mother over a week ago. The match was called off. Did she not tell you?"

Teodor stared at him. Anger bubbled to the surface.

"Why?" he spat.

"They thought you might lose."

"The point was the fight!" Teodor snapped. "I was going to show I could—"

"Fight and lose? What's the point in that?"

"I don't have to win!" Teodor's voice cracked. "In two days, I'll be king."

Tilson arched a brow. "Really?"

"And I'll be Commander-in-Chief of the Dome Militant."

"And you'll lead them into battle?"

Teodor hesitated. Would he charge a Scavengii raider with blades drawn? Could he?

Tilson stepped closer. "Do you think they'd follow you—if they saw you lose here?"

"Yes, but—"

"But nothing. What is it you want, Prince Teodor?"

Teodor blinked. The question hit deeper than he'd expected. What *did* he want?

He wanted to ride gorans. Eat breakfast with Princess Nuria. Get lost in maps of Known Space with his tutors.

"Well, what should I want?" he asked, waving at the palace around them—the wealth, the gardens, the watchful servants.

Tilson's disappointment was quiet but visible.

Teodor looked down, confused. *What was the question again?* Did he want to be King? Was that it?

"I have one thousand boys down the river," Tilson said. "And they all want the same thing."

Teodor shifted uneasily. The Domeside boys were fearless—deadly, loyal, relentless.

"If you don't know what you want," Tilson said, "that's your problem. Until you do, you'll keep losing. And no one follows a loser."

Teodor drew himself up, face flushed. "I will be a great King, like my father. And you will kneel before me."

Tilson gave a single nod.

Maybe he would kneel, Teodor thought. *Maybe they all would kneel. But would that make him a leader?*

"Until next time," Tilson said. "Remember: calm, Teodor. Control."

He always said that. Calm. Control.

Yes. Teodor would be calm. And he would be in control—especially this morning. He turned toward the palace, leaping blades still strapped to his feet. The golden gorans followed, flanking him like royal sentries.

Teodor bounded up the stairs three at a time and burst into his mother's suite, not bothering to knock. The gorans trotted behind him, their hooves clicking softly against the marble. Teodor made straight for the breakfast table and served himself without a glance.

It was only eight. He'd already had a full morning—and he was starving.

There she was. Regent Sayginn, ruler of Earth.

"My blades. Any day. Any time. Any place," Teodor cried. "Will you yield?"

"Don't say that!"

Teodor sighed. "It's what the Dome Militant blades fighters say."

"Yes, but you're not in the Dodecahedron."

"I like it, and they are our people too." He spun his blades across the palms of his hands.

"And stop that silly trick with the blades. It's dangerous. Now, say good morning properly."

"Good morning, Mother."

"That was a careless mistake this morning, Teo."

Teodor ignored her criticism and, instead, asked. "Why, Mother? Why did you cancel the Domeside fight?"

"The reason I cancelled the fight is because the Domesider they chose to fight you will beat you."

"I don't believe you."

"I didn't believe it either. But I have spoken to everyone. They all said the same – the security team here, your blades instructor. I've seen the tapes of this young man; the others have watched him train. They all agree he would beat you, Teodor."

Typical. Another thing he was not good enough at. His father had been marvelous, Erederon had been amazing, he – Teodor – could not beat another boy (a Domeside boy!) at blades. "He's probably sixteen and a full member of the Dome Militant," he snapped, rebuking himself as much as his mother.

"He's fifteen. He's a skinny thing. But he was fast, and he was smart. You would have lost."

"Oh, and suddenly I'm not clever enough?" Teodor shouted. "Do I not work hard enough, long enough?"

"Teodor!" Sayginn snapped.

"No, Domesider will ever beat me. Do you hear me? I won't allow it. And didn't the Emperor want to see me fight at blades?"

"Yes, yes, he did. But you can present your exam display, and he'll be impressed by the way you handle gorans."

"Tsk! You know they'll call me a chicken inside the Dome if I don't fight."

"Yes, well, the people can say what they want. At least they will not have seen their fighter knock you onto your backside."

"Mother!" Teodor was outraged; he knew she was referencing his four-year-old self. He picked another sugar roll from the breakfast table and bit into it. His mother was frowning. How many rolls had he eaten? Was it two or three? He sought to distract her. "May I come with you to the spaceport this morning to see Uncle Freddie?"

"You mean to come and greet Emperor Frederon?"

"My Uncle Freddie, yes," Teodor said, repeating the words with emphasis. *Let's remember who I am.*

For an instant, his mother looked confused. She might even have said yes, but then she checked her communicator.

"You mean," she cleared her throat – never a good sign – and continued. "We have to re-organise a rehearsal which involves one hundred children, all in costume, twenty adults – including the full crew of technicians – and all the security, the police escort and the drivers? Oh, I am sure everyone would be delighted with any change of plan." She paused. "Teo? That's almost two hundred people waiting for your arrival in the Dodecahedron Dome."

"Mum, I don't want to go." *Did he have to explain to his mother what he felt about the Dome?* The Dome, where his father had been going the day he died. The Dome

Militant, who should have protected him. The Dome that overshadowed their everyday lives and would never go away. Of course, he did not have to explain.

His mother nodded. "You will have your security." She checked her communicator. "Twelve cyborgs, six cy-wolves and, of course, your bodyguard."

Both looked out to where a cyborg and wolf patrolled the balcony. This one was Aengus. Well, he had once *been* Aengus. After the explosion, his family signed the papers for him to become a cyborg. A robotic processor had been wired into his human body.

"Aengus's skin is starting to peel," Teodor muttered.

"It's over two years since he lost his legs," Sayginn replied. "But he is one of those who tried to save your father that day."

"But one of the skin cracks across his face is so deep, you can see the bone, and last week I saw him pick up this big piece of skin which had fallen off his arm."

"Remember he's still human, and his heart is so loyal Teodor. No, I think we'll keep him, but I will ask the surgeons to look at his skin if it bothers you so much."

Teodor felt wretched then and forced himself to smile at Aengus. He knew it was not Aengus who was troubling him.

"Do I have to go into the Dome?"

"Teodor, what's this about? I thought you wanted to—"

"I had a bad dream," Teodor interrupted, and ignored his mother's surprise. "I was in the dark. I was trying to find my way out. It looked a bit like the catacombs we visited last year. A voice kept telling me it wasn't the catacombs – it was the Dome. I didn't know where I was. It was so dark. I was all alone. I was trying to find my way out. I kept trying to find a way out, only... I woke up."

Sayginn sighed and shook her head. "A dream, Teo. It was a dream. You have to go. It's an important weekend. I need to win the Dome Debate. You know that. Chart Segat has his supporters too, but we have to win them over. Your singing with a choir of Domeside children will be—already is—very popular."

She reached to run her hand through his hair, but Teodor backed away from her caress, scowling.

"It will look good on the news," his mother concluded.

"It will look good on the news, Mum! It was dark. I was cold. I couldn't find my way out."

"In two days, you will be old enough to be their king."

Teodor sighed. "Maybe. But you are the Regent."

"Only to make your life easier. Once you are sixteen, you may claim your crown at any time. Do you remember the words?"

Teodor felt his heart sink. *Not this again.* "I want to be a great King like my father, mother. I want to protect our people and our planets but..."

Behind his back, his mother recited. "I, Teodor, son of Serge." His mother tapped him on the shoulder. "Remember when you are eighteen, you will be Emperor—Emperor of all the Dodecahedral."

"If I survive," Teodor muttered.

"Of course, you'll survive," his mother snapped. "Just remember the words. I, Teodor, son of Serge..."

Turning to face her, Teodor recited the oath. "...do claim this planet and its dependencies. To rule as is my right, For the benefit of my people, As guided by our democratic institutions, And prescribed by our laws. So help me God." An eerie silence followed, as if a crowd somewhere was supposed to applaud but had forgotten.

"I do know the words, Mother. I do want to rule this planet. Only..."

"You're a good boy, Teodor. Your heart will tell you when the time is right." She kissed him one last time, then checked her communicator before heading off. She was gone.

Teodor looked at his communicator. *Time to go. They're expecting me at the cathedral.*

Chapter 5

Interlude. Diplomatic Exchange

From: Ambassador Nikato Valvanchi II, Earth

To: Captain Karl Valvanchi, Sas Darona

My dear Karl,

Just dropping you a quick line. I am experiencing a few difficulties organising a display of tribal dancing for an important forthcoming event here on Earth. Any intervention on your part would be much appreciated.

Your dear brother,

Nikki

From. Captain Karl Valvanchi, Sas Darona

To. Ambassador Nikato Valvanchi II, Earth

Dear Nikki,

No can do, Sas Darona is in lockdown following Mezzatorra.

Sincerely,
Karl

From: Ambassador Nikato Valvanchi II, Earth
  To: Captain Karl Valvanchi, Sas Darona
My dear Karl,
My dearest brother, I don't believe I fully explained myself in my last communiqué. I am organising what you might call an elegant evening at the embassy, as part of the Festival of Fashion and Sport, often referred to as Royal Ascot Weekend.

Unwisely, you may think, we settled on a Sas Darona theme many months ago – and we had already put in place all the necessary arrangements to have some specialty foods – Sas Darona sand lizards, no less – and displays of tribal dancing.

The council has decreed. It would be preferable for the Dome to be closed, as a precursor to a broader reconfiguration of the Dome Militant activity on Sas Darona. This entertainment is an important part of our plan to influence the humans. Regent Sayginn has promised to attend and I may even have persuaded the emperor himself – so you'll understand: the stakes are high, and failure is not an option.

From: Captain Karl Valvanchi, Sas Darona
  To: Ambassador Nikato Valvanchi II, Earth

Dear Nikki,
Please don't "my dear brother" me. You and I were never that close — and we both know it.

As for your entertainment, are you suggesting we break quarantine so your guests can dine on chilli lizards? Perhaps, for a truly authentic Sas Darona experience, we should send you a nest of Cy-sects as well? How about Sas Darona plague as a life-or-death experience? Would your guests find that amusing, I wonder?

Of course, I agree: The Dome must close. But, under the circumstances, I strongly suggest you make alternative plans.

Cordially,
Karl

From: Ambassador Nikato Valvanchi II, Earth
  To: Captain Karl Valvanchi, Sas Darona
  Cc: Ex-Ambassador Nikato Valvanchi I, Zarac 1
Dear Karl,
I don't know what you are suggesting. *Sas Darona plague on Earth?* Really?

All I am asking for is a consignment of sand lizards. Are you threatening me?
Nikki

From: Ex-Ambassador Nikato Valvanchi I, Zarac 1
  To: Captain Karl Valvanchi, Sas Darona

Karl,

Your brother copied me your recent communications. I am appalled that you threatened him with plague and certain death. Your brother, as you well know, is doing an excellent job in difficult circumstances.

As your father and head of the Valvanchi house, I command you to do everything in your power to assist him. It is a Council Decree. The Dodecahedron Dome must close.

I have written to your commanding officer and made our position abundantly clear. Your brother's requests are supported at the highest levels from within the Zaracan Council.

Your family expects,
Your father.

From: Captain Karl Valvanchi, Sas Darona
  To: Ambassador Nikato Valvanchi II, Earth
Dear Nikki,

The Dome must close.

I am on my way, together with the tribal dancers and sand lizards.

We expect to arrive Friday. Please make all necessary arrangements.

In my family I trust.
To the Council I obey.
Karl

Chapter 6

A Roar of Fire and Light

S o, it comes to it: the moment I have been dreading all week. Now there is no turning back.

Prince Teodor travelled within an eight-vehicle convoy from Buckingham Palace along the river, and into Domeside. Drones had been deployed to stop side traffic, and their vehicles sped on unimpeded, coming to a stop on the circular plaza under the cathedral, one of the oldest buildings in the entire city and said to be the beating heart of the Dome.

From the vehicles emerged a dozen fully armed Royal Guards in red and silver, and six huge cy-wolves, considered to be the bare minimum to escort and defend the Prince. Teodor was the last to emerge. He acknowledged his escort with a nod of thanks, then turned to look up the wide staircase leading to a massive door, where a bishop, and a crowd of others he could not identify, waited.

I am well protected, Teodor told himself. *Also, there was no cathedral in my nightmare. Tunnels yes. Cathedral no. 'Pull yourself together.'* That's what his mother would say. *'You must do this for your people; after*

all, they only expect you to sing.'
All at once, he remembered the alternative. Oh, why had his mother cancelled the blades fight? How would it feel to be making his way to fight in the Dome Militant gyms? Would he be afraid if he had a blade in each hand? Still, that was no longer an option.

Teodor had been inside the cathedral many times, but still he found the towering columns vast and beautiful. He was glad they had built the Dome around this sacred place. It was said to have been a church for over three thousand years. As with all truly ancient cathedrals, the altar was shielded from view by a single large tapestry said to have taken three hundred embroiderers three hundred days to create. On Sunday, the curtain would be drawn. The population would lean in to glimpse the priests and their rituals; instead, they would see Prince Teodor leading a choir of Domeside children.

"It will be spectacular," the art director had assured Teodor's mother. "It will also be emotional. You will see. They will call it genius."

Teodor was unconvinced. It was a trick that involved drawing a curtain (a vast curtain, for sure) but still a curtain. Nevertheless, the artistic team had their way. What had started as a small performance by a children's choir had grown into a no-expense-spared production, complete with lights, special effects, abstract art installation as a set, costumes by a top designer from Old Fleet Street, and high-definition surround sound.

A trick involving the curtain, Teodor repeated, with weary impatience. *Let's finish this show and be done with it.*

"Your Highness, we have a costume prepared for you," one of his hosts said.

Teodor nodded. All the children of the choir were wearing costumes, so he had no choice.

After all the rushing, Guy Erma found himself standing on the side of the altar in the cathedral—waiting. *Waiting, and what for? How long did it take for a prince to get dressed?*

All the other kids had their costumes on. Admittedly, they had arrived in the cathedral over an hour before the prince. But there was a buzz of excitement that the teachers were finding hard to contain. Guy was not in the choir of Domeside children. Guy was the prince's understudy and stand-in. Over the past month, he had taken part in a dozen singing rehearsals, where the prince himself hadn't even been present. He had enjoyed being the stand-in prince. He had even enjoyed the performance, maybe not exactly singing, but he liked the praise and attention he received by being centre stage.

Supposedly, all this made up for not having to fight the prince at blades. It didn't. Guy only had to close his eyes to feel the weight of his fighting blades in the palms of his hands and imagine stepping up across a fighting mat from the prince. Still, it was not to be.

At least as understudy, he did not have to dress up. The understudy had no costume. In fact, his role today was 'to be introduced'. Guy was due to meet Prince Teodor, before handing over the role to him. This was considered a great honour. Right now, he had been waiting twenty minutes for this so-called 'great honour'.

If only they would let me fight the prince, Guy thought. *That would have been great – to meet him with a blade in each hand*. Guy kicked the skirting board.

Gold shorts, a shimmering chiffon shirt and the wings of an angel. Teodor looked at the proffered clothes with dismay. Before him, the head designer of the fashion house Riffault was talking him through the intricate details of the outfit.

"Here you see an earlier design."

Teodor froze, because the youth who stepped forth—while maybe two inches taller than him—was otherwise identical to him in face, in stature, in hair and in manner. Teodor had heard of such models, young men—for there was no doubt this youth was older than him—who earned a living imitating him. Until today, he had never met one. He swallowed hard, but forced himself to smile and say, "Aren't those shorts - ahem - a bit short?"

"They are based on the fighting gear of a Dome Militant competition combatant," the designer said. "You are supposed to be a warrior angel."

Teodor nodded and stifled a sigh. It was years since he had given up trying to have a say on his clothes. He was forever told how hundreds, if not thousands, of jobs depended on his wearing Old Fleet Street Fashion. He had to live his life as a walking talking advert for the craftsmen and women of Domeside. "We have a changing room prepared for you," the look-a-like youth cut-in. "I can help you dress."

Teodor wanted to shout: *I can dress myself!* Except he could see the clothes had some complex buckles and fastenings, and the wings appeared to be stuck on by magic. "Thank you, that would be kind," he replied, forcing himself to meet the gaze of a face so much a mirror image of his own.

"Afterwards, the Press will want photos," the designer said.

This time, Teodor could not help himself. Involuntarily, he took a step back. *Did they expect to photograph me in that?*

"I can do the Press, if you like?" the lookalike said, waving him to the next room.

Teodor hesitated, he wanted to say yes. He hated posing for photographs – detested how it was never one photograph, but multiple shots with photographers shouting at him to smile, turn or do some such ridiculous thing.

The lookalike was watching him. "I don't mind," he added.

Teodor sensed genuine kindness behind this offer. This confused him. He felt himself liking the youth even though he knew all his advisors would hate this model on sight. He was a forbidden friend, and Teodor knew he should mistrust him. But his instincts told him something different.

"Someone might notice." Teodor replied.

The boy smiled, exactly the diffident smile Teodor allowed himself in public. *So, like me*, Teodor thought in wonder – *maybe no-one would notice?*

"Can you sing?" he joked.

"Yes," the other replied, before finishing in a burst of song. "Just not like that, not like that..."

Teodor thought he recognised a popular song, and he laughed. Obviously, a young man working as a model for one of the Old Fleet Street fashion houses would have good singing voice.

"All right, just help me with this costume - if needed, do you have these shorts in a larger size?"

"You'll be fine," the other replied.

"And the changing area has been checked for cameras?" Teodor heard himself ask, and immediately regretted it. Even to himself, he sounded fearful.

"Checked and checked again. Wed never leave something like that to chance. Only the finished costume gets photographed, not anything else. What do you take The Riffaut for?" The youth said.

"I see," Teodor said. "I had to check."

"Quite so."

"Have you been my understudy? They said I would have a chance to meet him?"

"Understudy, no. That's Guy. Guy Erma. You'll like him - you sing better than him." The lookalike winked, and pulled the door closed on the changing room.

Out of boredom, Guy moved closer to where he knew the prince was changing. One of the Royal Guards held up a hand to stop him.

Chocolate box soldiers, Guy thought, eyeing the red trim along the seams of the silver trousers. *What good would they be in a fight?* They were purely ceremonial soldiers, brought here to look impressive, not protect their prince.

Through the half-open door, Guy saw the prince dressed as an angel in tunic, shorts and sandals. The designers had said it was supposed to look like a blade fighting outfit, but Guy could not see it. *Not golden shorts like that—what fighter would wear those?* Also, Guy would have liked to see some evidence of the so-called injury that had precluded the prince from entering the blades fight. He expected to see a bandage on one of his knees at the very least. But no, nothing. The prince's legs were bare. Guy checked to be sure. The prince had cream, plump legs, and the designers had twisted the long laces of the golden sandals, criss-crossed from his ankles to his knees. *Was that top-grain leather painted in real gold*, he wondered. *Complicated and impractical.* And no sign of a bandage, bruising, redness or any sign of injury – none at all. *Maybe the prince was chicken after all.* Guy kicked the skirting board again. *And I'm going to be late for maths.*

Behind Guy, there was a commotion among the crowd of waiting children; this distracted the Guard, so Guy moved closer to where he could examine a neat pile of clothes on a chair inside the door. Those were the prince's clothes, the ones he had worn before putting on the angel costume. Guy found himself looking at the labels. The prince had been wearing a handmade designer shirt and suit, the best Old Fleet Street had to offer. His shoes were handmade too. As Guy peered down, he saw the prince's name carefully painted inside the heel. He felt a little sick. He knew how much handmade shoes cost, and he could not imagine spending so much on his feet. And it looked like he and the prince might be the same size. He moved his own boot-clad foot a little closer. Yes, he and the prince wore the same shoe size. *What must it be like to own – indeed to wear – shoes like that?*

He peeped through the door again. Photos—they were taking photos. Guy looked at the time and made a decision. Calmly bending down, he picked up the shoes and put them in his bag. As he went to swing the bag over his shoulder, he felt – rather than saw – someone watching. Instinctively, he turned and met the blue eyes of Teodor. The prince had seen what he had done.

Guy froze. At his feet, the prince's shoes were gone. He knew they were in the misshapen gym bag over his shoulder, but who else knew? Across from him, the prince said nothing just watched. Guy returned his gaze.

What should he do? To put the shoes back was to risk detection. Was the prince going to tell on him?

Guy scrutinised the boy standing across from him. The prince had golden blond hair – but otherwise, they were the same age; give or take a few days. Apart from that, what else did they have in common? The prince had the plump flesh of someone who never went hungry – probably had more clothes than anyone rightly needed, and he was surrounded with fashion designers, staff and press reporters – all of whom agreed to his every request.

All this, Guy saw, in less than the second it took him to rise and look up. Did the prince even need these shoes? Did Guy himself need patent leather, high-polish brown shoes? Whether the prince needed them or not, Guy did not think of himself as a thief. Should he? Then he saw something in the prince's eyes. Teodor had not moved a muscle. He had not even smiled, but Guy thought his eyes said. "It's alright, take them."

Someone was calling the prince's name. Guy briefly saw the concealed resignation before the prince looked away. Guy took his chance and bolted. Only the choirmaster called to him.

"Guy, Guy." Guy froze. Had he been caught? "Guy, we want to do the solo one more time while we wait?"

"Sir, I've got double maths."

"Come on, Guy, be a good lad. All the kids are waiting." It was true, the crowd of costumed children was becoming ever more boisterous – with hysterical laughter breaking out here and there. But Guy had a pair of stolen shoes in his bag - he needed to escape, yet he saw how bored and restless the other kids were, how some were making pleading gestures for him to do something. Anything.

"Always singing," muttered Guy. "I thought the first time I met Prince Teodor I would have a blade in each hand."

"Life's not fair. Hey? Still, we've not thrown you to the borgs – not yet anyhow."

Guy looked up and saw his teacher laughing. "C'mon, one last time, then you can go."

Guy set aside his jacket and his bag, and took his place centre stage, looking out over the innumerable rows of empty seating. He looked back once, but no one cared about his belongings. If it were not for the stolen shoes he knew—he would have felt elated. Instead, disappointment overwhelmed him.

I am a thief, he told himself, *no one here knows it except one person. I have let myself and my prince down. Why did I do that?*

Teodor stood to one side of the altar watching the shoe thief sing. No one had noticed that his shoes were gone; undoubtedly, there would be a fuss when they found out. But given there was a whole street of shops a short distance away, he figured someone would be sent running. Or he could call the boy out. If he was his understudy, they were due to be 'introduced'. Maybe he could say something casual like "Oh, and I'd like my shoes back."

He imagined how amazed everyone would be that he had even noticed. The only problem was, if he did that, this boy would be in trouble. Why had he stolen the shoes? Did he want to wear them?

Teodor looked at him. The shoe thief was wearing battered, hand-me-down boots, which might once have been part of a Dome Militant uniform. Similarly, he was clad in an old, washed-to-grey Dome Militant tracksuit – which appeared to be at least one size too big. And he was skinny. *Huh!* Teodor thought. His gaze followed where the boy shoved his sleeves up his arms to the elbow. His forearms were stick thin – bone and well-defined muscle. *Here was someone who trained for hours on end and was never once offered sugar buns for breakfast. Did he fight blades?*

Teodor looked for clues. If this boy trained with the Dome Militant, he would be wearing blades in a harness strapped across the small of his back. No, his clothes were too bulky for him to see. Still, he had the black hair and dark eyes of a Domeside boy. What was he doing here? Singing in the Cathedral?

He had a good voice, Teodor thought, *a little shaky on the top notes*. Why would a Dome Militant boy be chosen to play his part? Unless he was too young to be Dome Militant. Teodor paused – maybe that was it. Maybe this boy was fifteen, not yet sixteen – the minimum age for joining the Dome Militant as an apprentice, and maybe he took the shoes because he needed to sell them for money. What did Domeside boys do if they didn't enter the Dome Militant? Teodor knew the statistics well. Almost half of all fifteen-year-old Domeside boys dropped out of school. Many would be taken into the Dome Militant, as his father had intended, but more disappeared from school than were places in the black and gold. What happened to the rest?

Maybe that is why he stole the shoes. He must need the money. Teodor thought, *I don't need those shoes. And I need to speak to him. I need to compare notes, because while I know the songs, I am not sure of the moves or the cues.*

"Thanks, Guy," the choirmaster said. "That was great." Simultaneously, he half-waved, half-bowed for Teodor to walk onto the stage.

"This is Guy Erma," he said to Teodor.

So that was his name. Guy. A common enough name, normally short for Guillaume – after Teodor's great-grandfather; and Erma, the name given to all boys born without a father. So we are alike, Teodor thought. *This boy Guy has no father; my father was murdered. But is that the same? Is it worse to never have known your father, or to have loved him dearly – only for him to be blasted to pieces before his palace gates?*

Without thinking, Teodor frowned and when he looked back, Guy Erma was moving. Fast. Guy grabbed his bag - the one with the stolen shoes and a jacket. He snapped his running blades to his feet and bounded off. He dodged the many adults who tried to stop him. And with the running blades on his feet, he covered the space to the exit in mere instants. At the great wooden door, he paused and looked back.

Teodor – who had been watching – caught and held his gaze. Astonished, he saw neither fear nor reverence in the other's eyes – as he clenched his hand into a fist, which he briefly pressed to his heart in a parting salute.

"Guy," the choirmaster called.

Too slow. That one moves like the wind.

"Double maths!" Guy shouted back.

"Guy, don't you want to meet..."

You're wasting your breath, thought Teodor. The boy was headed out the door at a trot.

"...the prince?" the choirmaster said with a shrug.

"Double maths," repeated Teodor. "Impressive. Now I do want to meet him. What was his name again?"

"Guy Erma, my prince. Everyone knows Guy Erma."

"Guy Erma? Really? Everyone knows Guy Erma. Tell him I was sorry not to meet him."

"I will, my prince. Are we all set?" Then, he was distracted. "What is it?"

One of the men, who had been smirking a few minutes before, stepped forward to block Teodor returning to his place on the altar. "The prince's communicator is interfering with the sound system. He has a nice kit, but the equipment here isn't that sophisticated, and, well," The man was speaking fast, and if Teodor did not understand the detail, it was evident by the way he pointed and gestured what he meant. *Still, to hand over my communicator...* Teodor hesitated and glanced round.

In addition to the eight Royal Guards, there were two cyborgs he could almost touch, on this side of the altar. Another two were patrolling with cy-wolves inside the curtain. His bodyguard was sitting three meters away in the audience. The communicator did look strange with his costume. He went and placed it with his clothes. *Why did I let that boy take my shoes? Tsk. Now there will be a fuss, or I will go home barefoot. Why did I let him do that?*

"Prince Teodor, this way. Here, my prince!" Irritated, Teodor walked back and, in doing so, glanced down the tight spiral stair to the catacombs. He glimpsed a Royal Guard and a cy-wolf hiding out of sight. He took his place at the centre of the altar. Ignoring both the cheeky wink of one of the girls and an older boy cuffing a youngster, Teodor paused. From here the Cathedral was vast.

Why is my bodyguard so far away? Where are the Royal Guards? Where are the cy-wolves? Teodor moved uncomfortably. He was well-aware that the Royal Guards, in their designer red and silver uniform, were not a fighting force like the Dome Militant. It was a small security troop, which had been selected for their loyalty and family connections. No, the real muscle today was the giant cy-wolves – the largest and strongest of their kind. Taken from the wild, they were fitted with cyborg brains that made them easy to control; and metal fangs and teeth that made them impossible to withstand. Teodor wished for a moment that he had a cy-wolf at his side. Of course, they would never allow it: cy-wolves were dangerous.

He sighed. *Oh, I wish this was over.* He nodded to the organist, counted out his introduction in his head, and started to sing.

The sound was perfect. His voice, backed by soft organ chords ringing out across the Cathedral. Teodor stepped forward one step, moving with the song. His sandal caught on the trap door. *What was under there? No matter.* He carried on: *three steps, stop.* The choir of children would gather around him. *Where were the children? They should have been here by now.* He took a moment to glance over his shoulder. The choir was still not moving. Unless he was mistaken, the older boys were holding back the youngsters, but why? *Face forward*, he thought. *Never look back.*

Five, Six, Seven, Eight. Teodor took a last breath, as he counted the intro in his head. *At least this was the third verse. It was nearly over.*

Not long now. Not long until they discover my shoes are gone.

His train of thought was broken. The lights had gone out. All the spotlights, all the high-hanging Cathedral lights, all the side lamps. For a moment, he felt blind. He heard a youngster gasp. From darkness, thin rays offered grey light from high roof windows,

OK, not bad. A power cut. I can still see.

He heard two sharp bangs – and a clatter of wood. The three-hundred-year-old altar curtain fell shut in a rush of wind. Several children shouted out in alarm. With the curtain closed, Teodor could no longer see the great wooden door. To escape, he would have to run around or push under the heavy drapes.

His bodyguard and most of the Royal Guards were also on the far side. Behind him, some of the children were sobbing. He should comfort them. He must act like a Prince. He turned. An explosion engulfed him in smoke and light and sent him tumbling onto his backside.

An attack. His head rang, yet he could not hear anything. He tasted blood in his nose and throat.

Another bang and a flash. Now he was blind, dazed and disorientated. *Where's my bodyguard? Where's the door?* He tried to stand. He heard (*or did he feel*) heavy footsteps running in from several directions. Shots rang out above his head. He crouched to the floor, taking a sprinter's position, as he looked round for a chance to escape. *Who was shooting? Was it his guard? Who were they shooting at?*

Children ran and screamed looking for escape. Teodor watched a girl as a bullet hit her shoulder and spun her round, so a second impact exploded above her heart, and she fell. He realised other children were also down or injured on the stage.

The barrage of fire continued. A huge crash, and the altar shook. Teodor realised the giant tapestry curtain had been shot to pieces and fallen from its hooks to the ground. The resulting wind dispelled the smoke. He looked around, seeking safety, but instead, he saw men in black uniforms leaping towards him. Only they were not men; they were not even cyborgs. Teodor's attackers were the Battle Borgs of the Dome Militant.

Teodor kicked the first Borg's arm, as he reached to grab him. Even in the gloom, the Battle Borg's skin appeared grey; a deep black crack ran from the base of his thumb up his arm, gaping wide at the wrist, showing dead, rotten flesh; beneath, his robotic core. Another black mottled face loomed down on him. Teodor slapped the face in a spinning blade turn, satisfied to feel the paper-like cheek rip under the palm of his hand. A third Battle Borg grabbed him by the waist from behind and threw him over his shoulder. The sour-sweet stench of drying and decaying flesh filled Teodor's nostrils. A jolt, as he realised, they had jumped down through the trap door. *They are taking me.*

"I am your prince! Let me go!" cried Teodor. He kicked and beat his captor with his hands and feet.

The Battle Borg paused, threw him to the wall – letting him fall to the ground. There, the Borg kicked Teodor in the legs and belly, and slapped him hard around the head.

The prince covered his head and cowered; yet he still looked up and tried again. "In the name of the King, I command you."

They pressed a cloth over his face. Dazed, breathless and with blood in his mouth, he recognised the smell and tried not to breathe. So, they slapped him again, and he gasped. "I am Prince Teodor." The fumes overwhelmed his senses.

When the Borg threw him over his shoulder once again, Teodor was limp. He could not move, could not hear, could not smell, but he could see, and he could feel. He knew they were running.

Guy laughed as he bounded down the stairs of the Cathedral and sprinted across the plaza to where, on the far side, the market was in full swing. Guy ran between the stalls, where he could easily disappear, all the while taking in the bustle, colours and movement of the early morning trading.

The market was different today. After all, it was Royal Ascot Friday – the first day of Royal Ascot Weekend. The bakers were displaying special Ascot cakes, the florists hung bouquets of seasonal magnolia blooms, and the veg stalls had great bowls of the season's strawberries, red and plump, shining with juice. Guy felt a thrill to see them. Strawberries meant it was the end of winter. Everyone loved Royal Ascot Weekend.

"Hey, Guy! Over here, Guy!"

Guy stopped and turned to see a small, plump market stallholder running after him. He had only run a few steps, but he was flushed and out of breath. Guy knew what he wanted. Delighted, he ran back. "Juke! Hi, Jukona!"

"You're still ready to help me tomorrow? At Royal Ascot. I'll pay you, Guy."

"Yes, yes of course." It was the highlight of the weekend for Guy – to see the greatest racing gorans of the empire, running in the Royal Ascot.

"Okay, you have to be ready at five. Five, you hear me?"

If Juke were still talking, Guy was no longer listening. He had heard something. A shout! He looked towards the Cathedral. A shot? The entire market fell silent, only for the silence to be rent by automatic gunfire. Around him all the traders and customers turned at the sound of screams – children's screams. Guy looked at Juke then back to the Cathedral.

"I'd better go back," Guy said.

A great creaking crash sent birds flying round the square, as a cloud of wind and dust billowed out from

the Cathedral doors. Guy started to move past Juke –
only the trader caught him by the elbow and held him.
The bang of the explosion echoed around the square.

"No, Guy, no. Don't go there."

"But..."

The bang echoed inside his head.

"There's nothing you can do."

Guy and Juke watched them running. Dome Militant,
soldiers, some stallholders, all running across the square
towards the Cathedral. In the distance, sirens were
sounding.

Guy hesitated. "The kids." He meant his half-brothers
and sisters of House Jewel.

Juke gripped his arm. "Go to school, Guy. Go to school.
There's nothing more you can do here."

Chapter 7

The Emperor of all Dodecahedral

The white teeth of the one-year-old goran cubs had been stained black, and Sayginn flinched. *Who did that to cubs?*

Looking closer, she saw its juvenile teeth had also been shaped into pointed fangs. *No doubt, to match the black-varnished, sharpened fingernails of Emperor Frederon*, she thought.

It was not unusual for an emperor or prince of Dodecahedral to travel with goran cubs at their side. Imperial transports were long and wide, with the passenger cabin shaped like a basin, allowing yearling gorans to curl up calmly at their owners' feet.

However, these tiger gorans were not calm. One hissed and spat at Sayginn, another reached up, snarling, to claw her hemline.

From behind her, a claw-like hand with black nails grabbed the cub by the scruff of its neck and pulled it back. The cub hissed and spat. Emperor Frederon growled at the animal, revealing his teeth – which were also stained black and filed to sharp points. The goran beat a hasty retreat.

Black varnished nails, black filed teeth, beady black eyes, long black curls framing a narrow, cruel face, Frederon was Emperor of the twelve planets of Dodecahedral.

And my future husband, thought Sayginn. *How could he think he could ever replace Serge?* She had always thought herself lucky to have married Serge, but now the girl from the impoverished, yet ancient house was being considered as a possible wife for an emperor. *What did it matter that the emperor was sixty-two years older than her in these days of rejuvenation treatment?*

She turned to where Emperor Frederon was finishing an interview. Frederon could not be called good-looking. His nose was angular. His much-discussed hawkish look was a practiced mannerism. The Emperor would narrow his gaze, jut his chin out and peer at you with unfriendly eyes. His tall, slim body was the result of a careful diet and repeated surgery, not exercise. His hands were strong. He had a habit of clenching and squeezing his fingers around small stone balls, until the stone exploded between his fingers. And then, of course, were his famous black nails, shaped into points, which the Emperor himself referred to as his claws.

Chalky stones exploding between strong fingers tipped with black claws, a piercing look, and the power of life or death over all he met. Was it any wonder most of the court was nervous around him? And yet, they told Sayginn she had nothing to fear. He was to be her husband. Sayginn wondered if they had said the same to Frederon's eight previous wives, who were all abandoned – even those who had borne him daughters. Frederon wanted – no, needed – a son. He also wanted to seize the six planets that rightly belonged to Teodor.

Sayginn looked across at Frederon once more. He was chatting with a press droid which was hovering between them. The car was sound-proofed, so it was good for press interviews. And a weekend of entertainment at Royal Ascot was newsworthy. He would make the most of it. So should Sayginn. She smiled when the droid camera pointed towards her and squeezed the Emperor's hand when this seemed to be required.

As the interview ended, Frederon pinched the droid between finger and thumb and tossed it from the car window. Alone, in the transport cocoon, the Emperor relaxed. He dropped his false publicity-hungry grin and eased his shoulders into the leather of the seats.

Sayginn's communicator beeped. She glanced at it. Had she not switched it off for this short ride one-on-one with the Emperor?

"Sayginn, it is good to see you. You look well."

Oh, it was an emergency call. Alarm code 19997. She deciphered the digits '1', the code for the highest level of emergency; '999' was the emergency code for Attack; '7' meant Prince. '19997': High level emergency - An attack on the Prince. Prince Teodor?

"My Emperor, I'm sorry, I must take this." Sayginn said, checking her red-flashing communicator.

"Freddie – call me Freddie. Switch that off!"

"Yes, but." Sayginn protested. An attack on Teo? Was he alive? It was not a '15' code – that meant death. So, not dead. And he had his security: Royal Guards, cy-wolves, even the Dome Militant. This is the only time I will have alone with the Emperor. My future husband. "Yes, of course. I will take the message later at the palace," said Sayginn, rebuked. She turned off the flashing light.

"Have you thought any more about my proposal, Sayginn? You must marry me. We two must stick together; me, an old widower, and you, my nephew's widow. Apart, we wither, our houses wither. Together, oh Sayginn, we would be so strong! Have you read the contract my people sent you?"

"Four sons, Freddie?" Sayginn had thought it was a misprint and queried the clause. The answer had not pleased her. The Emperor expected her to bear four sons. Four sons and Teodor - one more than Baron Storm. She sighed.

"You will not mind? I know you will not, Sayginn. You understand, don't you? Our marriage brings power and influence. You give me these sons, and we will both be more secure."

"Yes, but what about Teodor? He is also your blood."

"My brother's grandson. So yes, my blood, but not my direct line. Teodor is already King of Earth. I predict that as King, he will be greater than his father. Maybe I can take him to court, maybe I can try and give him a backbone. Teodor needs to understand that only chaos and pain follow when power is weak. Until then, he is not suited to be Emperor. By his character, he isn't suited. Give me a son, Sayginn. No, give me sons. So we might choose which one should be Emperor. Now kiss me."

Sayginn looked around for inspiration but instead saw a newsreel running on a small screen with the sound muted. She saw shots of destruction and darkness in the cathedral, weeping children, a teacher shot dead.

19997. She remembered: an attack on the Prince. Where was Teodor? On the screen, the news reporter was talking while a droid showed images of the destroyed curtains, the blasted artefacts, trampled, blood-stained headdress and torn, scattered sheets of choral music. "You see this?"

A ticker tape across the screen was summarizing: at least ten die in cathedral explosion.

Frederon snorted in disgust.

He does not seem surprised, thought Sayginn. She checked the Emperor's face and then the screen. He knew about this!

"We would be stronger if we were married. This kind of nonsense would stop if I had more than one heir, if I had many, many sons."

Another headline flashed red and white. Prince Teodor missing, feared dead.

"What?" She could barely take in what the emperor was saying. Teodor dead? Could it be true? No, a single word was a scream inside her head. Her breath came out in pants. "No, no, no."

"Sayginn, just sign the contract. I will place all my power and influence toward retrieving your son."

Sayginn pulled her gaze away from the screen to look at the emperor in disbelief. "What?"

"He's alive; he's been taken – that's all."

"You did this?" suddenly the words of the Emperor became clear in their meaning.

"Teodor needs to understand that: chaos and pain follow when power is weak. It'll be an experience, that's all." the Emperor said and shrugged. "Be good for his character, give him a backbone."

"Backbone? Is this your idea of a joke?"

All at once, Frederon stretched across the car and shoved her up against the window with a claw-like hand around her neck. "You forget, Sayginn. Without your son, you are nothing. A wealthy widow somewhat past her prime – you should be grateful I considered you at all."

Chapter 8

The Valvanchi Diplomatic Corps

K arl Valvanchi had taken a simple personnel carrier to travel from Sas Darona to the second planet of the Dodecahedral Empire. Earth was temperate, with broad land masses and rich reserves of minerals – making it ideal as the "workshop" of the Empire. In recent years, they had even started mining asteroids, moons and gas giants throughout their solar system. So it was deemed a rich and prospering if still underdeveloped, planetary system.

During his reign, King Serge's principal concern had been that his governments – for there were a dozen or so local governments – manage the inequalities between the haves and have-nots of Earth society; something the Emperor had noticeably failed to implement across the other planets.

Serge's democratic ideals had brought prosperity and fast engineering development. Karl gazed in awe at the new spaceport. Designed like a vast space snowflake, it had six broad tunnels, the spokes of the snowflake, leading to a central transit hub from where shuttles sped down to the surface. Along each of the six branches, ships were parked, nose first – clustered by size, class and origin. As Karl approached the docking platform high in orbit above Earth, he started to wish he had chosen a more suitable craft.

Nikato would, of course, have lent him the family yacht if he'd asked. The yacht, at least, would have been ostentatious enough to stand out among the array of visiting dignitaries and celebrities. Earth's Royal Ascot Weekend was a must-see festival among some United Races Elites who liked the fact that money alone could not buy you access to some events. You had to be famous, to have influence – not just across Known Space, but also as far out as this remote primitive backwater. And if you were not 'known on Earth' then 'how splendid' to be 'totally anonymous' for two days, while spending vast sums of money on fashion and entertainment in the hope of being noticed.

Not that Karl was interested in impressing the United Races social elite. He was born Valvanchi. He had nothing more to prove. No family in all the United Races had more influence, and no individual had more access to such unlimited funds. Yet Karl had turned his back on this birthright when he had joined the Zaracan Space Rangers. For Karl, life was not that of a gilded prince working his way from one prestigious diplomatic posting to the next. Neither had he wished to join the financial units with their vast fortunes; he had no interest in the mysterious black arts they used to grow this wealth. He was not one to fly into Dodecahedral space in a glittering space jet and yet.

It was when he saw the row of parked Dome Militant carriers, that Karl wished he had a more impressive craft. His small military ship – with its proud Zaracan colours and Valvanchi flag of white and turquoise – seemed to shrink to insignificance, as it passed under the bows of the great Dome Militant troop carriers. The Dodecahedron insignia – twelve pentagons joined into one geodesic dome – was emblazoned in gold on their prows.

"Room for eight ships, would you say?" he said aloud to the captain, as he stood on the flight deck watching their approach. "Probable capacity 850 to 1,000 men and another four empty bays over there?" he pointed.

The captain nodded and replied, "I heard they had four trapped in orbit around Sas Darona – thanks to the lockdown."

"How many men do you think the Dome Militant have in training on Sas Darona?" Karl asked.

"You're asking me?"

"I had thought it was under a thousand, but."

They were passing a huge cargo ship, again painted in Dome Militant colours.

Karl pointed. "That's one of their supply ships, so you have to wonder how much more is going on."

"Maybe the Dome Militant have bases elsewhere in the Dodecahedral Empire?"

"No, the Emperor forbade it. In theory, the Dome Militant is a training scheme for the poor boys of the city. It was supposed to prepare them for the regular army. But the Emperor reneged on that promise as well. Any who transfer to the normal Imperial Army find they are little more than servants to the main troops and deprived of any form of advancement – however skilled they are."

"So, King Serge acquired his personal army."

"Indeed, King Serge had his own army of 20,000 blades – and all at once, he was a real threat, a true power. So, they killed him."

"Who?" the captain asked.

"Who knows? There's a truly short list of possible suspects. However, they didn't count on Chart Segat. He has kept the Dome Militant running in King Serge's absence. Oh, they cut his funding, so in turn, Chart Segat began large-scale mining of monazite-9 on Sas Darona. To do so, he needed the co-operation of the tribes. The tribes most eager to help were those with a grudge against us. So, we're left managing a war on Sas Darona, while the Dome Militant goes from strength to strength."

"They say he will be voted out at the Dome Debate."

"Yes, let's hope so. Regent Sayginn should retake control just as her husband once did."

"What difference will it make?"

Karl smiled as he thought about it. "The big difference is that the regent has signed a whole host of treaties with the United Races. She must curb and clamp down on illegal activities. And if she does not know about them, well, Nikki and I have a list."

The captain laughed.

Karl watched as he manoeuvred the ship into its docking bay. "No one to meet us?" Karl asked, looking out a side window into the empty reception lounge.

"We don't have all of the paperwork yet, so we stay on board until it arrives."

Karl ignored him. "There's nobody out there."

"It's still safer to stay on board, sir."

"I'll let the boys off. We've all been cooped up for too long."

"Yes, but..."

Their ship had been allowed to dock on an isolated gangway, distant from most other ships. Karl stepped into a utilitarian reception lounge with a row of folding seats, a pile of forgotten crates, a drinks machine and a bin. Because the lounge sat on the station's outer edge, the gravity was a little heavier than Karl expected. He stumbled as he headed to the large window to look down onto the planet below.

The Sas Darona dancers followed him off the shuttle. Out of the confined space, they burst into motion, turning somersaults and spinning. Distracted by their youthful athleticism, Karl did not notice the heavy tread of boots until they were on the far side of the door. As they came through the door, the eight Sas Darona tribesmen drew themselves into a line along the far wall. Karl sensed they were both in awe and in fear of the Dome Militant. For his part, Karl was curious to see the Dome Militant on their home turf. He was impressed by the pristine cut of their uniforms, the shine of the gold and yellow trims and details, the smooth faces, clean hands and polished boots. They were men of whom any commander would be proud.

He heard a low whistle and saw his ship's captain urging him to return on board. It was too late for that; the Dome Militant had already seen him. Their commander called to his lieutenant for a checklist and having glanced at the crate of sand lizards, he strode across to lift the chin and stare into the face of one of the tribal dancers. The tribesman blinked once in acknowledgement, and the Dome Militant commander turned on the spot and walked back.

He knows him, Karl thought. But were these dancers not from friendly tribes? He caught himself glancing at the eight slim youths at his side; had his careful checks been in vain?

"Fine-looking warriors," the Dome Militant officer said.

The Dome Militant Commander scrutinised Karl. He made a play of checking the paperwork twice. "And you are?"

"My name is Captain Karl Valvanchi."

The Dome Militant commander looked him up and down. A flutter passed through his men. Clearly, he recognised the name. Karl smiled to himself, pleased his name alone had drawn their attention. "May I ask your name?"

"I don't have to tell you. But you may call me Commander Tilson." Tilson tapped the clipboard in his hand. "We have no details of passengers on the manifest, so what are you doing here?"

Karl wondered whether he had to reply, but in the end, he decided he had little to hide. "I am travelling to see my brother, Nikato Valvanchi. He is the Ambassador on Earth."

"Well, in that case, we need identification papers: a visa, a letter of introduction, and are you claiming diplomatic status?"

Karl half-shrugged. He was not entirely sure.

"You will also need a letter of invitation signed by Regent Sayginn. Do you have that?"

Karl was momentarily distracted by how the captain of his shuttle shook his head and waved him back on board. Had he known this would happen? "I have my United Races identification card," Karl replied, with what he hoped was a winning smile. If he had meant it as a joke, he was taken aback by its reception.

The Dome Militant Commander barked back at him. "That isn't a valid identification on Earth or anywhere in the Dodecahedral."

"Of course not, it's only valid in all of Known Space, except for this backwater empire," Karl snapped. His brother Nikato had hypothesized that the humans liked to have their own identification procedures, so they could keep close tabs on all visitors from outside the empire – but whatever the reason, Karl was annoyed. Out of the corner of his eye, he saw the captain vigorously shaking his head in a warning.

The Dome Militant Commander smiled and said with some relish. "Under our laws, you are an illegal alien – I will therefore be taking you into custody."

Karl's mouth dropped open, but no words followed. Were the Dome Militant serious? Did they not realise who he was? That he should be a prisoner of the Dome Militant was unthinkable. Would they go through with this charade? "Let me call my brother," Karl replied, aware that the Sas Darona tribal dancers were riveted by this exchange.

"Hold him!" ordered the Commander.

In an instant, four Dome Militant immobilised Karl. The commander reached to remove his wrist-mounted communicator from Karl's forearm. "I'll take that."

"I don't need that device to speak with my brother," Karl snapped.

"Well, you can try, of course. But you'll find this entire spaceport is lined with mixed alloys, to protect our equipment from unwanted telepathic interference."

"Commander," the captain protested. "Karl Valvanchi is a senior member of the Valvanchi family; if you continue like this, you will face a serious diplomatic incident."

"Shut him up."

One of the larger Dome Militant soldiers stepped forward, blades in both hands. When he went to strike the Captain, he did not use the cutting edge but the blunt handle of his dagger – grasped within his fist. With one blow across his temples, the Captain was knocked unconscious to the ground.

Karl went to protest, except Commander Tilson continued. "Strip search, I think."

Karl wrestled against his captors. He knew of many simple strategies to prevent his clothes from being removed – but before he could employ any of them, the blades flashed in their hands and, with lightning moves, they sliced the cloth from his body.

"Leave his shorts," called the Commander. "I'm off to lunch after this, and I don't want to ruin my appetite."

Now Karl was spread-eagled against the vast window looking out over Earth, wearing only his underpants and his boots. His clothes were sliced to ribbons around his feet, and he was bleeding from numerous small cuts – where the soldiers had not been too careful with their razor-sharp blades.

Nikki, where are you? Karl sent a desperate telepathic cry, even though – in all likelihood – his brother would not hear him.

I'm here; I'm here. On cue, Nikato Valvanchi, prince of the House Valvanchi and Ambassador from the Zaracan Democratic Union to Earth, with four guards and an admin assistant, crashed through the double doors.

Running alongside her uncle wearing her house colours of turquoise and white was the fifteen-year-old Nuria Valvanchi, shapeshifted to her slim self – pale-skinned, black-eyed and with a mane of turquoise and white hair tied in loose bunches down her back.

Still panting, Nikato's assistant handed the necessary paperwork to the Dome Militant commander. "Karl Valvanchi's identification, visa, letter of introduction and a letter of invitation signed by Regent Sayginn herself."

Nikato drew himself up to his full height and shouted at the Dome Militant Commander. "You will release my brother at once. And don't think the Regent won't hear of this."

The Commander held out a hand to take the paperwork and scrutinised every page. Finally, he nodded to his men. "Lunch," he murmured. With a sharp salute, he and his troops disappeared as quickly as they had arrived.

Nuria skipped across the lounge and took her uncle's hand, heedless of his near nudity.

Karl bent to kiss her on the hair before turning to Nikato. "Nikki! How could you be late? How could you not have the correct paperwork?

"You gave me two days' notice. If you want to know, it's a miracle I have any of the paperwork. Fortunately the Regent had heard of you."

"The Regent knows me?"

"Yes, Regent Sayginn is interested in Sas Darona."

"But look at me. You were late and look at me. Look at him." he said, pointing to the captain, who was being helped to his feet.

Another crew member had brought Karl his luggage, and he rummaged inside for a change of clothes.

"Look, I'm sorry. What can I say?" Nikato struggled as he couldn't make his mind up whether to laugh or be outraged to find his brother in his underwear, with clothing in tatters at his feet. "The traffic planet-side was awful."

"The traffic planet-side was awful?" Karl repeated. He had found a shirt and pulled it on.

"Uncle Karl, Uncle Karl. It's not Uncle Nikki's fault," interjected Nuria. "It's not his fault. Really. The traffic was awful. You see, Prince Teodor has been kidnapped. An attack on the Cathedral. There has been a security lockdown. But they have taken him. He's gone."

Karl hesitated. He needed to take his boots off to put on his trousers. "Prince Teodor. You mean the heir? The heir to the kingdom of Earth?"

"And the heir to the empire," Nuria added. "Did the Dome Militant hurt you?"

"It's nothing. We'll talk in the car. Tell me about the Prince. What happened?"

"He was singing in the cathedral with a choir of Domeside children. Some of his poorest subjects."

"Where is this cathedral?"

"St Paul's Cathedral," Nikato replied. "They call it the beating heart of the Dome."

Chapter 9

The Cy-wolves of Empire

"**W**here's Dad?" Teodor murmured. His mind was hazy, his eyes were closed, his eyelashes were sticky and crusted with dry pus. He would need to force them open, but he was so weary.

My father will rescue me. No, he won't. Dad is dead. Deodran is dead. You're on your own. Grief, like a bitter drink rising in the throat, threatened to overwhelm him. He struggled to find a calmer voice. "Okay, so Dad is dead, but what was it he told me to do?" He closed his eyes as he tried to remember.

"One day, you will be their commander in chief," his father had said. "Whenever you enter the Dome to view the Dome Militant, you must remember that one day you will command them."

Teodor had gone with his father, King Serge, to inspect the new intake of Dome Militant apprentices. One of them was said to be a superb blades fighter, and there was to be a display match.

Teodor had stepped out of the car. Commander Tilson greeted him and his father. Next, the Dome Militant marched out to greet them. Teodor and his father took the salute. No falling on his backside this time, Teodor must have taken the salute over five hundred times – but still, the press replayed the image of his four-year-old self falling. As he walked along the line of Dome Militant apprentices, he wondered if they expected to see him or a baby. The youthful soldiers were not much older than himself, Teodor reflected. Sixteen when he was nearly thirteen. He noticed a smudge of white dust on the cuff of one of the soldier's jackets.

His father had told him to inspect the troops and not to hesitate to mention anything amiss. Well, a white mark on a black uniform was something wrong. Teodor stopped in front of the young soldier, and his father looked back at him, curiously.

Teodor looked up into the smooth face of the young soldier who was looking down at him. "You have something on your cuff."

He saw the youth glance at his commander, and when the commander nodded, he checked his arm to look.

"I'm very sorry, sir." He sounded embarrassed and dusted it off. "It won't happen again."

"What's wrong with your eye?" Teodor asked him.

"Oh," the boy raised his hand to his black eye "I got it in training. Eyes take the longest time to heal."

"I see. Well, that's talc on your sleeve," Teodor told him. "I use talc on my hands when fighting blades, myself."

"It stops the blades slipping," the other admitted. "I was practicing before you arrived."

"Oh well, that explains it. This soldier was practicing blades right up to the last minute. That's good, isn't it, father?"

"Yes, it certainly is."

As it turned out, the youth with the talc on his hands was the blades fighting star they had come to see. When he took out his blades and stepped onto the mat, he was breath-taking in his gymnastic training and accuracy of his spinning blades. Yet, even as he watched, Teodor remembered a quiet argument going on behind him – and of course, because they were whispering, he listened.

"Unregistered from Old Fleet Street?" his father had asked Chart. Teodor had heard the word 'unregistered', and his ears pricked up. The unregistered children of Old Fleet Street were infamous, as living reminders of the darker side of the glamorous fashion business, something his father had been keen to eliminate.

"But it does not matter who his parents are, we had to let him in."

"His parents should be prosecuted."

"What good would that do?" Chart had asked.

Teodor was surprised to hear Chart Segat speak so rudely to his father, without moving, he tried to glance sideways at the man, as his father replied.

"It's illegal. No child should be abandoned."

"And excluding him from the Dome Militant will help?" Chart had replied. *Did this man Segat not know his father was King? Why was he arguing?*

"It's breaking my law. There will be a fine."

"If I am prosecuted, I will challenge you in court. The law is unjust. It hurts the vulnerable most." Then Chart Segat had laughed then, a bitter grating sound.

"Maybe. But there are two children it protects. Two who are very dear to me."

His father was talking about himself and baby Deodran. Teodor winced. *And why? What further protection do me and my brother need?*

"Don't worry about the boy Serge - that one isn't a lost prince."

"There's no such thing," Teodor exclaimed. As both turned towards him, Teodor was embarrassed, but he was right, wasn't he? There was no such thing as a lost prince.

"Teodor are you listening to the grown-ups?" his father asked.

Teodor nodded, ashamed.

"Go and sit further forward. Chart and I are not finished. And no more listening!"

Teodor moved to the seat indicated, but nevertheless he listened even harder.

"Would that Erederon had given us a legitimate heir," he heard his father conclude. "As the heirs, my sons are in danger, of course, but more so because of these pernicious rumours of a lost prince. Damn them."

Later that evening, King Serge had come upstairs to wish Teodor goodnight.

They read a few pages of a book together and then Teodor said, "I want to fight blades as well as those Domeside boys do."

"Those boys eat, sleep, fight. They live for blades. You know that don't you?"

"Yes, if I'm the commander-in-chief." Teodor paused. That was not the reason. "I need to be able to defend myself."

His father smiled. "Aha, so you heard what I said about Erederon?"

"Erederon that was my first cousin, the Emperor's last surviving son?" His father nodded.

"The eldest Prince Frederon was assassinated, yes. But Erederon died when his flyer crashed. And then there was a baby, Sergeron he died just two months after he was born. But Erederon was the last one. Your uncle Freddie was seventy when he was born."

"He was handsome, too, and a hero..."

"Yes, he was all those things. Maybe a little too wild, it's not good when you always have things your own way."

Teodor nodded, then asked somewhat anxiously, "But when he died, he was **36**, he was old enough to have a son. Did he?"

"Well, there was this little girl - she might well have been, but when we tested her blood." His father shook his head. "It was very upsetting for the girl, her mother, everyone really."

"So, if there was a girl, are we sure there were no boys?"

Teodor looked into his father's face, trying to see the truth. *Was there something his father was not telling him?*

"Teodor, remember you are the anointed heir."

Teodor remembered nodding, but he also noticed that his father had not answered his question. What did that mean? No, there was no lost prince, so why didn't his father just say so. Yes, there is a lost prince, and we know who he is, and Teodor you are in danger. His father had not said either of those things. So, was his real answer 'I Don't Know'? Potentially the most dangerous position of all because it meant there was a lost prince, but no one knew who or when or when he might appear to claim the throne. The fact that his father had not said No, told Teodor everything he needed to know. In all likelihood, there was a boy somewhere who would challenge his claim to the throne.

"I must be able to defend myself," Teodor said.

Now it was his father's turn to look surprised, but he laughed before agreeing.

"You might have to give up some of the time you spend in the goran stables."

"Oh." Teodor had not thought of that. "Well, I suppose."

"No, seriously, every time I ask: where's Teo? Oh, he's goran racing. Where's Teo? He's nursing goran cubs. Where's Teo? Oh, he's cleaning out the stables. Where's Teo? He's grooming gorans. With you it's eat, sleep, gorans. You live with your gorans."

Teodor just laughed.

His father added with a sly sideways glance. "Where's Teo? He's hanging out with the stable girls."

"Dad! Stable girls aren't really 'girls.'"

"No?"

"No. Well, for instance, they ride gorans as well as jockeys, and they don't mind getting messy or cleaning up and stuff."

"I was madly in love with a stable girl when I was young."

"Dad! I hate girrrls."

"I guess I must have been fourteen or fifteen, but she was my first love, and I'll never forget her."

Teodor crossed his arms and shook his head in severe disapproval.

His father smiled. "You're sure you want to give up goran time to learn blades?"

Teodor sighed. "Well, I have to, don't I? But if you find me a good teacher, I'll work twice as hard, because the gorans are important too."

"Good plan – I'll find you the best coach in the city. I promise."

King Serge had ensured his eldest son Teodor knew how to fight. But what good had that done when the great Battle Borgs of Dome had attacked him? Nothing. He no longer tried to recall the name of the drug they had made him inhale, but he recognised the symptoms from his kidnap training. Loose, uncontrolled limbs; foggy, distorted vision; hearing so muffled he might as well be deaf; and no sense of smell at all. His head had been jolted to one side during the running. He was somehow holding it in place with one ear against his attacker's back, one eye on what happened behind. All he knew for sure was his captors were Battle Borgs from the Dome.

He'd thought they'd be running through catacombs and long-forgotten tombs, but these were long, narrow maintenance tunnels. So straight, he could see the Royal Guards chasing after him. They had released the cy-wolves, and the creatures of muscle, fur and steel were closing in. What would happen when they attacked? Teodor had no fear of the cy-wolves, they were programmed not to hurt him, but they would attack the Borg that carried him. He imagined the huge wolf leaping at his captor's head. He was going to fall; he had better be ready.

Instead, the Borg stopped, crouched and turned. Lifting his gun, he shot the nearest cy-wolf through the head, machine-gunned his companion before sending another volley of fire towards the Royal Guards – then he sprinted onwards. Teodor watched as one cy-wolf convulsed and died, the other, even injured, continued to chase after him, until with one last blast, the Borg shot it dead.

Teodor thought of his two golden gorans. How he had argued he should bring them to the cathedral. But if those beautiful creatures had been curling around his legs and prowling at his side, they too would be dead. Just as the two brave cy-wolves now lay dead and dying in this dark, damp corridor. It was almost a relief when the Borg turned hard right, and Teodor lost sight of the fallen creatures.

At the turn, the Borg threw something over his shoulder. Teodor recognised the 'snake', an automatic weapon, effectively a coiled rope of bullets. The Borg ran on. Behind him, guarding the corner, the snake rose like its namesake and unleashed a circle of fire, starting high and spinning low. Teodor watched the machine spit out its indiscriminate cyclone of death. He thought of the Royal Guards trapped in that narrow corridor. Nowhere to hide, would they retreat? Would they dive to the floor to avoid the bullets? But there was no escaping the exploding head.

Silence. The bullets were spent.

"Ten, nine," Teodor counted down, "eight, seven, six."

Bang. The snake-head explosive echoed along the tunnels.

"Damn them," Teodor cursed. "A five-second fuse. Why did they set a five-second fuse? Damn them."

Though distant now, the blast shook Teodor and his captors, his Borg stumbled but kept his footing. What about Teodor's guards, his rescuers? Teodor looked back at the clouds of dust. Had they survived? Could anything survive?

Out of the fog of destruction, bounding over the bodies of fallen colleagues, the Royal Guards were still coming. Fast as athletes, and strong too, they were closing the distance. Weaving through their legs to lead the charge two more cy-wolves raced forth, barking and snarling as they came. This time they would free him.

Only Teodor was falling. His captors had opened a drain in the floor to reveal a ladder. The Borg carrying Teodor had dropped him, a fall of perhaps ten meters, to where another Borg caught him, punched him in the abdomen and threw him over his shoulder. Even as the last Borg leapt down, to land on its robotic legs, Teodor had one glimpse of the drain door high above.

One cy-wolf sniffed down the drain and leapt back as shots were fired upwards. The fall was too high for the cy-wolves to jump. So the other sat and howled – a clear signal to the rest as to where Teodor had gone.

Stay there, Teodor thought, *stay up top and be safe*. He watched a Borg with robotic arm wrench the ladder from the wall. He saw another throw something up through the drain.

Another snake! Teodor heard its spiralling bullets and counted the five seconds to the exploding head. *What of his wolves?* Dust rained down on them, but the tunnel held.

Now the borgs were running again. He was tumbling against his captor's back. As they turned a corner his hand flew right, and his knuckles ripped against the rough concrete. He saw blood, but drugged as he was, he felt nothing.

How much more? These drugs have made me a coward, incapable of fighting back. I am not a coward, I know, but for now, all I can do is survive. Why do I even think? What long forgotten training was kicking in? I don't know but I will survive, and I will keep my eyes open to bear witness.

They were sprinting by torchlight down a dark sloping tunnel. Teodor heard a door being unlocked. *Keys,* he thought: this escape was planned. *Practiced even?* The borgs bounded down two further narrow metal flights of stairs, a corridor, another drain cover, and a ladder. At last, the borgs were running along a narrow ledge alongside a deep, turgid river of filth.

The city sewers, Teodor thought as his eyes started to burn and weep. At least he had no sense of smell. Yet the borgs did not stop, did not slow, agile as gymnasts, they sprinted along the narrow ledge. They sped around a corner, with him swinging out over the steaming brown liquid and then all at once they stopped.

Shouts echoed along the corridor.

Across the tunnel, on the far ledge, three more borgs waited. *What now? Were they going to jump?* It was a two-meter-wide gap, wide even for Borg. Teodor felt himself being dragged off his captor's shoulder.

I can't jump that far, Teodor thought. *Not now I'm drugged.*

No!

They tossed him!

With no control over his body, Teodor was like a ragdoll spinning and flying over the river of sewage. The cyborgs on the far side grabbed him by the waist and tried to get him to stand. His legs buckled under him, and he crumbled. Kneeling and swaying on the narrow ledge as, across from him, the first team of captors headed off at a run.

The new team took him by the hands and swung him out from the wall and dunked him in the sewage waters. Teodor found he could not close his mouth, though his eyes blinked shut. Were they trying to drown him?

No, they are yanking him out, and wrapping him in a sleeping foil. By the way, they joke-complained, and wrapped him from head to foot. He knew the foil was more for their benefit than his. Teodor could not smell himself, but he managed with effort to cough and spit to partially clear his mouth and throat.

His new captors headed off in a different direction to the original team. Teodor guessed the sewage dunking was to prevent any remaining cy-wolves from tracking his scent.

As they rounded the corner, he glimpsed the last remaining pursuers: one cy-wolf, two Royal Guards. Earlier there had been six wolves and twenty-four men, were all the others dead? Dead? What of these three? When would they realise they were chasing the wrong borgs in the wrong direction? Would they live long enough to discover this deception?

Teodor groaned. How could they all be dead? Who had wanted to take him so badly? He must survive, if not they would all have died in vain.

Again, he tried to clear his mouth by coughing or spitting. His new captors noticed. They smothered his face with a stinking drug-drenched cloth. Teodor's world turned to blackness, and he saw and felt no more.

Chapter 10

Regent Sayginn of Earth

G uy Erma came out of maths, switched on his communicator and found three urgent messages. There had been a terrorist attack in the Cathedral. Prince Teodor was feared dead.

And...

"Hi, Loulou, I'm alright."

"Oh, Guy. I put you on the missing persons list. Thank God, you're alright. I thought you might be injured. Weren't you at the front?"

"I was the understudy, remember? I left before the performance. I had double maths."

As he spoke, Guy realised what he was saying must be right. Prince Teodor must have been singing when they took him. He remembered the golden shorts and blousy shirt Teodor wore. How could anyone say that costume looked like a blade fighter?

"Can you come down to the clinic?" Loulou's voice crackled through his communicator. "I want to see you with my own eyes."

Guy shook away his daydream to focus. Teodor had been singing with a choir, his half-brothers and sisters from the attics of Old Fleet Street.

"I'm on my way. I'm nearly there. Were any of our kids hurt?"

"I'll tell you when you get here."

Going to my maths class saved me, Guy thought. *Maybe it was a sign.*

Regent Sayginn walked through the bloodstained confusion of the Cathedral. The captain briefed her as they went.

"When the curtain fell closed, we lost sight of the prince," he said, "so we shot down the curtain from its hooks and caught these images of the kidnappers."

Sayginn had seen the stills and a short video on her way there. She watched, as great Battle Borgs — Dome Militant Battle Borgs by their uniforms — had grabbed and dragged her son Teodor off down into some tunnels.

"How were so many children killed?" Sayginn asked. She had asked the same question three times. Each time, the answer was the same — and even less palatable.

"One of our men threw a grenade to open the hatch," the captain replied. "Others opened fire on the men attacking Prince Teodor."

"You're saying most of the Domeside children killed were hit by the Royal Guards?"

"Yes," he said quietly, "but not deliberately. With all the smoke, visibility was limited."

Sayginn's face hardened. "You know there will be an enquiry. The men may be prosecuted for murder."

"Imperial Prince Teodor was under attack," the captain insisted.

High above, flags continued to burn. One pole crashed to the altar, sparks flying out over the rescuers.

Time to go, thought Sayginn. But what should she do? She paused.

"What happened to the injured?"

St Paul's clinic was worse than Sayginn could have imagined. The youngest victims were mute with shock. An unruly gang of older children rushed through the wards chanting lists of names as they created a grim tally of their friends, living, injured or dead.

Amid the chaos, Sayginn realised she was, herself, part of the problem. She had arrived with four bodyguards and a host of press, so, despite her best intentions, her presence was blocking the entire reception area of the clinic.

A senior surgeon came charging up, yelling at the press. "I thought we told you to leave. Security! Security!" He was pointing the security guards to the press. Suddenly he recognised her. "Oh, Your Highness, I'm sorry, I didn't see you."

"No need to apologise, Doctor," Sayginn replied, then turning to her protection. "Men, help the hospital security remove the press."

The Surgeon nodded in thanks then said without prompting,

"I am afraid there are no teenagers, Your Highness," he said. "None of the right age, I mean."

"You mean among the injured," replied Sayginn; she knew he was referring to Teodor.

"No, nor among the dead," he said.

Sayginn already knew this; she had seen the films of Teodor being taken. "I came here to check on the injured," she said.

"If you like to accompany me, I am just checking on one very sad case." He pushed open a door into a private room just off the children's ward. Inside, it was warm – with a whiff of fresh blood in the air.

"This child is about six, unidentified. We think he was standing next to another child who was killed by a shot through the head. That's what he told us. He turned to look at his friend and saw him get shot. He was blinded by fragments from the other child's skull."

Sayginn rocked, as if she had been struck, struggling for balance. The child looked tiny on the oversized bed. It was as the surgeon had described, worse because except for the bandage across his eyes, he was perfect.

An alarm sounded on the surgeon's communicator,

"If you would sit by his side a little while — he has no-one else." The surgeon said, Sayginn nodded in vague agreement as he headed out the door. Slim and dark-haired like many of the Domesiders, the child's lips were moving, and Sayginn leant over to listen.

"Is anyone there?" the child asked again and again. "Is anyone there?"

Sayginn sat down on the side of his bed and took his hand. "I'm here."

"Please don't go. Please don't leave me."

Sayginn stroked his hair back from his face until the boy said: "It's dark, I'm afraid." Without warning, tears ran down her face, and Sayginn found herself gasping for breath, as she remembered Teo's words that morning. *It was so dark, and I was all alone.*

Guy arrived at the clinic just as Chart Segat was pulling up. He watched as the press were assembled so he could make a statement.

"The Royal Guards opened fire with live ammunition," he said. "A wholly unnecessary use of deadly force. Another example of Royal ineptitude and cruelty against the poorest people in the city. The Regent and Prince Teodor would be better protected by the Dome Militant."

Of course, the Prince would be safe with the Dome Militant, Guy thought, *if only King Serge had not died that day ...if somehow, we could have saved him...* Like all Domesiders, Guy felt deep shame at the memory of the day the Dome Militant failed. Never again.

Guy's communicator beeped. He turned to race up the stairs, and along the corridors to the ward where Loulou had sent him. He arrived as a nurse drew the curtains around the furthest bed. Guy slipped inside and greeted Loulou, only to see Marline bat away some of the drone cameras. Behind Guy, Chart Segat had pushed his way in.

"How many from House Jewel?" he asked Loulou.

"I think we have four injured and possibly another four dead." she replied before asking in a whisper. "Did you know about this?"

Chart Segat shook his head and muttered, "Why did the Royal Guards use live ammunition? Why?"

"Well, the prince." Loulou started to say but stopped.

"It wouldn't have surprised me if they'd shot him too. " All at once Chart Segat put an arm around Guy and hugged him. "But at least you made it out." Guy looked up at him in surprise, but Chart Segat pulled back and said to Loulou: "You need to return to the rehearsal, Loulou – you and this young thing." He pinched Marline's cheek. Guy watched as Marline giggled and pretended to be pleased. Chart Segat continued. "You need to lead by example for the other girls. Oh, and bring this chap to the drinks party tonight."

"You mean the Emperor's reception? It's a bit late." Loulou cut in.

"I'm sure he won't say no to earning a few notes at the after party. Will you, Guy?"

Guy was astonished. Chart Segat had used his name. Still, Guy had no interest in fashion work.

"How much?" Guy asked. Chart Segat laughed.

"How much indeed?" He patted Guy on the shoulder. "You'll be serving drinks. Don't worry! Those boys get good tips too." He chuckled. "How much indeed? You're a good boy, Guy Erma. You're one of us now."

He held open the curtain and the three stepped outside to leave the ward. They headed along a corridor towards the exit when a door opened.

Marline gasped. "Is that the Regent?"

Regent Sayginn washed her hands and face in the small basin. Sobbing would not bring Teodor back. *What was she doing in the hospital, anyway? What could she possibly learn here?* She checked her communicator. A notification. Someone she knew was nearby. *Him! Could it be? Just outside?* She stepped out to see Chart Segat coming down the corridor with his inevitable retinue of courtesans, and a youth. All froze.

"It's Loulou, isn't it?" Sayginn asked. "I always enjoy my clothes from House Jewel."

"Yes, and this is Marline, do you remember her?"

Sayginn looked at the young girl. Not just pretty, she was a true Domeside beauty, and young too and yet she was familiar; why? Loulou cut in. "Marline is a model, it's her first season," She added: "We're all so sorry about Prince Teodor."

"We'll find him. I'm sure he's not gone far." Sayginn replied, but she knew she had to change the subject. She looked away from Marline and saw Guy. "Is this your son?"

"Well, he's House Jewel." Loulou replied.

"Cheer up, young man." Why had she said that? His skin was paler than most. His eyes were piercing blue, his black curls were pure Domeside. Sayginn thought she would have them trimmed. Plus, he had the typical slight, slim, tall frame. *Destined for the Dome Militant I bet*, thought Sayginn. *Well, he will have a better future with me at the helm than he would have had if the*

Dome was under the control of Chart Segat. "You are so familiar; do I know you?"

"No, Ma'am."

Loulou cut in with a note of pride. "It was he who was going to fight Prince Teodor at blades."

"Aha, so that's why I recognise him! The little blades champion, yes, well done, young man. I have to tell you, Teo was disappointed to cancel the fight."

Why had she said that? It was she who had cancelled the match. She could still hear Teo's aggrieved complaints from that morning.

> Why do I have to sing? *A good question, why did Teodor have to sing?* She remembered her reply. "It's about the Dome. I'm taking it over this weekend. It's not a popular move, so you must sing." So, to protect herself, she had sent her unprotected son into the Dome alone. Only he had not been unprotected; there had been twelve Royal Guards soldiers. Twelve and it was not enough.

The young man had said something. "Sorry, I didn't catch that."

"My blades. Any day. Any time. Any place. Will you yield?"

"Don't say that" Sayginn whispered, only she wasn't talking to Guy.

> *"My blades. Any day. Any time. Any place. Will you yield?" Teodor had cried, as he bowed to her at the end of his blades practice.*

*"Don't say that!" Sayginn had scolded him.
"It's what all the blades' fighters in Domeside
say."
"Yes, but you're not from Domeside."
"I like it, and they are our people too." Teodor
finished with an angry spin of his blades
across the palms of his hands.
Contrary, opinionated — Teodor was right, as
always.*

Sayginn focused on the youth in front of her. He looked startled.

"Sorry, I didn't mean you." *Were those tears? No, not tears*, Sayginn pleaded with herself. Fortunately, Loulou spoke.

"Guy!" scolded Loulou. "My lady, please excuse Guy his manners."

"My blades are yours to command, Regent," he repeated, more sober now. But Sayginn heard another voice.

*"My blades are yours to command, Mother. I
still like anytime, any day, any place, better."
Oh, Teodor!*

Resolutely, Sayginn turned to Chart Segat. "A word in private." She batted away a droid camera from in front of her face. She nodded to her security, which started to pinch and throw the cameras away. Sayginn pushed open the door to the private room. Chart Segat stepped through. The door was closed behind them. The small boy was sleeping. Sayginn smoothed a curl back from his face. Chart Segat stared down at the boy from the foot of the bed, the blood on the eye bandage had worsened. As they stood on opposite sides of the bed, Sayginn reflected they must look like the child's parents. She noticed the helpless anger on Chart Segat's face. Sayginn realised it was now or never.

"Do you have him, Chart?" Chart Segat did not move. Sayginn asked again. "Do you have my son?"

Chart Segat replied with anger. "Oh, that's right, the men were wearing Dome Militant uniforms, so of course you think."

"It's not what I think. I know you control everything that happens in this damn Dome of yours, or do you deny it? You have done this. I don't know why you even deny it."

"Stop it! If anyone has done this, it is you. You, Sayginn. With your Dome Debate. You, Sayginn — closing the Dome. You. Calling me a murderer. Threatening everyone and everything here. As if I would murder Serge, murder Prince Deodran. No. Sayginn, you brought this on yourself."

Sayginn had heard it all before. "You know I don't mean to close the Dome."

Chart Segat looked at her. "Finally," he said. His voice was deep and satisfied.

Sayginn did not reply. She knew that though she had kept her plans secret, many speculated that if the Dodecahedron Dome shut at all, it would only be for a matter of days – because what else could you do with all the men, women and trainees in the Dome except keep them going? It was the outcome that Sayginn needed to change. So that the Dome was no longer a training camp for mercenaries, but a military force to protect and defend Earth and the other five planets of the kingdom.

"You want rid of me," Chart Segat murmured. "Have you forgotten we were once friends?" He sounded sad, as if in mourning for being so firmly cast aside.

Sayginn could smell Chart Segat's raw energy and passion. She remembered him well as the sexy, flamboyant guest at Buckingham Palace. As mayor of Domeside, he was an unavoidable part of the public life. Always with a compliment for her, flirting, occasionally hugging her, and whenever Serge looked, he would make a joke of kissing her hand. "The most beautiful girl in the empire!" he would shout. Serge would laugh; flattered that another man should admire his wife. After all, how could Chart be serious when he always had impossibly young girls on each of his arms?

"Not friends, Chart." Sayginn replied. "Maybe we were political allies. We shared the goal of revitalising Domeside, and we succeeded. So, yes, we worked together. But he was my husband, Chart. We don't know who killed him. And today it's my son. Someone has taken my Teo, and he's all I have left. He's everything, Chart."

"Sayginn. Let me stay on at the Dome. You want overall control; you can have it; just give me something. I did not kill Serge."

"I don't want to hear about that." Sayginn turned away and pressed her forehead against the cold wood of the door. "Where is my son, Chart?"

He paused then replied, "Give me back my power. You know the evidence against me is inconclusive. Say something. I want my authority back. Then, maybe I will be able to help."

Sayginn jumped. *Had he said he knew where Teodor was?*

"My son? Chart? Do you have Teo?"

"Help you find." repeated Chart. "Whatever mad firebrands have pulled off this stunt."

Sayginn shook her head. *So it wasn't him, then. Could that be true?* She could not speak. *Firebrands?* Of course, there were rumours of ultra-militant factions within the Dome Militant. If they did exist, it would mean Chart Segat had lost control. Maybe he was right. Maybe it was her fault. She had wounded him and as a direct result, she had brought this attack on herself.

"They come back from Sas Darona." Chart Segat whispered, "changed."

"What are they even doing on Sas Darona? It is supposed to be a short-term training camp."

"Sayginn, how high is the ivory tower you live in? You and your barons own everything, have everything, and want more. What kind of democracy is this, where your people have nothing? A Dome guard earns one thousand four hundred a month. Your shirt costs more than that, your handbag ten times that amount. Your shoes, palace, gorans, more than the entire budget of the Dome. Through your greed – yours, the Emperor's and the barons' – nothing is left; or almost nothing. What crumbs you do leave on the table, like the Dome Militant, there is such intense competition."

"Save me the lecture on poverty and inequality," Sayginn sneered. "My government has done more to increase routes to prosperity than any other legislature in the Dodecahedral. More even than Serge – but if the barons do not reap their rewards, they will not take the necessary risks. The risks that are needed to expand the empire."

"Why expand the empire? To have more poor people? Ever-expanding desperation? You should be praying I do have your son, because at least I look after my boys."

"Chart Segat, I am giving you one last chance – give me back my son and I will speak for you in the future."

"What? When I face charges for murdering Serge? I didn't do it, Sayginn – will you not hear me? I didn't do it. Listen to me, just let me keep the Dome. Call it whatever you like. We could work together, like the old days, building Domeside. What do you think?"

"You disgust me. Your politics, your whores and the blood of my husband on your hands. Give me back my son. Or you will never have a part in the future of the Dodecahedron Dome. Do you hear me? Never."

Chapter 11

The Battle Borgs of Dome

Teodor woke. It was dark. It was cold. He was shivering all over from the last vision of his dream. He had seen a snarling goran roaring in his face and slashing him with her claws.

"Impossible," his rational brain told him. "Nothing like that happened. Cream Carolina—she was a sweet goran. She would never attack me."

"Teo, Teo, wake up, Teo."

He had woken in his room; it was still dark, and his father was leaning over his bed.

"Cream Carolina is having her cubs. If you want to choose one, you need to be there."

Teodor had slid out of bed and pulled on the clothes he had laid out at his bedside. Moments later, he'd run down the stairs; his father had a small cart waiting for them at the back door.

With his heart beating fast, Teodor entered the stall of a birthing mother goran. A misjudged step or word could anger the goran, and the stall left little room for evasion or escape. However, for a jockey to bond with his ride, the telepathic connection had to be made at birth.

"You will come with me, won't you, Father? You'll stay with me?"

"Of course. I have to stand behind you, if you want to make the connection."

"Yes, I know, but promise me you'll be there."

"Teo, my son, I am always there for you."

Teodor remembered standing beside the great female goran, calming her with his thoughts while watching for the newborns. He had a fresh towel hung over his shoulder and was wearing rubber gloves. He would pick the cub up, clean and cuddle it, and then make the connection.

He looked over his shoulder; his father was two steps away. With a nod, his father directed him forward.

The cub is coming, thought Teo. It is almost time.

The crucial moment—when Cream Carolina would either let him touch her newborn cubs or snarl and slash at him to chase him away. To gain the cub, you had to reassure the mother. He had ridden Cream Carolina for tens—almost a hundred—hours; surely, she trusted him?

He checked once more with his father, then stepped forward towards the giant mother. He remembered how, when he picked up a cub, his father had patted him on the shoulder.

"See, you didn't need your old dad after all."

"Yes, I did," Teodor had replied. "I always need you, Dad."

I need you now.

As the dream faded, he felt the pain grow. His body crumpled around him – his knees under his chin, his feet twisted up at odd angles, one arm behind his back, one curled in his lap. He wanted to free his body, but realised he had been dropped into a narrow tube. He moaned. His head ached, and he was thirsty. He tried to cough and managed to spit a foul taste from his mouth; then he gagged at the smell. His clothes, his body, his hair, all caked in the filth from the sewer.

I have to escape.

In a blind panic, he placed his feet on the floor. Ignoring the pins and needles that cut into his calves and thighs, he pushed himself upwards – impatiently pulling his right arm from behind him and shaking it back to some sensitivity. Only he couldn't stand; his head crashed against a flat surface. He reached up with his hands and realised the tube had a lid. At his feet, he kicked to make sure the base was also sealed.

He wanted to stand up straight, but the best he could achieve was a three-quarters crouch, with his feet flat on the floor, the top of his head pushed up flat against the top. He drew his hands up and turned on the spot to feel the smooth curved walls. The diameter of the tube was so narrow that he barely managed to turn around. At the top of the tube, there was a small grille under the lid. He pushed his fingers through the meshed wire and pulled himself upwards. Try as he might, he could not see through the narrow gap.

He started to shout. "Help me! Is there anyone out there? Give me a hand. I'm in this tube!" He beat and thumped the walls of the tube. Made of metal, it made a vibrating echo. He heard footsteps – the heavy tread of a soldier. Teodor redoubled the amount of noise he was making while craning his neck to put his eye up to the grille. "My name is Prince Teodor, let me out of here!"

Surely, they would know he was missing by now. Surely, they would be looking for him. If he could make himself known.

All at once, he heard metal on metal snap together. The top of the tube lifted up. Teodor followed it, standing up to his full height, and – looking up – he saw it was not a man, it was a Battle Borg. If this cyborg had once been a man, it was a long time ago. The man must have been dismembered in battle. It had robotic arms and hands. Its legs had been amputated at the hips and replaced with steel legs and wheels. The eyes were mechanical, the neck reinforced; its last remnants of humanity were its face, body skin and hair. Even his head was balding, mottled black and grey, his skin cracked and cratered, a large scab having fallen away from his face to reveal its mechanical inners. This Battle Borg would be used in the vanguard, sent forward to die a heroic death. He was perhaps the most frightening thing Teodor had ever seen, yet at his core, also a machine.

All Battle Borgs were programmed to follow orders, and at the top of the chain of command was the King. This machine had to do as he commanded.

"Thank goodness. It's you." Teodor pushed his weight upon his hands to rise out of the tube, and so he did not see the blow that struck him hard across the temples and sent him tumbling back down. "No, please, you must help me. My name is Prince Teodor. I am your commander in chief. You must obey me."

The Battle Borg had pulled a cloth from a satchel and pressed it across Teodor's face, pinching his ears hard when he saw him trying to resist. "Sleep, Prince Teodor, sleep," he hissed down at him. Teodor tried one last time to lash out, but his strength was too slight, his captor too strong, the drugs too potent. His legs crumbled and he slipped down into the tube.

"No, please. No, I am your prince. Please, no. You have to help me."

"Calm, Teodor, sleep now." The Borg threw the cloth into the tube so Teodor could not escape its vapours. The lid closed on top of him again. Teodor heard the metal clicking into place. He clawed at the tube one last time, hoping to the very last to climb out, but the footsteps were already fading away – and in the distance, a light went out. Teodor valiantly held his breath as he reached the lid, using his fingers to look for any weakness, punching it with his knuckles to push it upwards. His legs had turned to jelly, and he slipped, as if broken, to the floor of the tube. His eyes were still open, looking up at the grille, but all his movement had stopped. His hearing gone, as well as his sense of smell, but he still had time to think. *Not long*, he guessed, *but a few seconds.*

Here he was alone and in the dark, a captive somewhere. Was he still in the Dome? And he could not escape. As he had dreamt. Well, not exactly, but clearly his dream had been some dark premonition. He thought how he had woken in a cold sweat that morning, how scared he had been in his comfortable bed. That fear had passed in a couple of seconds. How afraid was he? He felt so dozy; part of his brain was chronicling his sensations. He was wet and cold. His limbs were twisted and bruised. There were untended cuts and grazes. What worried him most was the lack of voluntary motion, and the darkness. He knew he would soon lose the ability to blink.

Wearily, he closed his eyes. He was alone inside his head. *Why hadn't the Borg obeyed my command? Most cyborgs couldn't be reprogrammed. Were Battle Borgs different? These Battle Borgs of Empire, who did they obey?*

"War is a terrible thing," his father had once said. "When you are at war, you have to accept that dreadful things will happen – and in turn, you have to fight to survive. The Battle Borgs are our greatest weapons."

Teodor had been accompanying his father on yet another inspection of the military facilities within the Dome. Chart Segat had been there, demonstrating some new weapons that could only be hoisted aloft by a small number of Battle Borgs with the right kind of reinforced mechanical arms.

"But are they still human?" Teodor had asked. His father had not replied as Chart Segat had spoken.

"We have over a dozen volunteers for this upgrade."

"I don't want men who have working arms to sacrifice their humanity to use these weapons," Serge had replied.

"No. I know that. But losing their arms doesn't reduce their humanity. If they have over sixty per cent brain function, they remain human."

"How can you be so sure?" Serge had replied. "I don't believe your humanity resides in your brain."

"You mean, how can a man remain human when he has superhuman powers?" Teodor recognised a familiar debate.

"Precisely," Serge replied.

"Are they human, Dad?" Teodor had repeated.

Chart Segat had smiled down at him. "The point is, they are dead, and we control them. Human or not, in battle, they are under our control."

Under whose control? Who controlled these Battle Borgs? Chart Segat?

"This weekend is all about the Dome Debate," his mother had said, "I plan to take control, and it's not a popular move."

The Dome Debate? Is that what this is about? What had his mother said? Something about the Dome Militant becoming her army, after the Dome Debate. His brain was becoming fuzzy. He saw himself riding a white snow goran, with the Dome Militant running besides him, blades at the ready, riding across the plains of Sas Darona – to fight who?

Who was he fighting? He heard his mother's voice. 'He was fifteen. He was a skinny thing, but he was fast, and he was clever. He would have beaten you, Teodor.'

No, no! Not when I have my gorans and my army. He will not beat me.

Chapter 12

Whatever Chartsie wants

Thud. The blade had embedded itself deep into the wood. Guy Erma who was standing at the furthest point with his back to the target, spun around and threw a second blade. This one embedded itself at the twelve o'clock position on the target.

Maximum points, he thought to himself – *a twelve and a bull's eye, maximum points*. The target accelerated towards him on a wire. Guy retrieved his blades with a smile. He polished them on his sleeve, then stepped aside for the next boy. He put his blades back in his holster, snug up against his kidneys. He then walked back through the gym. The Dome Militant were coming in at the end of their duties, and the training mats were filling up. Training robots were set aside, and an instructor was calling a vast crowd of soldiers into formation for a warm-up routine.

Guy rolled his shoulders as he walked, easing the stiffness he had built up during training. He and the other boys had the run of the gym between school's end and six. Then they had to clear out, but it was these minutes of handover that Guy lived for. He would hang about on the edge of a blades mat, shyly watching some champion or battle-hardened veteran spinning blades with breath-taking precision or counting the ranks of Dome Militant chanting their way through a hard-learnt battle routine.

Guy heard a cheer. Des Parks had appeared across the gym. He was being congratulated every step he took. For the third consecutive year, Des Parks was senior blades champion. He was dark-haired, slim and fit, but he was also deeply tanned. And it was the tan they applauded.

"Back from Sas Darona," Guy heard one of the men mutter.

"How the heck did he get back?" said another.

"Sas Darona has been locked down for three months," said a third.

As Des reached the central training area, the ranked men stopped in their routine. They parted and fell back to the edge of the blades mat. It was something of a tradition among the Dome Militant. A returning hero was given a moment to shine, and Des did not disappoint.

Without hesitation, he performed three consecutive back somersaults – before taking off into a corkscrew spiral kick, landing in a high backward kick that would smash the face of any opponent. The crowd roared their approval.

Guy grinned and set off at a sprint around the perimeter of the gym, pausing at a water fountain before squeezing and squirming his way through the crowd with a cup of water in his hand. "Hi Des, here – take this!"

Des grinned down at him, downed the water in one gulp, threw the cup aside and embraced Guy in a bear hug. "Hi, kiddo! You still training?" Guy nodded, speechless with delight. His hero had remembered him. Des took Guy by the chin and lifted his face up. "Hey, Guy, you still live in the House?" Guy nodded. Des had grown up in House Jewel too. "And you see Loulou?"

"Every day," Guy said and smiled.

"Ok. Ok. I might have a job for you."

"Oy, Guy Erma. Out." It was an angry shout from a Dome Militant apprentice – the same one Guy had beaten that morning in training.

Des whispered, "Go. I'll catch you later."

"Not so fast, fill up my water bottle first." The apprentice held out his flask. Guy took it and in light leaps, headed back to the water fountain. Unbeknownst to him, Des' eyes followed him. Once Guy had his back turned, fixed on the water and the tap, they jumped him. There were four or five apprentices, including the youth Guy had beaten at blades that morning. Oh, Guy reached for his blades, but they grabbed his arms and pushed him through a double door. Guy tried to kick out, but another teenager threw himself across Guy's legs, pinning him to the floor. With the doors shut, they were no longer visible to either the instructors or trainers. The punishment started. A hard volley of punches to his belly and chest, and last of all, a hard slap across his face.

"Do you yield?" the youth sneered. "Do you yield?" He lifted a fist closed around the handle of his blade. Guy winced in anticipation when a familiar voice rang out.

"Stop that this minute." It was Des, of course, and with him two other seniors. They made quick work of pulling the apprentices off Guy and confiscating their weapons.

"What do you think you're doing?"

"He had it coming. What with the girls like 'Ooh Guy Erma', and he's Chartsie's pet and Loulou's too and "Oh

I don't want to be a fashion model." Who does he think he is?"

Des pushed the fighter against the wall and shoved his arm up his back. "So that justifies you going at him six against one? Does it? I have a good mind to tell your commanding officer. Your prospects won't look so good with a report of cowardice on your file."

"Leave off, will you? He's not hurt."

"Get out of here!"

The six apprentices raced back into the gym. Des nodded to the two other seniors, who also left. He bent to help Guy up. "You ok, kiddo?"

"I guess. My ribs hurt."

"Ok. C'mon." Des put an arm around him and, using his pass, led him into a private elevator.

"Where are you taking me?"

"To be checked at the clinic."

"I'm not yet Dome Militant."

"True, but I'm with you, and you were injured in training."

The doors of the elevator had opened into a narrow metal corridor. An officer waited at the door of the elevator. Des saluted him, fist across his chest to his heart, and when he looked at Guy, Des pointed to the blood running from his nose. The officer nodded. Along the narrow corridor, there was one admin assistant carrying a box of silver Dome-medallion awards. Des led Guy through the double doors and into the spacious military clinic. The receptionist took their names, an orderly took one look at Guy and found a hover chair, and they were taken straight through to the treatment room, a wide room with over twenty beds and clustered monitors. A young doctor came over, checking his screen as he came.

"Des Parks? This boy isn't Dome Militant."

"He got these injuries in a Dome Militant gym," Des replied.

"How's that?"

"Six apprentices decided they didn't like the look of him."

"Is that true?" the doctor turned to Guy.

"Yes, sir," Guy said.

"Did you do anything to upset them?"

"No, sir."

"Well, we're not busy, so I'll take a look. But in future, you should stay away from bullies. Do you hear me?"

Guy nodded, all the time thinking how useless the advice was.

The doctor continued. "Take your boots off, and your shirt."

Guy tried to comply but his ribs were too painful. Des helped him sit on the edge of the bed, then bent to undo his boots. "Here, let me."

The young doctor brought a scanner over to check Guy. Des eased Guy out of his shirt, revealing a nasty red mark on his skin.

"Six of them, hey?" the doctor remarked. "You're Guy Erma, aren't you? You were due to fight Prince Teodor, weren't you?"

Guy just nodded.

"You're the kid, who beat all the apprentices last year? I watched you beat a seventeen-year-old the size of a Borg. You were so fast you were a blur on the screen. Those six, huh? They were cowards. I'm guessing you've beaten each and every one of them many times?"

Guy nodded.

"This feels good," he ran his hands over his ribs. "When can I fight again?"

"Give it a week?" the doctor said. "Unless your life depends on it." He laughed.

"I need to fight," Guy insisted.

The doctor paused and gave him a look.

"Chart Segat said I need to, it's a demonstration," Guy said and clenched and unclenched his blades hand.

The doctor glanced at Des who shrugged and spoke. "Whatever Chartsie wants."

"Okay," the doctor said, shaking his head. "I have something, but you'll need to do these exercises as well."

"Do as the doctor says. Okay?" Des urged Guy as he helped him back into his clothes. His skin had returned to its healthy state, and the doctor had given him a sheet of physio exercises to be completed each hour.

"Will you train with me?" Guy asked.

"I don't know when. Are you working at Ascot tomorrow?" Des replied. Guy nodded. "There's some training space there - so when I take my break, maybe?"

"Yes please," Guy agreed – he would never pass up the chance to train with his hero. "And you want me to give a message to Loulou?" Guy knew this to be an odd request, even though Des was also an orphan from House Jewel.

"Well, no. And yes. Tell her I love her, as always."

Guy nodded. "But I need her to talk to Chartsie – tell him I'm back from..." He hesitated and pointed to his tanned forearms. "Well, you know where. I need to speak to him in private."

"Oh?" Guy asked.

"What with Royal Ascot Weekend and the Dome Debate, his office says I can't see him until Thursday."

"Next Thursday?" Guy repeated astonished.

"I need to speak to him. It's important. Look, if she says 'no', then say Mezzatorra. Tell her it's about Mezzatorra."

"Mezzatorra? Wasn't that a battle on Sas Darona? What are you doing here, Des? How did you get back?"

"Tribal Dancing!" Des sighed, and then added. "Valvanski ordered dancers for his party."

"Killer Valvanski?"

"No, his brother. Nikki Valvanski. He's ambassador to the Kingdom of Earth."

Guy nodded. He had thought all Zaracans were Valvanski, but maybe not. Maybe only if they were brothers. Had Killer Valvanski a brother? Des was still talking, Guy forced himself to focus.

"So I was the only one fit enough to learn the moves. Someone had to get back here."

"Serious, huh?"

"I was at Mezzatorra," Des hesitated, "I should not be talking to you."

"Please, Des. Please tell me. Who would I tell?"

Des shook his head. "I should have realised with Royal Ascot Weekend. But I have to warn Chart Segat about Mezzatorra."

"Please tell me."

"You know I can't. But I have an urgent message for Chartsie. Tell Loulou. Tell her. No, beg her."

"I will. I'm sure Loulou will help. She spoke to Chartsie about the Dome Militant for me."

Des gave Guy a hard stare. "She asked Chartsie? And?"

"He said no. Not with the Dome Debate, but he said there would be a fight." Guy trailed off; he was confused by the whole thing.

"Did Chartsie say he'll let you into the Dome Militant or not?"

"Loulou said I should be in the Dome Militant, and Chartsie said there might be a fight – if I won, I'd be in. Then Loulou said I had to do what he said. Exactly what he said."

Des sat still for a moment. "That's what she said to me too."

Guy froze, his hands and face were cold. He had known Des all his life. He remembered the ambulance. Loulou screaming. The blood dripping from the black boots. The adults had shooed him and the other kids up to the attic, out of the way. In the dismal shared space, they did not know what injuries Des had sustained, so what they had imagined was worse. Guy swallowed hard.

"She said what to you?"

"Loulou said there was to be a fight, and Chartsie," Des stopped.

"He didn't throw me to the borgs, did he?" Guy asked. "I mean, that's just a Domeside joke, right?"

"A joke? No, it's not a joke. Not on Royal Ascot weekend. The VIP guests, they like their fights bloody."

"Yes, but Chartsie said he won't do that to me."

"I hope he don't, but c'mon Guy, it wasn't that long ago. You remember, don't you?" Des lifted up his left foot and pushed down the synthetic skin to reveal the injury he found so easy to hide, for while Des had a human lower leg and ankle, beyond the heel, the foot had gone, the skin was fake, and underneath was a hideous claw-like prosthetic.

"I always think about how Chart Segat took my foot two days after my sixteenth birthday."

"But he gave you the Dome Militant."

"But he gave me the Dome Militant. And it cost me. Remember, Guy – you have to do whatever he says."

"I know, Des. I know. But he won't do that to me."

Des sighed. He hugged Guy a moment.

"Let's hope so, kiddo," he sighed again, then repeated: "Don't forget to talk to Loulou for me. Mezzatorra. Urgent and important. Got that?"

Chapter 13

3D Models and Avatars

"So, who is Erederon?" Karl asked. He was lounging on a low sofa in Nikato's study at the Zaracan embassy. Nuria sat on a stool across from him. She had a pen and paper and was drawing a family tree of the Dodecahedral Imperial House.

"Oh, Uncle Karl." Nuria scolded him.

"Just call me Karl."

"Well, you see Unc— I mean Karl,"

"You need to be neater than that, Nuria," Karl said in a robotic monotone, mimicking a tutor-droid. Nuria laughed – she knew she was the teacher here.

"There are two," Nuria replied. "First, Old Erederon – or Erederon the Great. He was the emperor before Frederon. He was the only one to survive the Hundred-Year War. He was the last son. He was raised and lived in Domeside before they called him to the imperial throne."

"Ok. Old Erederon is Frederon's father. He's dead, so Frederon is the current emperor."

"Yes. The second Erederon is Prince Erederon, who was the last surviving son of Emperor Frederon. He's dead."

"Died in a terrorist bomb?"

"No, Prince Erederon crashed his flyer, died instantly."

"Ok, Erederon the Great (dead), father to Frederon (emperor – alive), father to Prince Erederon (dead)."

"And how is Teodor related to them?"

"Frederon had a brother, Sergeron. He had a son, Sergeron called Serge, hence King Serge. King Serge had two sons, Teodor and,"

"Don't tell me! Sergeron?"

"No, Deodran. He was the baby prince who was killed by a terrorist bomb in the car along with King Serge."

"Ok. So, Frederon (emperor)," Karl summarized, "is the brother to Sergeron. Is he dead?"

"No." Nuria said, so Karl continued:

"Sergeron is missing, presumed dead, he disappeared seventeen years ago. He was father to Serge (dead.) Grandfather to baby Prince Deodran (dead) and finally, Teodor – the last surviving male heir."

"That's right." Nuria said, clapping her hands. "That makes him the emperor's great nephew."

"Will you two be quiet? The regent is about to speak." They all looked.

"Good evening," the newsreader said. "The six o'clock news will be broadcast after a message from Her Royal Highness, Regent Sayginn."

The information screen went blank. The chords of the Royal anthem started up, and the screen displayed the regent's coat of arms.

Karl whispered. "And how does Regent Sayginn fit in – is she related?"

"No. Regent Sayginn married King Serge, but she was born of one of the lesser families. There are twelve baronial households in the Dodecahedral Empire. Five major baronies, the Imperials and six more minor families. But what minor means is that there have been no marriages between them and the Imperial family for several hundreds of years."

"So, Sayginn, lesser family, but Royal and very old, was she lucky then, to marry Serge?"

"Yes, very lucky. Except of course."

The head and shoulders of Sayginn appeared. Behind her on a stand was a painting. King Serge, Sayginn, Teodor and Deodran, with Prince Teodor standing to the fore.

"Hush, you two," Nikato said.

"Serge is dead," Nuria whispered.

Karl nodded and stretched out the full length of the small sofa, taking care to keep his boots hanging over the armrest. Nikato raised a disapproving eyebrow, but Karl ignored him. Nuria sat down on the floor near to Karl's head and used the armrest of the sofa as a chair back. Karl stroked her hair. All three concentrated on the screen.

"Citizens of Earth, my people," Regent Sayginn stared into the cameras. "This evening's news broadcasts, and your evening papers give details of the violent kidnapping of my son Teodor, as he was undertaking charity work in Domeside. My son was taken, but another dozen children are dead, and more are injured. A terrible crime was inflicted on both me and my people. It is to you, my people, I do declare my first duty."

She paused, then continued, "You can be sure that while my son is in captivity, I will not compromise the economic prosperity or safety of this planet. Any decision taken now, and during this period, will be reviewed by Prime Minister Patrice Macey and the planetary committee. He will continue to do so until Prince Teodor is returned to his rightful place, here in Magnolia Palace." Another pause, then the regent adopted a new and angry tone.

"To the kidnappers! I remain the head of the Royal Guards. I will employ all my powers to find my son. Release my son, unharmed. For you will be caught, I promise. So, help me God." In a deliberate break, Sayginn took a sip from a glass of water. The camera zoomed into her face as she became more persuasive. "To the people of Domeside, some of you know a great deal about the horrendous act that took place today. The video files are being scrutinised for evidence. There will be prosecutions after what happened in the cathedral. No man is above the law. And if you (the word 'you' was accented, so it sounded like pleading) come forward with information that leads to the release of my son." The camera switched to the portrait, "I will ensure you will avoid prosecution for kidnapping, and you will receive a reward that reflects my gratitude to see my son returned here, alive and well." Another slight pause. Sayginn, who had dropped her eyes, returned her gaze to the camera. Her voice was soft.

"Finally, to Teodor. My Teodor, I love you very much. You know of my love for you." Her emotions were strong. "Everything I do is working towards your freedom. From now until the next time I hold you in my arms, I love you, Teodor. We all do." The screen snapped to a photograph of Prince Teodor grinning and hugging a young goran cub, and a repetition of the final bars of the anthem.

"Not a dry eye in the house," Nikato commented. He picked up the control and switched off the screen.

"How old is she?" Karl asked.

"Thirty-three, so older than you, little brother."

"I'm thirty-one. Is it true she will be forced to marry the emperor?"

Nikato frowned, then said in the mild tone he always used for rebukes. "Not forced, but many of the barons think it would be desirable."

"She can say 'no'?"

"Yes, but she will also try to gain some advantage for her son."

"What advantage?" Karl asked. "Prince Teodor is heir to two crowns, the Kingdom of Earth and the Dodecahedral Empire."

"Yes, but deep down, the emperor still wants his son to succeed him. Even if it was an illegitimate son, a lost prince."

"So Teodor might not become emperor?" Karl asked.

"If the emperor died tomorrow," Nuria said, "Teodor is the only heir."

"He was due to be named King on Sunday," Nikato added. "And Saturday is the Dome Debate. So the timing of this kidnapping..." He let it hang. "Anyway, we leave for the Dome in an hour. Will you be ready, Karl?"

"To see the inside of the Dodecahedron Dome. Yes! Do I need to change?" Karl was wearing combats and a t-shirt. "I've got this jacket." He held up a light, leather, flying jacket that Zaracan troops wore when off duty. Karl thought he saw a flicker of amusement pass behind Nikato's eyes, but all he said was, "You have read the schedule for this weekend?"

Karl thought he sounded a little waspish, so he lied.

"Of course, it all looks great."

"Uncle Nikki?" Nuria asked with a sceptical raise of her brows.

"Your uncle Karl is who he is," Nikato said. Then to her. "Whereas you," he pointed to the door.

Nuria smiled as she rose to leave. Karl took this as his cue.

"Nikki, would you mind?" Karl nodded toward the library next door.

Nikato gave a single nod of approval.

Karl had spread himself over most of the ambassador's once-tidy library. His intentions were clear. All across the space were plans and screens of information, as he pieced together the detailed structure of the Dome. Called a mini-city, the Dome was huge. Karl had lost all sense of time, as he scrolled through screens and leafed through the maps. When he heard a small cough, Karl turned to see Nuria stood in the doorway wearing a gown.

"Oh, it's you." Karl said as Nuria crept in and stood alongside Karl at the centre of the 3D graphic of the Dome. "Have you seen this?" He asked. Nuria shrugged and nodded to the windows.

"It's just over there, Uncle. It's hard not to see it," and she laughed.

"Yes, but did you know they had a one-hundred-thousand seat stadium for ball games. There're six swimming pools – from small training pools to massive competition pools with seating for a further ten thousand, then there's further arenas with seating of seven to fifteen thousand. An entertainment complex here, and all these layers of in-person shopping."

"And cafes and restaurants!"

"Yes, but have you seen this. Here and here. All these hidden floors. It's a massive sports complex but it's almost exclusively used by the Dome Militants. I reckon there are barracks for one hundred thousand men, and a transport hub – including all types of land and hover transport and an extended runway to allow the small fleet of military shuttles to transfer to the space stations. Underground there are further gyms. Room after room is given over to weapons, as well as a military kitchen, storage, cellars and refrigerated units. This is massive Nuria, I wonder if Nikato knows, it's much bigger than I would have expected."

"The humans have the right to defend themselves." Nuria said, pulling a chair up to get a better look at the 3D projection of the Dome.

"See this," Karl said. "The verticals and horizontals of the Dome are hollow. The massive structure needs to be strong, but there also has to be access, so..." Karl adjusted the settings of an avatar to see how large you could be to climb through the maintenance network.

"They will rescue him, won't they, Uncle Karl?"

"They will try."

"What would you do if it were me kidnapped in there?"

"I think I would be dismantling their Dome even as we speak," Karl said with a growl.

"Really?" Nuria looked shocked and delighted.

"Fortunately, there are other methods. More than ninety-five per cent of the Dome's infrastructure is monitored by cameras. I expect there are video streams, audio streams, comms. Everything will be checked; should they find anything suspicious, pretty soon someone will have a Royal Guard knock on their door. Of course, whoever kidnapped Prince Teodor is aware of the methods that will be deployed to retrieve him, so that leaves the black zones and the quiet zones."

"Black zones? Those are the areas without camera coverage, aren't they?"

"Yes, and in the Dome, we're talking about Chart Segat's admin suite," Karl waved over several areas of the map that was blacked and crossed out. "Here in the so-called Cap of the Dome, and a variety of areas here linked to the military training facility, all likely to be heavily guarded. I found a document saying this building included a prison block and munitions store."

"Prison? Won't they be keeping him there?"

"You would think so. But it was searched by the Royal Guards this afternoon, and they didn't find him."

"Tsk."

"They will be moving him around, to keep ahead of the searches – but every time they move him, they could end up in the visible zone. See those screens there?" Karl pointed at more video feeds on large screens. "Those are video feeds for the corridors here, here and here."

"The corridors outside the black zones."

"Yes, that's where we are likely to have first sight of him, unless you can think of anything else?"

"Me?"

"Yes, you have a young brain – where do you think they might hide him?"

"In a cupboard."

"Droids can check those; they should be finished soon. They'll start over just in case."

"They could be hiding him in a box or something. I mean, look at those deliveries."

Karl looked at one of the access points; they could see large boxes being delivered and moved around the Dome."

"It's a fashion show. They have been moving stuff in and out all day. I could run an algorithm. What we need is something that would show us where something is hollow and large enough to hide the prince."

All at once, a large stack of crates lit up orange on the display.

"Ooh, orange, so why are those boxes orange?"

"Because they meet the criteria of the algorithm. They are large and hollow, and the prince might be inside."

"Really?"

"No," said Karl. "Look at the signs on the boxes; it's a delivery of melons, but I will send a mini-droid to check just in case." Another room was flashing on the map.

"Where's that?" asked Nuria.

"It's one of the rooms in the Cap of the Dome. There's a party there, but it's a black zone, as well. I don't have the plans, but I found this catering plan for tonight's cocktail party."

"Everybody is having parties tonight," Nuria said. "It's Royal Ascot Weekend!"

Karl nodded. "The algorithm is saying that those cocktail tables are hollow, and the space inside is. Oh, that cannot be right!"

"It must mean the bases, the columns." Nuria leafed through the catering plans to find a photo of the silver cocktail tables. "But they look narrow."

"Well, Prince Teodor isn't much bigger than you. Algorithm, give him space to breathe at least."

At once, all of the tables on the layout turned from orange to black. "Oh!" Nuria exclaimed.

"Ok, so not the cocktail tables." Karl said then added. "Good, there are at least a hundred of them."

"Can you not send roaches to check? Just in case." Nuria asked.

"The cocktail party is in the black zone. Our roaches might get noticed. No, I'll put it on the list for when they move them. It will be under a heading. Nuria's idea."

They laughed, though Nuria stopped first.

"I hate the thought of him being locked up somewhere, all alone."

"Yes, but he'll know they're looking for him – but it would be easier if I had met him."

"How so?" Nuria asked.

"Well, I might have made a telepathic connection with him."

"Would make that a difference?"

"Well yes of course, because I could use my telepathy to sense him."

"I made a connection with him," Nuria said, "When we rode his gorans, he connected his mind and memories to mine."

"That's great! Why did no one tell me," Karl said. "Don't let go of it."

"No, of course not, I keep reaching out for him."

"You have to be in the right place," Karl nodded to the graphics spread across the carpet.

"You think?" Nuria said and glanced out the window to where the Dome dominated the city. "He'll be ok, won't he? I mean he's only fifteen, the same age as me. What if they hurt him?"

"Nuria, Prince Teodor rides two-meter-high gorans. Anyone who does that must be pretty brave. He knows they're looking for him. Most likely, he's curled up fast asleep somewhere."

Chapter 14

Do you think I look like him?

"Oy, Guy! Hey, Guy Erma!"

Emerging from the military complex, Guy looked over and smiled. Running on blades, he covered the distance between them in three bounding leaps.

"Hi Seb. You okay?"

Seb, short for Sebastian, short for Sebastian of Riffault was the lead model of that great house, the muse of its lead designer The Riffault, and the most perfect look-a-like for Prince Teodor on Earth. Even off-duty, Sebastian still looked like Prince Teodor.

Now he sat perched a little too straight, and a little uncomfortable on the corner of an ornamental pot plant. As if he was indeed Prince Teodor, even though the real prince would never be perching on the edge of a planter in the atrium of the Dome.

But today, something was off. As Guy approached, Sebastian concealed the smoke inhaler within his sleeve, then behind his back. Of course, Prince Teodor didn't smoke, but Guy knew if Sebastian was hiding it, he shouldn't be smoking it. Guy wondered whether he should say something, when suddenly he was roughly pushed aside by two men. Guy caught a glimpse of the uniform, and he bit back a laugh. Sebastian showed the men his ID; they nevertheless insisted on a blood sample as well. A few minutes later they hurried away.

"Fifth time today," Sebastian muttered, holding up his index finger, and showing the multiple pinpricks where blood samples had been taken. "You'd think they'd never heard of me."

Sebastian was not just a model; he was a celebrity. As Prince Teodor's twin, he appeared in photo shoots, attended parties, galas and much more. Guy knew he was one of the best-paid models on Old Fleet Street, yet today he was being made to pay for his success in an entirely different way.

"You should be glad you're not him," Guy said.

Sebastian looked at him. "Sorry, I forgot – you were there too, weren't you?"

"You were too?" Guy said.

"No, I missed it. Someone lost the Prince's shoes, so I had been sent off," Sebastian paused as Guy paled, so he changed tack. "Anyway, what about you?"

Why had he stolen those shoes? Guy wondered. He felt sick as he remembered the sound of the explosion, the sight of the dust cloud materialising at the cathedral door, the blood on the pillows of the children in the clinic. But the shoes, he shook his shoulders minutely, yes, they were still in his bag. *What was he going to do with them?*

"Oh god, I'm sorry Guy," Sebastian said, misreading his distress.

"No, it's all right, I left early – I had double maths." Sebastian didn't seem to believe him, so Guy added. "Dome Militant entrance exam?"

Sebastian didn't reply, instead he looked a little bored. "Well, don't just stand there. Take a pew. I'll look less like him if I have a Dome Militant guard at my side."

Guy smiled. Sebastian was cool. He tried to perch alongside him, hoping his face could look calm and aloof as well. Before them was a scene of chaos. The central square of the Dome was being remade in advance of one of Royal Ascot Weekend's great set pieces: the annual Festival of Fashion. For three days, the great fashion houses of Old Fleet Street would present new collections, throw open the doors of their secret studios and workshops and unveil new talent – be it models or designers. The whole event started on the Friday of Royal Ascot Weekend, with a dinner which featured displays and catwalks from the eight main houses and up to a dozen smaller concerns.

Today was Friday afternoon. The last technical rehearsal was in full swing. And they were running late. Guy watched as another array of lights was hoisted upwards. In the rafters above, technicians in black jumpsuits scrambled scrambled to secure and manually adjust the spotlights. Finally, the head designer of the Riffaut walked along the catwalk, pausing at intervals and shouting out colours. "This is the cold white. It has to hit here." The circle of light moved. "And I need the warm white here. No, I said here."

"Oh, there you are, Guy!" Guy looked around. Marline. Guy frowned. Of course, he knew what she wanted.

Guy checked his communicator. "It's not time yet."

Marline replied. "No, but soon. Loulou said I was to look out for you, make sure you weren't late." She turned back to Sebastian.

"Hi, Sebastian." She nodded towards the stage. "I thought we'd have time to rehearse – a proper rehearsal."

"Nah, we'll have five minutes at the end, if we're lucky." He sucked on the smoke tube. "Hey, don't look so worried, you'll do fine. You're a Domeside beauty – you know that, don't you?"

Guy smiled at the compliment and looked up at Marline; she shrugged. "They say I need to get a big order, at least one big one. I don't know what that means."

"It means you need to be your beautiful self and make some rich customers want to buy your look," Sebastian replied.

"They say that if I don't make a sale, they may demote me or even fire me."

This is fashion model talk, thought Guy. He had nothing to say, but Sebastian spoke.

"Cheer up. Have faith in your old friend Sebastian. Even though you are House Jewel, and I am the Riffaut, I'll give you a tip. First, don't listen to those who say they won't serve a Valvanchi. She's coming to House Jewel, isn't she?"

"Yes, the other girls say they won't talk to her because she is the niece of Killer Valvanski. They say modelling for her is like helping the enemy."

"Ok, the situation on Sas Darona is messy, but technically they are our allies. So, listen, she's an only child, her mother is dead, and her father never says 'no' to her. Money is no object, and I mean it, money is no object. So, remember, the Valvanchi always like to know the history of a piece, the name of the designer, the origin of the fibres, the story of the seamstress."

Marline still hesitated. "Valvanski?"

"Val-van-chi," Sebastian corrected her. "Ask Guy here. What would you say, Guy, if Marline sold a wardrobe of clothes to Nuria Valvanchi?"

Guy looked up, first at Marline, then at Sebastian. "Well, better House Jewel," Guy said at once, then as an after-thought. "Marline is, after all, the most beautiful girl in Domeside."

"See?" Sebastian said. "Even the Dome Militant agree. So don't be an idiot – but if that does not work, remember the name Baristella. Very new money and lots of it. The son came into the salon this morning, and I showed him the gold and platinum hand-carved communicator, told him there were only three in existence and that Prince Teodor had one, and he bought it. Eighty-five thousand, just like that, and he bought the belt and cufflinks to match. Then we started on shoes – four handmade pairs, one brown, one grey, two shades of black, and after that the clothes. You have no idea, over three hundred thousand in two hours."

"Yes, but I can't model for boys like you," Marline said.

"There's a sister. Amber Baristella, and I could tell her family had plans for her."

"Plans?" Guy asked.

"Like, Prince Teodor—type plans," Sebastian explained.

Marline raised her brows. "Really?"

"Prince Teodor is sixteen," Guy interrupted, but Sebastian ignored him, as he continued.

"What with those pictures of him and the stable girl, the Riffaut was saying the young girls of the court have suddenly become a lot more interested in him. I met him, you know?"

"Who, Teodor - did he come to the shop?" Marline asked.

"No, I helped him dress this morning at the cathedral." Marline cut in. "What's he like?"

"Nice, a proper gent, very polite. Hated the costume though, absolutely hated it. Not something I would have chosen to be kidnapped in, either."

"What? He was wearing the gold shorts and the wings and all that when they grabbed him?" Guy asked.

"They found the wings - the borgs took a shaft that led to the sewers. That's where they found the wings."

"The sewers?" Marline repeated with a wince.

"They're old – the deep sewers go everywhere under Domeside. Wings of a Fallen Angel, you know all that. It was in the news. He wasn't even wearing proper shoes, just these lace-ups—one step up from flip-flops."

"And no communicator either?" Guy added. "Someone had it all planned, separate the Prince from his effects, and he was totally vulnerable."

"I had not thought of that," Marline said. "Poor Prince Teodor!"

"Yeah, well, if he's still alive. I don't know what I'm going to do if they've killed him." Guy glanced at Sebastian. He was so close in looks to the young prince – the most perfect of all the lookalikes – his presence at events fooled or misled many who claimed to know the prince well. "At least I could stop taking the height inhibitors, and, I don't know, grow a beard. Do you think a goatee would suit me?" Sebastian turned to Marline, stroking his chin as he did. This reminded Guy, that despite his outward appearance, Seb was older than both him and the Prince. *Wasn't he the same age as Des, what almost eighteen or something? So, they gave Seb drugs to keep his Prince Teodor look? Height inhibitors? And what else?*

"Surely they're going to find him?" Marline interrupted – she was still talking about Prince Teodor.

"Are they even looking? Hey, Guy, you've been inside. What says the Militant?"

"Well, I was training there. Loulou said I could go."

"What she actually said," Marline corrected him, "was that she couldn't bear you fidgeting anymore and would you please go and burn off some excess energy."

"Well, I have to train to join them."

"Yeah, yeah," Sebastian said, silencing them both. "Listen, what's going on back there? Did you hear anything?"

"Not really, some of the guys are saying there's bound to be a general recall – but right now, everyone is still on leave. It's Royal Ascot Weekend."

"So, the Dome Militant are not looking for the prince?" Marline asked.

"Some of them are asking why the Dome Militant should help when the Royal Guards killed and injured all of those Domeside children."

"That's rubbish; that's not the reason." Sebastian shook his head impatiently then nodded across the space to a large banner. "That's the reason; I tell you. That over there."

Marline and Guy both looked where Sebastian was looking.

"Oh," Marline whispered.

Five more years.
Chart Segat for the Dome.
Five more years.

"They're going to kill him. I know it, I just know it," muttered Sebastian.

"Oh, Sebastian, and you're topping and tailing the display tonight," Marline exclaimed. She was referring to the fact that Sebastian had both the first and the last outfit of the Riffaut's catwalk. As Teodor's lookalike, he was the star of the show.

"A last hurrah!"

"Not necessarily." They all turned at the familiar voice. "Hi Sebastian. Long time, no see."

"Des!" Sebastian hugged him. When they were standing side by side, it was easier to spot that Sebastian and Des were similar in age. Not an innocent, not an ingénue – Sebastian was a seventeen-year-old model who knew his craft. Through hard work and determination, he always appeared identical to fifteen-year-old Prince Teodor.

"Let's go and grab a beer," Sebastian said. "I need one, or maybe three."

"No way! As Marline said, it's your show tonight. I'll buy you a bite and a coffee if you like. And put that away." Des took the smoke stick off him. "You need a clear head tonight."

"No, no. You don't need to buy me anything." Seb looked embarrassed. "I had a good client." He said.

"I don't care about that. I'm your mate, and before you get any ideas, I'm not taking you for three courses at Bistro Jewel. C'mon."

Marline and Guy were left standing, watching them leave. Simultaneously, their communicators beeped. "That's us," Marline said.

"You go. I've got these." Guy showed her his running blades.

She shook her head. "No way. You'll only get me into trouble if you're late!"

Guy shrugged. He was watching Seb and Des. Des had led him to Juke's food van and had purchased a large cup and a roll – a combination Guy knew was the cheapest meal in all Domeside. Des was sharing the drink with Seb and had ripped the roll in two. They perched themselves across from each other on high stools. Guy could tell Des was already deep in a tale from the savannah of Sas Darona.

"Guy, c'mon," Marline was pleading now. "We better go." Guy nodded and followed. Again, he wished he was older – that he and Des might be true friends. Then he felt a deeper pang; he would have liked to have just one friend. Just one other with whom he could pass the time of day and share everything.

"Wait no!" Marline said and stopped. Guy looked up at her. "What was that about this morning?" Guy frowned. What was she talking about?

"You mean the Prince getting kidnapped?"

"No, no, not that. Loulou, she made you take a blood test. What was that about?"

Oh that – of course, Marline had been there. She had seen. Guy winced as he remembered Loulou passing the test to Chart Segat. "Please don't use it unless you have to," she had said. If she was his mother, then why had she said that? "I need to be registered, to have a mother at least, to be accepted into the Dome Militant."

"Yes, but Loulou is my mum," Marline said.

Guy looked at her. Of course, he knew that. He had always known that. "Yes, but..." *Okay so how could that be?* He and Marline were the same age, born on the same day.

"Look, it even says here on the Press Release, when they launched me last month. Marline, the beautiful daughter of legendary model Loulou, whose lovers allegedly include the artist Lord Baltimore, the singer-songwriter Et Van Dore and Prince Erederon of Dodecahedral." Marline showed him the information on her communicator. "I am her daughter."

"And they used to say Prince Erederon was your father, I know - but you had the tests, and they were negative."

"They were inconclusive," Marline interrupted him. "One test said I was his child, one test said Loulou was not my mother." She shook her head in disbelief. "Pah! Then they made the test illegal. That test, you had this morning, it was illegal. You know that, right? I don't know what you want to prove. I am Loulou's daughter. I know it. I've always known."

Guy stood a moment. He felt lost. If Marline was Loulou's daughter, then who were his parents? And without parents. Unless. "Maybe we're twins," he blurted it out in a moment of inspiration. They stood looking at each other. The same dark eyes, the same pale skin, the same black curls.

"No. No, that's not ok." Marline replied.

"It could be ok," Guy replied taking her hand. "That would mean you were my sister. My real sister, and neither of us are orphans."

Marline shook her head. "No!" she said, and then her communicator beeped. "Oh God, we're late!"

They set off at a run. It was not far. A large gym had been converted into a green room. There were racks of clothes at the centre, surrounded by clusters of mirrors – one for each of the houses of Old Fleet Street. Within their area, hairdressers, stylists and make-up artists worked up a frenzy preparing their models. Guy and Marline slipped through the crush until they found themselves standing at Loulou's shoulder, as the make-up artist finished her work. She smiled to see their reflection in her mirror. "Thanks for getting him here, Marline."

Marline nodded and headed off. Loulou reached up to stroke Guy's cheek. "Good boy, you remembered to wash your hair. Dana here will dry it. She's the only one I let touch my hair."

The make-up artist, Dana, smiled and gave Guy a wink. "Hey, gorgeous, you make my life too easy."

A golden-haired youth passed by their section wearing a tweed jacket.

"Who's that?" said Guy. "Is that?"

"No!" Loulou replied. "It's another one of those lookalikes from the Riffaut. They won a contract to dress Prince Teodor this season, so they have all these teenagers made up to look like him."

"But..." Guy protested.

"Fake the hair, adjust the skin tone, and insert false lenses. I think two had surgery to shape their noses and cheekbones."

"I thought Seb was the only one," said Guy.

"No, it was too much work for one person. And Seb is a bit too old, really. These newbies are younger. There are eight lookalikes now. Remember, if they are good, they could make a whole career out of imitating the prince."

"I guess." Guy remembered Seb's assertion that the prince was most likely dead. He thought of Seb and Des sitting together, eating rolls. Wait a minute, what had Des said?

"I saw Des today. Do you remember Des Parks?" Guy asked Loulou.

"Has there been a shuttle from... I thought it was locked down," Loulou whispered. She did not say Sas Darona aloud, though that was what she meant. Sas Darona had been in lockdown for three months. No Dome Militant had got in or out. *What was Des doing here?*

"He says he needs to speak to Chartsie, but the office won't offer him an appointment until Thursday. He asked me to say. Will you talk to Chartsie?"

"Hush!" Loulou shushed him and held up a hand, index and thumb firmly closed together.

"Please, Loulou. He said I was to tell you it was about Mezzatorra."

"Mezza-what? Okay, tell him I'll let Chartsie know he's back. Mezza-what?"

"Mezzatorra."

"Mezzatorra. Got it."

All at once there was a piercing squeal – someone was pointing at a screen. All the screens had switched to showing the Imperial Coat of Arms of the Kings and Emperors of Dodecahedral.

"What's that?" Dana said.

Loulou and Guy looked up on the screen above them. "Is it like an emergency broadcast?" The screen switched to show Regent Sayginn sitting at an ornate desk.

"Put the sound up," Loulou added.

"I speak to you on the eve of a terrible day. To you, my people, I do declare my first duty." Sayginn started.

"She doesn't mean that!" interrupted Dana. "What about our kids?" There were shouts of agreement from around the green room. It was now clear that most of the children who had been killed in the cathedral had not been killed by borgs but by the Royal Guard, who had been caught unaware as Prince Teodor was snatched from under their noses.

"Murderer!" Someone else shouted. There followed such a lot of noise and shouting that Sayginn's words from the screen were barely audible. But suddenly, a photo of Prince Teodor appeared – first wearing one of his uniforms and then the golden angel costume.

"Shhh," shouted Loulou. "Put the sound up!" All around they quietened, maybe influenced by Loulou, maybe shocked as they tried to imagine what might have happened to the Prince. The Regent was concluding her speech with her very last appeal.

"To Teodor, my Teodor, I love you very much. You know of my love for you. I am thinking and working towards your freedom from now until the next time I hold you in my arms. I love you, Teodor. We all do." The last image was one of Teodor – some years younger but ecstatically hugging a young goran cub.

There was no way you could look at such a photo and not feel a pang at the danger the boy now faced.

Guy leant in close to Loulou and whispered. "Will they kill him?"

Loulou shrugged her shoulders and kissed him. "Poor Sayginn, I know I couldn't bear it."

Guy nodded and blushed; he knew she was talking about losing him, her only son.

"Loulou," Guy whispered – now he had her to himself. "Do I have any brothers or sisters, half-sisters maybe?"

"You have a loft-full of half-brothers and sisters in the attics of House Jewel," Loulou laughed.

"No, that's not what I meant."

"Guy, I know. But you know that a model isn't supposed to have children, or lovers – she is meant to be beautiful and alluring, unfettered and unattainable."

Guy knew this, he didn't need to be told. "Yes or no, please?" he pleaded.

Loulou looked at him. "If I answer this, then they'll be no more questions?"

Guy was about to agree but then he remembered. "It's about Marline."

"Ah," Loulou said and stroked his cheek. "The answer is no, but Marline was born on the same day as you - so I have tried to look out for her, just as I did for you."

"Why? What happened to Marline's mother?"

"I said no more questions, Guy. I am mother to all the children in the attics of House Jewel, you know that."

Guy nodded. What exactly had Loulou said. No? No brothers or sisters, is that what she meant? So did that mean he and Marline were not related, not twins. Yet Loulou also said she was mother to all of his half-brothers and sisters living in the attics. All the models said the same, but Loulou had also said she had looked out for Marline. Why? Did she know Marline's mother? If they had their babies on the same day, they must have been pregnant together. Loulou must have known Marline's mother, but where was she now? Why did Loulou feel like she had to look out for Marline?

"C'mon Guy. Stop daydreaming. You have to change." Loulou pulled Guy onto her chair in her place, and

– kissing the top of his head – she said, "What do you think, Dana? This one could never look like Prince Teodor."

"No, but he could easily pass as a young Prince Erederon," Dana replied. "He so totally has the look."

"Oh, Dana! You're right. Blow dry his hair in Erederon's style. I'll look for that black eyeliner he preferred."

"No, no! Well, ok, but no eyeliner," protested Guy.

"What's going on?" Marline said. She was beautifully dressed and made up with glittering red eye-shadow, that matched Loulou's signature look.

"Oh, c'mon, Guy. Do you want the Riffaut to take all the Imperial glory?" Loulou joked.

Marline watched closely while they styled his hair and make-up. She snorted. "Oh, please. Don't tell me he's supposed to be the lost prince?"

"Hush, Marline. Don't say that. Guy has no idea who his parents are." Loulou looked into his eyes. "Do you?" Guy smiled up at her beautiful face. She was his mother, and he would refuse her nothing. "The Great Emperor Erederon, father to the current Emperor Frederon, lived in hiding in Domeside for part of his childhood," Loulou told him, a tale he knew well, as she painted on the black eyeliner. "And the reason he did so was because, unlike Prince Teodor, he could pass unnoticed amongst the local children. He had the original Domeside look."

"Who cares about old Emperor Erederon!" Marline cut in. "It was his grandson Prince Erederon who was your paramour, wasn't he Loulou?"

"Marline, we never talk about our clients."

"Or our consorts." Marline whispered to Guy.

"Marline!" Loulou said, "A true Domeside beauty knows when to be silent." Marline pouted and rolled her eyes, as Loulou continued. "I mean look at Guy. Black hair, dark eyes, skinny build, tight muscles, a Domesider through and through. You look good." Loulou concluded.

Guy gave Marline a knowing look, and with his fingers he mimed. "Together". If they were twins then of course they would both look alike, they would both look good.

Marline shrugged. "No, I don't see it. He's too skinny, he misses too many meals. As for his muscles - what else does he do except fight blades in the light and shadow of the Dome?"

Guy was hurt by her words. She did not want to accept they might share the same mother. Neither one of them knew rightly who their parents were, so why might they not be twins? Well, he would just ignore her. Why should he care what she said about him? He scrutinised his reflection – skin-tight black trousers, a white silk shirt and a sparkling red waistcoat. Then the stylist offered him a black jacket. He pulled it on, turned the collar up at the neck and flicked back his hair.

"Nice," he murmured to himself. As soon as the word escaped him, he was embarrassed. All round, there was a chorus of remarks from the women and girls.

"Well?" he asked Marline.

"I guess he'll do," Marline said to Loulou.

"He'll do," Loulou agreed, and she led the others in applause. "Ladies, for one night only before he abandons us to join the Dome Militant - who knows why? I give you the latest face of House Jewel. Guy Erma." The girls laughed, cheered, hugged, squeezed and kissed him. The make-up artist stepped in to shoo them away and fix the damage.

"Perfect!" she said.

Guy looked in the mirror. He might not want to be a model, but as he tweaked his collar once more, he knew he was a success.

Chapter 15

Diplomatic Prep

"Okay, we're ready."

From the corner of the library in the Zaracan embassy, Karl turned to where Nikato was standing in the doorway. He sighed and he dragged himself away from his maps of the Dome. What was his brother talking about?

"You look very nice, Nuria," Nikato said.

Karl looked at his niece. She was wearing an extravagant gown. A single sheet of cloth draped from her shoulders to hang to her knees, and it was the colours of flames. She had shifted her long silver mane to hot oranges and deep reds rippling like molten fires.

Nikato had also changed. He wore a purple silver fur trimmed cloak, hanging open to reveal a lilac brocade suit, and embroidered and polished boots. "Don't forget your jacket, Karl," he said with a smirk.

It dawned on Karl that something was amiss. "Where are we going?"

"You remember, Karl," Nikato purred. "The Festival of Fashion. The reception party? I have organised a Sas Darona-themed party with tribal dancers and fried chilli

Sand Lizards. We have to promote House Duet – you know, the Zaracan fashion industry?"

Karl felt sick at this rebuke. After all his protests and the sheer effort of bringing the tribal dancers and Sand Lizards, he had forgotten. Or maybe he had never realised. The party was tonight – his first night, and it was a fashion party. And Karl was wearing combats?

"I'd better change," he said.

Nikato checked his communicator before he replied with a hint of victory, "I'm afraid we no longer have any time to spare."

"Why do I think you have been waiting all day to say that to me?"

"I dare say they will recognise you, uniform or not. You may have kept your shadow war off the main newsfeeds, but the Militant remember."

Karl picked up his jacket. The creased, off-duty Zaracan uniform felt scruffy, out of place, and somehow defiant. "You know Nikki, you're right. I don't need fancy clothes to remind anyone who I am. I will wash my face, though." Karl nodded to the attendant mini bathroom off the library. Anger flashed in Nikato's eyes.

"The cars are downstairs. Don't take too long."

As Nikato and Nuria left, Karl reran the algorithm. The cocktail tables, previously blacked out as too small, now glowed faint orange. One descriptor stood out: *grille.* Large enough to hide a body. Just.

God.

"There's air in the tubes." Karl muttered. He stared at the screen. "Maybe."

Chapter 16

A Festival of Fashion and Shadows

"**S**o, what now?" Sayginn was restless. "I have cleared my entire diary. For God's sake, give me something to do." Regent Sayginn and Prime Minister Macey were watching the viewing statistics for the broadcast earlier that evening. Over 78% of the Domeside population had seen the broadcast. It was being repeated on every channel. Saturation coverage was only moments away.

"We need to look again at your diary, but you're not going to like it."

"Patrice, no. I'm not going to any party. What about the press? How can I attend a party when my son has been kidnapped?"

"I'll manage the press. You need to go back to the Dome."

"I've already spoken to Chart Segat."

"His inner circle, Sayginn. You need to speak to each of them and, eyeball to eyeball, ask them directly."

"But how?"

"The Festival of Fashion? I guarantee they will all be there."

"Oh no!" Sayginn protested, only to be distracted. One of the screens was showing footage from the viewpoint of a cy-wolf as he raced along a narrow maintenance corridor chasing Teodor. The animal had come so close to freeing the prince in those first vital moments after the capture. But it was all in vain, the Battle Borg had been fast, accurate, and unafraid. The cy-wolf was torn apart.

Sayginn watched the film playing on a loop. These were the last and best pictures of Teodor from that morning. Alive, yes, but drugged. His limbs hung loose, his eyes glazed, *and yet, and yet*. His fingers were twitching as he tried to reach the cy-wolf. He was trying to escape. He had been well trained. He knew he had to fight, whatever horror came his way. Here he was fighting, trying to escape, until unconsciousness overtook him.

"Oh, sweet Teo!" she muttered. "Hang on, my darling; Mummy is coming."

The three identical turquoise and white hovercraft cruised silently around to the pentagonal entrance. At their approach, the milling crowds paused to look and point, for these were the special vehicles of the Zaracan—alien ambassadors of the 1,000-planet-strong Zaracan Democratic Union. As the vehicles came to a halt, first Nuria, then Nikato stepped out, followed swiftly by Karl Valvanchi.

If there was some applause as the women recognized the princess, it faded at the sight of her uncle, the ambassador, and was followed by gasps as the crowd recognized the uniform of the third. A group of younger Dome Militant had stopped to stare at the aliens.

Nikato, Nuria, and Karl, having paused to take in the vast structure, were now being lured inside by music, the clink of glasses, and the scents of fine foods.

"Welcome to the Dodecahedron Dome of Earth," Nuria murmured, clinging to Karl's hand.

"Take a good look," whispered Nikato. "It's a whole other world."

"I'm sure," Karl replied. He sounded like he was determined not to be impressed. Yet the sheer scale of the Dome was certainly impressive and the number of Dome Militant so numerous that, even in his combat jacket, he felt exposed.

The entrance atrium had been converted into a vast festival of fashion and flowers. There were ten-metre-high floral displays, gilt and velvet catwalks, unbelievably beautiful men and women, and astonishing, unforgettable clothes. The embassy had sent a large contingent to represent the Zaracan Democratic Union, including many of the young female staff who were all dressed up for the occasion. They were an intimidating clan, Karl realised, these ten tall Zaracans – all with long, sweeping multi-coloured manes – entering the party dressed in the finest Old Fleet Street fashion. Ten tall Zaracans and him – the tallest and most impressive of them all. His casual combats were gaining him more stares than all his colleagues, and as he passed, his name – sometimes mispronounced as Killer Valvanski – echoed at his back. A single voice cried aloud:

"Go home, Killer Ski!"

Karl raised a brow and turned to look, even as Nikato swirled around to glare. But the young men just laughed and sprinted away.

"Tut!" Nikato said.

"They fear you uncle," Nuria said.

Killer Ski indeed! They had not seen him cradling a dying Dome Militant, willing him to live, applying the best antidotes the Zaracan Union could devise. Could it be that the humans knew not how most of their losses on Sas Darona came about? That their young men had orders to commit suicide rather than surrender? That the Dome they loved and the medallions they so admired, when worn by their soldiers on Sas Darona, were instruments of immediate death? The entrance atrium had been transformed into a riotous festival of fashion and flowers. Ten-metre-high floral arrangements loomed over catwalks and seating pods. Beautiful men and women strode through the space, dressed in couture Karl could only describe as performatively absurd.

"It's nothing," Karl replied. "We should keep moving."

The Zaracan delegation was here in force—young, statuesque, and impossible to ignore. Yet even among them, Karl's presence drew stares. His off-duty military garb made him stand out—perhaps intentionally.

They had barely taken more than a dozen steps when Karl spotted him.

"Chart Segat," Karl whispered. He nodded to where the mayor of the Dome was surrounded by a circle of enthralled sycophants who hung on his every word and laughed at his jokes. He was waiting for someone. Who? Karl found he wanted to hear what he was saying. Nikato pinched Karl on the upper arm as he saw him edge closer into Chart's orbit.

"He's expecting Sayginn," Nikato muttered under his breath. "This is political theatre. She arrives late, and he gets to walk her to the Emperor's table in full view. Him, the man most likely to be holding her son, yet She has to pretend she does not know this."

Karl's gaze sharpened. "So, we just stand and watch?"

"We're diplomats, of course we stand and watch, for now it's all we can do."

"It's not ALL we could do," Karl rebuked him.

"Karl!" Nikato hissed silencing him with a look, and waving for him to watch. Karl turned to where Chart Segat gestured broadly toward the entryway, glancing meaningfully at a man holding a comms unit. Segat was ready to move. The escort tightened their formation. Beyond the pentagon archway, a fleet of land vehicles bearing the Kingdom of Earth heraldry drew up before the entrance.

The crowds pressed forward, and Chart Segat was shouting orders, Dome Militant and Battle Borgs took up positions. The Valvanchis found themselves pushed backwards and that's when Karl noticed, then, all at once, his attention was yanked away—toward a nearby display. At first, he thought it was a fashion tableau—mannequins maybe. Then the truth hit.

There were eight models. And they were all identical to Prince Teodor.

"Nuria," he whispered. "You have a link to the Prince?"

Nuria nodded. She too was suddenly staring at the young men.

"Use it."

Karl held his breath as she looked from one to the next. None of them reacted.

"No. He's not there," She said at last.

Karl exhaled sharply. "It was a long shot."

They both turned to the sound of cheers. They saw Chart Segat leading the applause, then pausing to bow.

She had arrived.

The entrance guards snapped to attention. The crowd, uneasy and vigilant, parted in silence. Regent Sayginn stepped forward, a garland of blossoms looped over one arm, her chin held high. Her people knew she walked into the lion's den not for politics, but for her son—her stolen son, their golden, future king.

"Over 3,000 guests," her aide muttered. "They've extended the plaza façade and doubled the atrium space."

Sayginn ignored him. She had seen him.

Chart Segat bowed, a politic smile already in place. "Regent Sayginn. This way, please. The Emperor is waiting."

A line of Dome Militant closed ranks behind her Royal Guards.

"This is unnecessary," she said under her breath.

"For protocol," Segat replied. "You understand."

She didn't reply. The escort moved swiftly through the crowd, clearing a path through the shimmering gowns and jewel-toned suits. Sayginn walked with steady grace, her gown brushing the polished floors like whispering silk. At last, they ascended the dais where the Emperor watched.

"You're late," Frederon snapped. "We waited, but in the end, you missed the first course. Sit. Wine! So, still no news about Teodor?"

Sayginn shook her head and sank into the seat beside him. Her throat tightened. She reached for the nearest glass and took a long swallow, turning away from the Emperor—someone was staring at her.

Not by the crowd. Not by the press droids.

Him.

Tall, slim, in a military jacket. Yes, she recognised that uniform.

He approached without hesitation, dropping to one knee at her side.

Who?

"My blades are yours to command, Regent," he said in flawless Old Fleet dialect. "Let me help you find your son."

His voice was deep, sure. He kissed her rings.

Sayginn felt a jolt—like static through silk—at the touch of his lips. She looked down at him and met his eyes, and for a moment, it was like the world had hushed around them.

The name came to her unbidden. Karl Valvanchi.

He felt her gaze the moment his lips brushed her knuckles. Her fingers were trembling slightly—maybe he should not have knelt. But as he had seen her, so he had sensed her distress and peril, a mother lost without her son, surrounded by enemies. He could not help it, he had to share some of his strength with her.

Behind him, Karl could feel Nikato's disapproval burning a hole in his back. He didn't care. The gesture was sincere, calculated, and deliberate. He wanted her to know whose side he was on.

He looked up. *Let me help you*, his eyes said.

Sayginn's face was composed, but her eyes... her eyes were searching. Measuring.

"Killer Valvanski," the Emperor hissed behind her, gleefully expressing years disdain. "I trust you enjoyed the Dome Militant stretch—exquisite for the spine, they say."

Sayginn's fingers tightened on Karl's hand. Karl saw her blink just once, a simple 'yes', but then she coughed and, clearing her throat, she spoke.

"Freddie, Karl is here on a diplomatic visa," she said. Her voice was brittle. She turned to Karl and whispered just loud enough to be heard, "You should leave. Now."

He rose slowly. "I offer my services freely," he said. "I've fought the Dome Militant before. I know how they move. How they hide."

Sayginn flinched. *Not Sas Darona, not now.*

"That is a lie," she said aloud. "There are no Dome Militant on Sas Darona."

This was theatre. For the Emperor, who would not want the Dome Militant to be too strong. For the press droids, who would broadcast to the wider empire. For the watching crowd who would know she was lying, because their sons and husbands were on Sas Darona, but also would approve of her defiance. Sayginn knew all this. She knew she was right.

Karl understood. The Zaracan themselves denied anything beyond 'mere disturbances on Sas Darona', they also minimised the ongoing conflict and tensions.

This is the game we play, he thought. Now a boy's life at stake, is it worth the risks? He held Sayginn's gaze until he saw tears pearling in her eyes.

Her hard-suppressed tears. All the answer he needed.

He bowed and stepped back.

His eyes locked on hers, and despite the din of the atrium, he sent the thought deliberately: *I am ever at your service, sweet lady.*

Sayginn turned sharply to look at him.

Karl Valvanchi hadn't spoken aloud. Sayginn was certain of it. And yet, the words had landed in her mind like a whispered promise.

I am the only one who can save him.

She turned—but he had already vanished into the crowd.

Was that alien telepathy?

Could the Valvanchi so easily enter her thoughts, brush his intent against her mind like silk.

She drew a breath, suddenly aware of her own stillness. The world felt altered, as if the centre of gravity had shifted. She touched the rim of her glass, grounding herself—but already the atmosphere around her was changing again.

The music surged. Lights dimmed. Catwalks descended overhead like golden vines. Tables rotated in synchrony, making space. Guests gasped, clapped, pointed.

Sayginn blinked, disoriented, as a new spectacle unfolded.

Then she saw them.

Eight boys. Identical to Teodor.

Descending in slow, deliberate motion from the upper platforms like celestial beings. Gleaming skin. Gold-threaded robes. Her son's face, duplicated and commodified, made fashion.

She stood so suddenly her chair tipped with a clatter. "Is this a joke?"

The music stopped. The crowd stilled. One of the boys turned—smiled—winked.

It was not him.

But her heart didn't know that.

"It's not him," Sayginn whispered.

"His name is Sebastian, My Regent," One of the organisers started to apologise, "We'll stop the show."

"No, no," she said, catching her breath. "It's a good likeness. There's no harm done."

She turned her back on the catwalk and walked back to where the Emperor offered her a glass of fizz with a sad smile. "Poor Sayginn. Poor, poor Sayginn. Let me protect you."

He bent down and kissed her. Sayginn groaned inside but dutifully stood for the kiss. All around the people were applauding, and the news people jostled for pictures. As he released her, Sayginn stepped back with a fake look of delight. She knew that if she must marry Frederon, then – in the eyes of the press – the marriage must be a success. She would have more power if people thought the Emperor loved her. So, she yielded to a third kiss, even though she recognised the angry glint in Frederon's eyes. He, for one, knew she was play-acting. Sayginn tried to defuse the situation, by taking Frederon firmly by the arm, and leading him to a nearby alcove where a human tableau of fashion displayed clothes and talent.

"Look, House Jewel," Sayginn said, nodding towards the latest catwalk. "Do you remember the beautiful Loulou?"

Frederon gave a small snort. "Of course, Loulou. She's older now of course." Sayginn glanced at him, puzzled by his tone—only for Chart Segat to lean in.

"Yes, and rumour has it one of those two youngsters—maybe both—are her love children."

"Loulou had another child?" Sayginn asked, then immediately regretted it. As Regent, she wasn't supposed to know models by name, let alone follow gossip about their illegitimate offspring.

As the scent of amber resin tinged with strawberries drifted from the stage, so Loulou lay reclined at the centre of the scene in a red, glimmering gown, draped across a low sofa. To her right sat a teenage girl in white lace with a red ribbon trim. Three other models stood artfully placed, but it was the youth at Loulou's elbow who caught Sayginn's eye. He wore black and white with a bold red sash and held out a bowl of strawberries.

"How old are they?" Sayginn asked quietly.

"Both Guy and Marline are working, so they're sixteen," Segat answered too fast. Sayginn clocked the lie instantly. Still, the teens didn't look unhappy.

What is he hiding? Apart from my son... Her throat tightened. Unbidden tears rose. She stared ahead, hoping the men would mistake her silence for fascination with the fashion. Breath by breath, her emotion eased. The models launched into a short performance: the youth offered strawberries to Loulou, who refused them. The girl beside her accepted—only to have them snatched away with a flourish of juggling and mock-scolding. Laughter rippled across the floor.

Sayginn's eye was drawn back to the boy. Something about him—the sharp cheekbones, the way his hair gleamed in the light—felt familiar. She turned away, unsettled—and caught sight of Segat. He was pointing subtly toward the youth. Frederon followed the gesture. No words passed between them, but something about the exchange—its intimacy, its secrecy—twisted in Sayginn's gut. *What are they doing? What are they seeing?*

Before she could form a question, the lights shifted. The spotlight fell on House Jewel. On cue, two young men strutted down the catwalk. A dozen models followed in rhythm. But the youth still hung back.

He's not keen, Sayginn thought. Then suddenly—he launched forward in a burst of movement, a whirlwind of somersaults and handsprings. Gasps rose from the crowd. He reached the end of the catwalk and spun, blade-like legs slicing the air in a flurry of stylised combat.

Astonishing. Sayginn stood with her mouth slightly open. Teo had learned those moves. But this youth was...

better. Is that disloyal? She looked again. Of course. It was the boy from the clinic. With Loulou. And Chart Segat. She'd felt protective of him then. But now... what about Teo?

Teodor! He reminds me of Teo. Her hand trembled. The glass slipped. She caught it—but the drink spilled. Her head spun. She realised she was leaning. No, someone was holding her. Frederon. He steadied her, concern etched in his face.

"Are you all right, Sayginn?" he asked. "You're not, are you?" He pulled her into a sudden hug, stroking her hair, pressing her cheek into the warm curve of his neck. "If we were one," he whispered, "then when they attack you, they attack me. Let me help you bring him home."

Sayginn couldn't speak. She nodded.

The Emperor stepped back and raised his voice just as the music paused. "Teodor must be rescued. Even if it means keeping the Dodecahedron Dome open." He turned slightly toward the crowd. "He's my heir. And I refuse to countenance any harm to him."

Sayginn blinked. Heir?

Almost half the room heard him. Frederon, ever the performer, saw his cue and repeated louder: "He is my heir. And let it be known—I will have no harm done to him. Let it be known!"

A cheer rose. Applause rippled outward like a wave. The music faded entirely. People stood, fists pounding tables, voices rising. The words hung heavy in the air. A claim made so loudly, so publicly, yet Sayginn noticed how Chart Segat concealed a conniving smirk.

Teodor is not the heir—not yet. What does he mean?

But Frederon wasn't done. He rose higher, arms raised. "He is my heir. No harm to him. Hear me—and obey!"

The ovation became thunderous. Sayginn had no choice but to rise. She applauded with them, as did Segat. She could feel the eyes of the room on her, even as her mind reeled.

Has the Emperor declared Teodor his heir—right here, right now? Or is there some second meaning I've missed?

Segat seized the moment. "My Emperor! Tonight, we celebrate the future of our Empire. Come! I have something special in mind." He mimed a clash of spinning blades, then turned to her. "My Regent, you should come too."

No more parties, Sayginn thought. She had seen enough. She needed to be where the real work was happening—where they were fighting to save her son. But still, she found herself apologising. "Maybe later," she said. "I need to stretch my legs." She gestured vaguely toward the exhibitions.

The Emperor shrugged. "Lead on, Chartsie."

Sayginn watched them go, forcing herself not to sag in relief—even though she knew the two men should not be alone together. But how could she stop it? That friendship—unpalatable and dangerous—had been forged long ago. She'd known Frederon and Segat were allies, but now it felt like something else. Something worse.

If Chart Segat really had Teodor... What was he doing with the Emperor? I need my friends, Sayginn told herself, then with sudden doubt, *but who?* Her eyes rove around the celebrating crowd, her gaze fell once empire on the tall Zaracan.

Karl Valvanchi.

He hadn't moved far. Just enough to let the spotlight pass. But still, he was watching her. He was a tall

Zaracan warrior, clad in his casual uniform, which barely disguised his power and menace, and despite being alone and surrounded by hundreds, no thousands of Dome Militant, he maintained an offhand nonchalance and a calm composed courage. Sayginn surmised, he knew his own strength yet deigned not to release it. Sayginn met his eyes, and a terrible, thrilling certainty swept over her: if anyone could bring her son home—it was him.

Killer Valvanski! A voice boomed out. Sayginn jolted. Who dared say that?

"Karl Valvanski." The booming voice was unmistakable. It was an intentional insult in the mispronunciation. Chart Segat had seen them.

The mayor of the Dome with the Emperor at his side, paused in his progress alongside the Zaracan aliens and greeted them with a theatrical flourish, flanked by glittering sycophants and orbited by a modest force of Dome Militant. His eyes gleamed.

"And another 'Ski? Is this another of your brothers? And, oh, look! A mini-'Ski. Are you enjoying the party, 'Skis?"

Ambassador Nikato stepped forward in silence. He bowed stiffly—whether to Chart Segat or the Emperor was unclear. His household shadowed him.

"My brother has diplomatic protection," Nikato told Emperor Frederon.

Karl had not bowed. Nuria, seeing him stand resolute and defiant, moved swiftly to his side. He ignored the

Emperor and simply glared at Chart Segat, tracking the man's every breath, every twitch. He didn't need to read the man's thoughts. The stench—beer, sweat, adrenaline—told him enough. Power clung to Chart Segat like cheap cologne, and it reeked of desperation.

"Of course, Karl! A warrior Valvanchi." Segat was still performing for his entourage, cracking jokes laced with innuendo. "We love warriors here in the Dome, and I'm sure any of our girls would be happy to welcome you," he said, leering. "They'll just charge you double and expect to be paid in Zaracan currency."

Karl continued to stare, willing Chart Segat to blink and back down.

"Don't antagonise him," Nikato whispered via their mental link.

"He stinks of lust and low living... And something else," Karl replied. "A hunger for power."

"That's what makes him dangerous."

Nikato was bowing again, as were the others. Now he reached to take Nuria's hand and tug on Karl's elbow, dragging them both into a bow backwards.

"Come. Enough. We've seen enough."

As the Valvanchi retreated, so the rest of the crowd parted for the procession to continue, Chart Segat was leading Emperor Frederon himself through the festival floor. With them, a train of fashion models in red and jet-black—some of them strikingly young. They approached a raised platform, where Chart and the Emperor, flanked by Dome Militant and an array of models in black shimmering red, stepped up onto a circular disk.

"Now the private parties begin," Nikato murmured. "Look, they're taking the disk-jet to Chart Segat's office."

The platform shimmered and rose, lifting Emperor Frederon, Chart Segat, and eight others into the air. No cables, no rails. Just pure lift and sleek motion.

Karl stared, stunned.

"Whoa," he muttered. "Disk transport. I didn't know the Dome had that. It's not on any of the plans."

"Must be new," Nikato said. "Because clearly, they do."

The disk floated up into the upper levels of the Dome, heading toward the Cap—the topmost, restricted section.

Karl's mind raced. He had pored over schematics for hours. There was no public record of any private lift system, let alone one capable of this level of access.

"What's up there?" he asked, trying to keep his tone casual.

"It's called the Cap of the Dome," Nikato said.

"Any diagrams I found were entirely blacked out," Karl replied.

A gust of air rippled across them as the second disk rose. The crowd was roaring, caught up in the spectacle. High above, the entrance to the Cap irised open, like the petals of some dark flower.

Nuria grabbed Karl's arm.

"I felt him," she said, eyes wide.

"What?" Nikato spun around.

"Oh nothing," she muttered, but Karl gripped her hand gently.

She looked up at him, trembling.

"It was just for a moment," she whispered. "As the door opened—up there—I could feel him. Teodor. He's there. Or near there. I swear it."

Karl turned her to face him. "What did you sense?"

"He's alive. I know it. But he's drugged... I tried to send something—just a thought—but the door shut before I could reach him properly."

Nikato looked horrified. "What are you saying, Nuria?"

"She felt him," Karl said firmly. "And he felt her. That's enough."

Karl's gaze turned from the blacked-out aperture above to the crowd below. And among the sea of colours and flickering lights, his eyes found Sayginn, standing alone, watching him.

And she was no longer undecided

Sayginn saw the disk vanish into the Cap of the Dome, carrying the Emperor and Chart Segat to some secret meeting high above the city.

Patrice would have told her she should have gone with them.

That's not the answer, she told herself and turned away.

She moved into the crowd, shielded by her guards, protected from the calls of reporters and the jostle of press droids.

She knew where she was going.

She had seen him.

Karl Valvanchi.

He and the others were headed toward the House Duet installation—no guards, no entourage, just his niece at his side and Nikato trailing behind, his expression thunderous.

I sometimes wear House Duet, she told herself. *That's my excuse.* She found her feet already moving toward the Zaracan Fashion exhibit, a recreation of a tribal Sas Darona village, with flower decked tipis, fibre-matted flooring, their densely embroidered silks and intricately woven woollens. Made once to last a lifetime, a frugal lifestyle born of necessity, adopted by these aliens as an aspirational philosophy.

With whoops and cries, the Sas Darona troupe burst onto the stage in a flurry of colour and motion—whirling beads, swinging braids, leather boots pounding rhythm onto the platform.

Sayginn paused. *What was she doing here? Mingling in the VIP area of a foreign pavilion, among dancers and dignitaries?*

Nikato reached her first, sweeping into introductions with practiced grace. She smiled and greeted them each in turn. Her gaze paused briefly on Nuria, whose hair rippled through oranges, golds and gleaming yellows—a telepathic glow Sayginn had seen only in documentaries. In person, it was breathtaking.

"Please excuse me," Nuria said, bowing quickly. "I don't mean to be a bother. It's just—Karl's son turns five soon, and I wanted to invite Prince Teodor to the celebration. It's an important milestone for us."

Sayginn blinked. "Karl's son?"

She glanced toward the dancers. Karl was watching them intently, arms folded, posture relaxed but alert. Sayginn took the moment to walk over, Nuria trailing beside her, still chattering.

"My cousin—Karl Valvanchi the third—his fifth birthday's next month," Nuria said. "Prince Teodor was so kind to me earlier. I thought... maybe he'd like to come to Zarac 1 for the party."

Karl turned as they approached. He bowed. "Regent Sayginn."

She nodded, then followed his gaze toward the dancers. "How many are there?"

"Seven," Nuria answered first. "I think. No—wait."

All at once, a new dancer vaulted into view, leaping into a spin, the motion so fast it blurred.

"Eight!" Nuria gasped. "There are eight of them!"

Karl smiled faintly. "Good."

They watched in silence for a few beats more, the dancers a blur of power and grace.

Then Sayginn spoke. "Nuria tells me it's your son's birthday?"

"My younger son, yes," Karl replied. "Karl Valvanchi the third. He's turning five next month."

He turned to Nuria with a small, knowing smile. "Your son made quite an impression on my niece."

Sayginn nodded, then after a hesitation. "I wasn't aware you had children."

Karl shrugged lightly. "I was married. It was a five-year contract—my family insisted. The marriage wasn't renewed. We parted on good terms. She gave me two sons. They're at school on Zarac 1."

Sayginn studied him. Contract marriages. Not so different from her own proposed union with Frederon, except hers would be until death—or worse. Permanent. Political. Irrevocable.

She glanced again at Karl. Tall. Sharp-featured. Thirty, maybe. Younger than her—but not naïve. His words about the contract hadn't just been casual. Was he telling her something more?

Single. Available. Her? Karl Val...She caught herself. Focus.

She took a final glance around the Dome to be sure the Emperor and Segat had gone. Then she leaned in, her voice barely a whisper.

"Karl, I need your help to free my son."

"My lady, it would be my pleasure."

"Please. My car is outside. If you come back to Magnolia Palace, I can brief you properly."

"Nuria, come," Karl said, already turning. "We'll need you."

Sayginn raised a brow. "Why?"

"The prince showed her how to ride gorans using telepathy," Karl said. "There's a connection. She can still feel him."

Sayginn's breath caught. Patrice had been right, but not in the way he expected. These two were the keys. Karl and his niece Nuria, they offered the possibility of Teodor's release.

"She must come," Sayginn said.

As they left together—Sayginn, Karl, Nuria, Nikato, passing out of the atrium, free at last of the great Dodecahedral Dome's shadow, Sayginn didn't look back.

Not at the Festival still raging behind them.

Not at the Cap of the Dome high above.

Don't look up, she told herself. *Just don't.*

Fifteen minutes was all it took to leave Domeside, cross the river, and arrive back at Buckingham Palace.

"This is our theatre of operations," Sayginn said.

Karl stood beside her on a high balcony overlooking what had once been a ballroom. Now, scaffolding and wires snaked up the walls, framing a command centre of rapid improvisation. Screens covered the walls, each flickering with fast data, split feeds, thermal views, and map overlays. Analysts clustered in islands of desks below, faces grim and focused.

Impressive.

"This is fast," he said quietly.

Sayginn nodded. "It had to be."

They descended the sweeping staircase into the centre of the makeshift war room. Karl noted the scent of solder and antiseptic—a blend of tech and triage. Below, stacked in uneven pyramids, were thirty large dog cages. Nearby, a pair of white-coated technicians were preparing a sleek table more suited to surgery than strategy.

As they approached, a massive wolf leapt onto the table and rolled onto its back.

"Cy-wolves," Nuria said with a gulp, but Karl's eyes gleamed with interest.

"It's our own tech," Sayginn said. "Inspired by yours."

The white coats slotted memory chips into the wolf's rib cage. It sprang up, alert and ready, and leapt down. The next wolf followed.

"What else do you have?" Karl asked, circling the cages.

"Cy-rats. Cy-roaches."

On a smaller table, rats were passed down an assembly line, having circuit boards fitted neatly into small hollows at their napes. One technician opened a crate of cockroaches—each already fitted with a glittering 360° camera and a third metallic antenna.

"We give them a pulse," said an analyst.

He slotted a chip into a control box and pressed a sequence. The roaches twitched once, then began crawling in coordinated lines.

"Thousands of them," Sayginn said. "We're not just relying on them. Every video feed from the Dome and surrounding districts has been pulled in. We've plotted the activity of every known resident. Now we start building exception reports."

Karl scanned the top-level monitors. Threads of location pings, biometric traces, movement patterns—some of the best surveillance tracking he'd ever seen outside Zaracan fleet protocol.

Sayginn turned toward a group of desks where eight analysts huddled.

"This is suspect analysis. We've narrowed it to three key figures. Once they're tagged, we move outward—friends, colleagues, family, connections."

"What's the Dome Militant doing?" Karl asked.

Sayginn hesitated. "We haven't asked for their help."

"It is every citizen's duty to aid their prince," Prime Minister Patrice Macey muttered behind them.

Karl looked up at the high screens again. Every light, every signal, pulsed with urgency.

Sayginn crossed to a corner table where a whiteboard map showed the Dome, crosshatched with red and blue indicators. On a nearby monitor, one of the few untouched diagrams blinked with the title: **New Management for the Dome.**

Nikato Valvanchi had followed, now he froze when he saw it.

"What is this?" he said sharply.

Sayginn turned. "It's a working plan."

"I thought the Dome was going to be shut down. Permanently."

Patrice came alongside. "Let's speak privately."

They moved into a nearby study, a quiet room just off the ballroom. The door shut behind them. Sayginn and Patrice sat across from Nikato, Karl, and Nuria.

"Let's talk about who has taken my son," Sayginn began.

"It's obvious," Nikato said. "This is about the Dome Debate."

"Yes," Sayginn said. "But we believe Chart Segat is working with the Emperor."

"Chart Segat should be in jail," Nikato snapped.

"Once he's deselected as Dome administrator, we'll begin proceedings." Patrice said smoothly.

"But not until after the Debate," Karl said grimly. "And in the meantime, they'll use the Prince to influence the vote." Karl paused. " Why not delay it. Delay the vote?"

"Then they would only hold him longer," Sayginn replied. "They might..." She stopped herself. She did not want to speak aloud what they all knew. In all likelihood, if Teodor's captivity lasted more than a few days, he would certainly be killed. "Maybe we should share our plans. About the Dome."

"You said it would close," Nikato said.

"It will. For twenty-four hours at least."

"But not forever?" Karl asked.

Sayginn shrugged. "We can't. It employs thousands. Families. Youths. It generates too much..."

Nikato leaned forward. "The Zaracan Council was led to believe a 'yes' vote meant permanent closure. Disbanding the Dome Militant in perpetuity."

Patrice stepped in. "That will be decided democratically."

Nikato's voice dropped. "If the terror movement on Sas Darona isn't curbed, we may consider sanctions. Against Earth."

Sayginn didn't reply. The implications of that single word—sanctions—could collapse Earth's economy.

Karl stood. "We have provided support. We fight the Dome Militant in the field."

"And yet..." Nikato reached into his pocket. "We found this on the body of a terrorist." He dropped a medallion into Sayginn's palm.

A Dome Militant emblem. Spattered with blood.

Sayginn stared at it. Cold metal. Dried blood. Then she looked up. Her aide was sprinting into the room, an envelope in hand, face pale.

"A bike brought this," the aide said breathlessly. "It's from the Dome. Addressed to the Regent."

Patrice took the envelope and opened it carefully. Inside was a white plastic blood test stick—both ends stained dark.

Karl's stomach tightened.

"What in the name of God?" Sayginn breathed.

"It's a blood sample?" Patrice said, confused.

"I have a drone that can test it." Sayginn pulled up a command on her device. A white pod like medical drone zipped into the room, landing on the table without a thud. With a handkerchief, Patrice placed the wand inside its scanning chamber.

The drone's first result came quickly.

"Inconclusive," Patrice read aloud. "Not related to Sayginn."

"Try a DNA trace," Karl said.

"That's illegal," Sayginn objected. "Serge banned all tests."

But Patrice had already spoken the command. A moment later, the screen flashed with a profile.

Loulou Jewel.

"Who?" Nuria asked.

Sayginn's mouth had gone dry. "She's a model. I saw her earlier tonight."

Karl stepped forward. "The blood—was it male?"

The drone began scrolling a new readout. Patrice read it aloud.

"Male. Estimated age 16. Sample taken within the last twelve hours."

"It's not Teodor?" Sayginn whispered.

"No," Karl said grimly. "It's a message."

The drone chirped again. A new image appeared. Sayginn gasped.

Prince Erederon. The Emperor's dead son.

"Those are the parents?" Karl asked. "And the blood sample is from their child?"

"It can't be," Patrice muttered. "Loulou and Erederon, we knew but, her child was a girl."

Sayginn stepped back. "They're telling us they have a lost prince."

The drone was presenting genetic matches.

Sayginn felt the walls shift around her. She stared at the two photos displayed on the small medical pod's display. Loulou Jewel's image, still radiant in a photo from a decade ago, lips parted in a model's pout. Then, beside hers—Prince Erederon, Emperor Frederon's only son, long thought dead in a flyer crash.

"The drone says," she whispered, barely believing it, "This boy was alive this morning. Taken less than twelve hours ago."

"It's a threat." Karl said.

"Why?" Nuria cried. "Why would they send this?"

Sayginn clutched the handkerchief Karl had given her and began to twist it, knotting it into a writhing coil between her fingers. "Because if they have this child, they don't need Teodor anymore."

Patrice looked grey. "They have an heir by blood. The Emperor's grandson."

Karl stepped forward, eyes narrowing. "If Frederon meets this child—Teodor is dead."

"No," Sayginn breathed. "Oh God, no."

"But this was supposed to be about the Dome Debate!" Nikato interrupted, aghast. "About the vote."

Sayginn turned her head slowly. "It is and it isn't."

On the wall screen, the news flickered: images of the Dome, then a photo of Teodor, smiling and radiant in his gold-and-chiffon angel's costume from that morning.

"It's political," Patrice said, trying to cling to something he understood. "Chart Segat is playing a complex game, but I know him—he's not as clever as he thinks. Somewhere, there'll be a mistake. A loose end."

Sayginn's eyes drifted toward Karl. Not toward the crown, or the council, or even the throne room. But to the one man in the room who was already moving—already planning. The one who might actually bring her son home.

Karl straightened, his decision already made.

"Send me in," he said. His voice was calm but rang with absolute conviction. "I'll search the Dome. Find the Prince. Bring him home. If I can do that before five o'clock tomorrow, then—by all means—the Debate can proceed."

"I'll go too," said Nuria, stepping forward with the confidence of youth. She reached for Karl's hand, standing in his shadow. "Together we'll find him."

Nikato drew himself up like a storm.

"There is no way I will allow you to pursue such a reckless course of action," he snapped. "Your father would not hear of it!"

Then to Karl, more tightly: "Such an action would go against diplomatic protocols."

"But I felt him," Nuria squeaked. Her voice cracked. She looked down, then up again, eyes blazing. "I do have a telepathic connection to the Prince."

"What?" Nikato demanded, aghast. "What did he do?"

"Nothing! Nothing like that!" Nuria cried, red-faced. "He showed me how to connect with his gorans. That's all. And now—I can still feel him."

"You could feel him?" Sayginn stepped forward and gripped Nuria's hand with sudden strength. "You mean he's still alive?"

"Yes. Yes," Nuria nodded, tears in her eyes. "We have to save Teo. Please let me go back. We could save him tonight."

The silence that followed was long and heavy.

Outside the tall windows of the study, the lights of London glittered, but inside, only the drone hummed, and the low, flickering glow of monitors lit their faces.

Nikato's voice was quiet now. "I should utterly forbid it. *Absolutely forbid it*," he said. "But if Nuria truly has the connection, then... maybe. Just maybe." He took a breath. "Be sure to keep our involvement out of the press."

"I couldn't agree more," Patrice murmured.

Sayginn turned to Karl.

"Do you really think you will find him?" she asked. Her voice was tight, trembling with unexpected hope.

Karl smiled gently. "The Dome is large. But yes."

He turned slightly and rested a hand on Nuria's shoulder.

"Together," he said, looking Sayginn in the eye, "we'll find him. Find him—and bring him home."

Sayginn said nothing. She only reached for the medallion still in her palm—the one found on a dead boy on a distant planet. She looked at it once, then tucked it away.

And without another word, she nodded.

Chapter 17

Canapés in the Cap of the Dome

The disk sped up from the Dome atrium towards Chart Segat's private offices. From an early start on the blades mats of the Dome, Guy listed his day: breakfast with Loulou and Marline, Chart Segat's money roll. The cathedral – and the Prince's shoes! He winced. *Double maths. Yes,* but he still saw the dust escaping the cathedral doors as the people ran towards the horror. Later the clinic later. Marline in curlers. The Regent. *Ah the little blades fighter!* Des spinning and turning. *Mezzatorra, you got that. Tell Loulou. Tell Chartsie.* And whatever Chartsie wants. *You do it!* Now here he was at a party in the Cap of the Dome.

"Quite a day!" Guy thought. "I just wish it didn't end with me serving drinks, dressed like this." Nevertheless, he perked up when he saw the Dome Militant in full dress uniforms. They were wearing military jackets with golden buttons and braid. Designed on Old Fleet Street – by House Jewel, no less. Even as he admired them,

Guy remembered with horror his appearance. Yes, he was wearing House Jewel: a sparkling waistcoat, shiny red boots, tight trousers like leggings, and a jacket cut short like a girl's. Together with his make-up and hair, which he had been instructed to keep long for Royal Ascot Weekend, what did he look like?

I look like a fashion model, when what I want is to look like them. Guy thought with a note of panic. *What if they see me?*

Guy fell back behind Loulou. He knew he would be unnoticed behind her beauty and style. Here, he could hide – or try to. He hung his head only to be overcome with vertigo. The uppermost sanctum of the Dome had the most extraordinary view of the entire city, a three-sixty panorama. The architects had made every surface transparent: the floor, walls and ceiling. Through the floor, all the sports facilities, all the entertainments, restaurants and shops, all the broad tunnel avenues and small interconnections, all were spread out like a giant model spread beneath their feet.

Giddy with tiredness, and hungry, Guy had the impression he was floating in space; then a finger lifted his chin.

"Don't look down. You'll make yourself sick." Loulou had come back to where he was glued to the spot. She smiled into his pale face. "C'mon, Chart Segat asked for you," Loulou said, "and I'll make sure he notices you; then you can go. You're dead on your feet." She reached to a nearby waiter and poured two glasses of fizz, then she handed the tray to Guy. "Here, take this. Go serve the Emperor."

What? Guy wondered. *Serve? Loyal to Empire*, he reminded himself. *So I will serve my emperor*. All in full view of the best soldiers of the Dome Militant. He couldn't think of anything more humiliating. Still, Loulou was smiling at him with that beautiful smile.

Guy held a silver tray of drinks high on one hand and placed his other hand on his hip to balance and strode towards the Emperor. *Let's do this.* The Dome Militant held the crowd back. Out of the corner of his eye, Guy saw Des hastily straightening his jacket. *Why was he late?* Their eyes met and Des nodded. The other Militant might smirk, but Des at least understood. Three years before, Des would have done anything to secure his place in the Dome Militant.

The party wasn't bad, thought Guy. A large conference space transformed with silver palm trees, lights and chrome furnishings. *Fancy cocktail tables too*, designed to look like palm trees with broad silver columns mounted with round tops.

As Guy approached the Emperor, he noticed something odd. A Dome Militant cyborg, one of the big Battle Borgs, had removed the top off one of the tables. Chart Segat and Emperor Frederon looked inside the column base.

Clever design, thought Guy. *Was it a storage unit as well as a table?*

"You will have a full pardon for Serge's death," he heard the Emperor say, "and you will have the Dome, but for God's sake clean him up. I'm pretty sure she'll cave in, if not tonight, then tomorrow."

Guy was close now, curiously, he peered in to see what they were looking at.

He gasped. *What?* The glasses on his tray rocked. *Who?* His mind went blank. *Why?* Then with a hint of panic. *Don't drop the drinks*. He froze.

The Emperor spun round and stared at him. His black eyes, like spears, cut into him.

"How long have you been standing there?"

Beside him, the Borg snapped the tabletop back into place and glared at Guy. Standing there with his tray of drinks, Guy dared not move. He stared directly ahead and found himself mesmerized by the borg's grey and black face. It was riven with deep cracks from under the eyes to its chin lines. The Emperor poked him. Again Guy jumped. The glasses bounced. Chart Segat swooped in and caught both, as the tray finally clattered to the ground.

"What did you see?" the Emperor barked. He glared at Guy. The tray lay at his feet. Should he pick it up? The emperor pointed a finger – one with his famous black claw-like nails – into Guy's chest.

"Nothing." The lie was effortless. First the Borg, now the Emperor, Guy was so scared he could not remember anything. "I saw nothing."

"Don't worry about this one," Chart Segat passed Frederon a glass. "He's a good boy." Chart Segat tapped the Emperor's glass in a toast, and with a flourish he downed his drink in one, nodding for the Emperor to do the same. But all Guy saw was his other hand, and the finger and thumb mime that was telling him to keep his mouth shut. Guy nodded. *I saw something I shouldn't have seen. Now I have to forget. And keep quiet.* He started to back away. *Who would I tell?*

The Emperor had also finished his glass. "Wait!"

Guy looked up, startled. First the Emperor, then Chart Segat, handed him their empty glasses. Without the tray which still lay on the floor, Guy was trapped holding the glasses like some broken robot. The Emperor stared at him.

"That face? Is this the one you told me about?"

The Emperor stared at Guy, who hardly dared breathe.

"Guy's House Jewel, my Emperor. Some say Loulou is his mother." Chart Segat said, sounding pleased with himself. Guy glanced at him. *What was this about?*

Frederon stood a moment, completely still. Guy had never known such scrutiny. He could not help himself, just glanced down at his body. No, he was not naked. Nor was the Emperor impressed.

"Working, is he? Fashion model?" Frederon said with distaste. He reached to lift Guy's chin with the point of his blackened index finger. He was looking closely at his features. "Sixteen is too old probably. Where has he been? Could it be surgery, Chartsie? Expensive surgery? Has he been tested?"

"The tests are illegal on Earth," Chart Segat replied with a shrug. "The Regent said Prince Teodor was the rightful Son of Empire."

Frederon snorted. "He could be too if she would only let me have a hand in his education. But this one looks like a fashion model, and if he has been working." Frederon looked down on Guy a little sadly.

Guy took a deep breath and found his courage. "I'm not a fashion model. I'm sixteen today. I want to join the Dome Militant. I am old enough."

"The Dome Militant, better and better." The Emperor said. "Sixteen today?"

"Yes sir, it's my birthday."

"You have an honest face, at least." The Emperor sighed. " Dome Militant? He's still too old," then he turned to Chart Segat. "Oh, you may as well bring him to my yacht to test him."

What were they talking about? To enter the Dome Militant, Guy had to pass tests in maths and blades. *What new tests? And why on the Emperor's yacht? Was it a fight?* A heavy hand landed on his shoulder, and Guy looked at Chart Segat for a clue. *Nothing.*

"He's not too old. He's not too young either." Chart Segat and Frederon exchanged glances. Guy had no idea what this meant. "He's a good boy. He'll do as he's told. You know me, Freddie. He'll do as he's told. If not, I'll throw him to my borgs." Chart Segat ran a hand through Guy's hair. Guy couldn't help squirming a little. He glanced around to see if any of the Dome Militant had noticed. Des was watching and made a 'calm-down' gesture. Guy stood still again.

All at once, Frederon had a hand around Chart Segat's jugular. His black nails were spearing his arteries. "I want him back; do you hear me? And don't you dare touch him. I want him back unharmed. I am paying you to hold him. Keep him until the time is right. Then you will be rewarded."

The two men stood face-to-face, glowering at each other, as with a theatrical flourish, Chart released Guy and waved him away. He backed off, swiftly walking behind the line of Dome Militant who scrutinised him as he passed. He lowered his eyes, until he heard a voice he knew.

"Here, let me take those." It was Des, he took the two glasses off Guy, handed them to an adult server and led Guy away. "Loulou says I have to get you out of here. Come."

Guy dared not look back. He followed Des out of the bright lights into Chart Segat's bedroom suite. Raised on a platform, at the centre of the room was a bed wide enough to sleep four or five adults. Its headboard was three vast statues, stretching five meters up at the head of the bed, two gowned women and a man, their three bodies touching, and arms and legs crossed and intertwined.

"What?" Guy protested. He had heard of Chart Segat's bedchamber and had no intention of going there.

"The main doors are locked and guarded; you'll not get out that way. Come."

All along the far wall was the bathroom, with a large jacuzzi, a wall of showers, three parallel baths, behind a glass wall. A group of young girls were giggling on the edge of the jacuzzi, goading each other to strip off and enter the whirling bubbles. He recognised Marline. She was still wearing her white dress, but she perched on the edge, her feet and ankles splashing in the bubbles. It looked like her hem was soaked through. She saw him looking, smiled and blew him a kiss, and with a wink stretched one of her legs down into the water, squealing as the bubbles rose around her knees. Guy looked away.

What was Marline thinking?

Des pushed Guy down a narrow corridor at the back of the bathroom that led to one of the great pillars of the Dome. There Des unscrewed one of the panels. He reached into one of his pockets and pulled out a head torch. He handed it to Guy and helped him put it on.

"You're not too exhausted to climb?" Guy shook his head and glanced back.

"Will you be..." Guy nodded towards the girls. "Partying?"

"No. I'm on duty."

"Oh, okay. Will you keep an eye on Marline? Make sure she's okay?"

"Marline? She's here?"

"Over there. She's only sixteen."

"I know, but Ascot Weekend should be for her. Marline knows what she wants, but yes, I'll keep an eye on her. And I'll see you tomorrow. We need to train."

"I'm working tomorrow at the races."

"Well, that's good. I'm there too. Look, you need to climb down two sides from here, but then at the junction, take the horizontal maintenance tube heading west. You should count six or seven grilles, and you arrive at the changing room on the seventeenth level. The grille is loose. Be careful to jump clear of the benches, it's a bit of a drop."

"I know where you mean. I've done it before."

"Not at this time of night, you haven't. It's late; you're tired, be careful."

"I'll be fine. Thanks, Des."

Chapter 18

Alone in the Royal Stables

S ayginn strode aimlessly across St James's Park until she reached the stables in Horse Guards. She knew the combination; the stable door slipped open. Inside, the beast stretched out its full length across the stall. The first successful cross-breed created using the genes of the ice cats of Sas Darona—where else?—Blue Barbarina had inherited their ice-white colouring and tufted ears and brows that Sayginn refused to have barbered to improve the goran's aerodynamics. She also retained their innate ferociousness. The ice cats of Sas Darona attacked all other males, including their own grown-up offspring, to defend territory. Blue Barbarina was a true match for her competitor at the Ascot Races: Frederon's Tiger. Despite its incredible strength, the tiger was a breed of almost impotent domesticity, so it would be whip-provoked to a pre-race fury.

Blue Barbarina opened one eye to gaze at her. Sayginn knew the goran had already identified her smell and sound. She knelt down in the synthetic hygiene fibres and stroked the goran's head. "You'd stand no nonsense. Would you, my beauty? You'd go in there and kill 'em."

The purring stopped. Instead the goran growled. A jockey was standing in the doorway with a torch.

"Hi Paulio. Why aren't you asleep? Big day tomorrow."

"Oh, it's you, Your Highness; I always sleep above the stable, the night before a race. Yes, you're right, a big day. She'll win, you know."

"The pair of you will win," Sayginn assured him. The man looked uncertain.

"Ma'am, I wanted to speak, but they wouldn't let me. I'm your best jockey for sure, yet Barbarina never runs at one seventy for me." Paulio sounded tense and unhappy. "We know she's fast. Why, she's surpassed one-seventy three times for you! With me, never! Not even one six eight; I don't think tomorrow will be a first either." Sayginn stared in dismay at her first jockey. Why hadn't she been told? The jockey continued. "She knows you and loves you. If you rode her, victory would be sure. Ma'am, I believe it. I'd put my life savings on it. They say the Emperor's Tiger Imperial Rina's highest speed to date is one six-eight." He looked up and shook his head. "We can beat her, but only if we are fast."

Sayginn ran her hands through the beast's mane. It was lush and silky. The huge goran rolled over for her to scratch her belly.

"Look how she loves you, ma'am."

"So, you think I should ride her?" asked Sayginn. "You're so sure you'll lose, Paulio."

"I've lain awake now every night for a week and despite all the training. She's in perfect shape, but under me, she just does not perform. Yes, I think I'll lose."

"Maybe she should lose!" Sayginn exclaimed. Then she turned to look at the beautiful creature. "But why should you suffer? None of this is your fault." Sayginn turned thoughtfully to her jockey. "Thank you Paulio, I'll think about what you have said."

Chapter 19

Alone in the Dark

Teodor woke as he tumbled within the rolling tube. At first, his instincts were all wrong. He threw his hands out to stop himself, but his fingers caught and twisted back hard.

Ouch. He felt the nails on his third and fourth fingers rip. He instinctively closed his hands into fists. Now it was his knuckles and joints that were scuffed and scratched amid the uncontrollable rolling. He fought to brace himself with his feet. For maybe half a turn, he held himself in a stiff, plank-like position—then he tumbled onto his back, his legs kicking out to find the floor again, his knees scraping against the sides until blood ran down his legs. He was turning and tumbling, rolling over and over. There was nothing for it. He wrapped his arms over his head and tucked his knees under his chin. Rolled up in a tight ball, he moved with the tube. It felt a bit better, though he was still out of control.

Who's rolling the tube? Did they not know he was inside?

On impulse, he banged the wall with his fist and shouted. Nothing. No response. If anything, the rolling seemed to accelerate—whoever was pushing the tube had started to run. Once again, he braced himself as best he could with his knees and elbows, even placing a shielding hand over his head. He closed his eyes and tried to pray. His head rang like a bell, so he could not hear much, but he could smell the sweaty fear of his body, the scent of his own piss, and taste the dust and grime where his mouth had been thrown against the metal of his prison.

Oh God, oh God, why hast Thou forsaken me? No, he thought. *Not those words. It was not that bad yet.*

He was not dying. He was dizzy, and in pain, and thought he might be sick. He retched, coughed, and spat, but nothing came up.

When did I last eat? he asked himself. *Don't know. What did I last eat? Easy. Sugar rolls and fruit. Who did you eat with? Easy. Mother and Nuria. Wrong. Nuria had left before. She was going to have breakfast with her uncle. Which uncle? Why do I care which uncle? You don't. It's just something to think about. Something that's not being trapped in a metal tube. Not knowing how to get out. Not wanting to know who's out there. So... think. Which uncle? Karl Valvanchi! Karl Valvanchi had shown Nuria the great gorans on the plains of Sas Darona. I wanted to visit Sas Darona. I wanted to meet him. First, I have to escape. Ha, ha—escape from the Dome to meet Karl Valvanchi. Yes. Maybe I can do that.*

The rolling had stopped.

It was easier to feel hopeful now that his metallic world was no longer moving. He forced himself to breathe. He shook out his legs and arms as best he could. He stretched up to look out through the narrow slit at the end of the tube. He had to press his entire face and cheek flat to the metal end cap. He closed one eye so the other could focus. Coloured lights pulsed across a pane of glass.

Was that a window? It was dark outside. So—nighttime, he said to himself. *What does that mean? It means I've been captive all day. Not all day. Think. It's important to be accurate. How long exactly? What time was I at the cathedral? Ten a.m. How long before the kidnap? I don't know. Think. About five minutes? No, not five. There was all the fuss about the costume. And the photos. Oh no—the photos. Had they given those to the press? Was the press reporting him as wearing a golden angel costume when he was kidnapped? No uniform. No hidden weapons or tracers. No communicator. How stupid had I been to listen to those idiotic designers with their silly ideas. An angel dressed as a golden blades fighter. Didn't they know that I'm not allowed to fight?*

"That Domeside boy would beat you," his mother had said.

Well no, he wouldn't. I won't allow it. If I get to fight him, I will jolly well win. The fight was due to take place on Saturday night, after the Dome Debate. A bit of fun, they had thought—to entertain the Emperor after all the politics of the Dome. But the fight was cancelled.

Yes, I know. But the Dome Debate is going ahead. The Dome Debate... No. Wait. Would the Dome Debate still go ahead, if I'm held prisoner? Why not? Because the Dome Debate is about the future of the Dome and the Dome Militant. Wasn't it battle borgs that took me? So—was that it? His kidnappers were Dome Militant.

What would they want as a reward? Something for the Dome? Something to do with the Dome Debate? What?

"Chart Segat must go," his mother had said.

I have to get out of here. I've been gone for hours. It'll have been on the news. People will be looking for me. How hard can it be? I have to get free.

Teodor kicked and banged on the sides of the tube, each impact sending a jolt of pain through his bruised limbs. The metal shrieked and groaned in protest. With a guttural cry, he slammed his heel into the top, the echoes bouncing off the curved walls like a death knell. A sliver of light appeared. *Hope*. He kicked again, harder—the pain a distant thrumming compared to the raging fire in his chest. Those gold sandals, useless adornments, slipped and slid. Bare toes found purchase, metal yielding to flesh. With a triumphant screech, the plate tore free. He scrambled out, gasping for air—only to crack his head against the unforgiving metal. Stars burst behind his eyes, pain a blinding white flash.

Trapped again.

Desperation clawed at him. He thrashed, a wild animal in a cage, his body screaming in protest. With a final, guttural roar, he tumbled out onto the platform, landing hard, his breath whooshing out of him. He looked around, heart thundering in his ears. Doors to the left. Supplies to the right. A way out. He stumbled toward the doors, each step a victory. A startled cry. A figure emerged from the shadows.

"What—?"

"Help me!" Teodor gasped, his voice raw and desperate. "I need to escape!"

But the man's eyes widened in terror, his gaze darting to the figures closing in. Three hulking Borgs, their mechanical eyes glinting like predatory beasts.

"Please," Teodor begged, his voice barely a whisper. "I need your communicator."

The man shook his head, face pale. "It won't work," he choked out. "Too deep."

Teodor's heart plummeted. He turned and ran, the Borgs hot on his heels. He dodged, weaved—but their metal hands closed around him, inescapable.

"Let me go!" he screamed, kicking and flailing. "I am your prince!"

A cry behind him.

The truck driver lunged at a Borg, his face twisted in defiance. A sickening crunch. The man collapsed, lifeless. Teodor's blood ran cold. He was next. A cold dread settled over him. A hand clamped over his mouth. A cloying sweetness filled his nostrils. He fought, but his body grew heavy, his vision blurring.

"No," he choked, voice barely audible. "Please..."

Darkness engulfed him. Then—a voice. Soft. Familiar. Impossibly distant.

Prince Teodor...

Nuria? His heart fluttered weakly.

"I said you could call me Teo."

Teo, please. Where are you?

He tried to answer, to reach out—but his body was a leaden weight.

"The Dome, Nuria," he managed, his voice a mere whisper. "I'm trapped in the Dome..."

Chapter 20

Alone on the roof

Returning to House Jewel, sent home by Loulou to sleep, Guy didn't feel tired. It was still his sixteenth birthday.

Sixteen.

He should have joined the Dome Militant today. He'd trained, studied, waited. But no black-and-gold uniform, no medallion with the deadly Dodecahedral gem, no salute, no dormitory bunk awaited him. Instead—nothing. Confusion gnawed at him. Why hadn't the exception been made? Why weren't the rules bent, just like they were for the others?

He tried to push the thoughts away as he climbed the columns of the dome, but the weight of uncertainty hung over him, heavy as the night sky. Normally, the attic felt warm, a retreat. Tonight, it was stifling. He shrugged out of his day clothes, grabbed his backpack, and slipped out through the fire escape to the roof.

The cool air hit his skin. Two leaps up the sloped tiles, and he was perched at the widow's peak—a small hexagonal platform overlooking the city. From here, the

Dome sprawled out below him, a giant heart pulsing with light, drawing in every road, every thought, every future.

Except mine, he thought bitterly.

His gaze slid over the river to the dull lights of Buckingham Palace. The Prince. Teodor. The rehearsal this morning. The gold sandals. The blood. His stomach churned. He sank down on the cold tiles, pulling his backpack into his lap. The shoes—the prince's shoes—rested inside. Why had he stolen them? His hands trembled as he pulled them out, turning the soft brown leather over in his fingers. The image of bloodstained sandals flashed in his mind. *Could it have been Teodor at the bottom of that cocktail table?*

The memory was so vivid, it blinded him to everything else.

He had been standing there—one fist on his hip, the other balancing a silver tray—serving champagne to Chart Segat and the Emperor. They had stood apart from the crowd, shielded by the Militan guards. Guy remembered that clearly now.

Then the Battle Borg had ripped the top off the cocktail table.
Both the Emperor and Chartsie had looked inside. And so had Guy.

There was a figure — crumpled, unconscious — concealed and restrained, head down, inside the gleaming, narrow column. Guy might not have recognized him at all, if not for the bleeding toes, the scabbed ankles, and the gold-and-leather sandals twisted and strapped up his legs.

How could he not recognise them?
Would he have forgotten, if he hadn't had another pair of shoes in his own bag?

He knew whose legs those were.
He was looking at the feet of a fallen angel.
Teodor.
Prince Teodor.
A prisoner.
Why hadn't the Emperor done something? Why hadn't he?

The creak of the fire escape broke through his thoughts. Marline climbed up to the roof, her silhouette framed by the glow of the Dome. She was wearing... well body shorts and a faded vest. What had happened to the white dress? And she had wiped her face clean, though Guy thought he glimpsed a glint of glitter at the corner of her eye. The last reminder of an overly glamourous party.

"They sold me," she said softly, her voice barely audible over the wind. "Simon Sorrow. Fifty thousand."

Guy's throat tightened. "You don't have to say 'yes'."

"What choice do I have?" Marline's voice cracked, but she held her chin up. "If not him, it'll be someone... well worse. I have debts., you know how it works. I have to at least try to pay them off."

Guy took a step towards her, feeling like the ground was falling out from under him. "You can't let them do this."

"They already have," she whispered, and her voice trembled as she moved closer to the edge of the roof, her eyes fixed on the distant lights. "If I say no, I'm done."

Her hand reached for the railing. Guy's heart pounded as she stepped up, balancing precariously on the narrow ledge.

"Marline, stop!" His voice was sharper than he intended, but he didn't care. He jumped up to the railing beside her, his arms spread wide for balance. "You're not doing this."

She turned to him, her face streaked with tears. "If I don't do this, what's left for me, Guy? What's the difference between falling now, or later, after they've taken everything from me?"

"You can't give up." He edged closer, trying to steady his voice, trying to steady her. "There has to be another way."

"Like what?" she snapped. "Who's going to save me?"

For a long moment, they stood there in silence, the cold wind whipping around them. Guy's grip tightened on the prince's shoes.

"What if I had a way out?" he said, his voice barely above a whisper. "What if I told you I knew something—something worth a lot of money?"

Marline looked at him, frowning. "What are you talking about?"

Guy hesitated. Blood stained gold and leather sandals and the fate of an empire unconscious and crumpled – the memory of what he had seen pressing down on him like the dome above. He shouldn't say anything. But the bleeding toes was an image etched to the back of his eyeballs.

And the Emperor saw him too. And Chartsie...

Slowly, he held up the brown shoe, showing her the name etched inside the heel.

Her eyes widened. "You know something about Prince Teodor."

"I do," Guy admitted, his voice hoarse. "But if I told you, it could be dangerous. For both of us."

Marline blinked, her hand trembling as she clung to the railing. "Dangerous how? What do you know?"

"I saw him," Guy said, the words tumbling out before he could stop them. "Today. At the Dome. He was there, and something was wrong. Something's *very* wrong, Marline."

She stared at him, the realization dawning in her eyes. "What are you going to do?"

Guy didn't answer right away. His gaze drifted out across the city, where the lights of the Dome cast long, jagged shadows over the streets below. It felt like the whole city was being swallowed by that thing—by the Dome. By the secrets inside it.

The weight of it pressed down on him, on Marline, on everything.

He wanted to save her.

He wanted to save the prince.

He had to.

But how?

His fingers tightened around the prince's shoe, the leather soft but heavy, like holding someone's life in his hand. For the first time in hours, his thoughts cut through the fog of panic. There was no time left. He had to act. Had to tell someone.

But who?

If Chart Segat was behind it all, there were no safe options. His throat went dry at the thought of speaking out. If the wrong person heard him, he wouldn't just be ignored. He'd be crushed.

But maybe... Loulou.

She had power. She had pull. And she wasn't afraid to break the rules.

He turned to Marline, his voice coming out in a low rasp. "I think Loulou might be able to help."

Marline's face twisted with doubt, her eyes wide with fear. "Are you sure?"

Guy's heart hammered in his chest, his pulse echoing in his ears like a countdown. He wasn't sure. Not even close. But what choice did he have? The weight of the Dome was inescapable, its presence looming larger than ever, its lights pulsing like the beat of a massive heart, like it was alive, breathing, waiting for him to slip up.

His hands trembled, but he spoke anyway, his voice low and steady. "I have to try. For Teodor. For you."

He forced himself to look away from her and out towards the Dome. At that exact moment, a black-and-gold spaceship roared up from the city below, its engines blazing as it shot into the night sky, disappearing into the stars. Guy's chest tightened, the sight of it sending a jolt through him.

That was the dream. To join the Dome Militant. To wear the black and gold. To fight for his planet. To be something—someone. His one dream, how could it appear to be so far from his reach? Or maybe he'd been wrong all along.

He swallowed hard, feeling the sting of that truth.

I do have to try, he told himself, the words ringing hollow in the back of his mind. *For Teodor. For Marline.*

His jaw clenched, his breath shaky, as the truth slammed into him like a fist to the gut.

For me.

S A   M E L I A
SON
OF
EMPIRE
DODECAHEDRAL SPACE EMPIRE 2

Now Read On

Discover the next first chapters of Son of Empire.

Chap 1. An Early Call

"Guy Erma, get yourself dressed and get to the yard!"

Guy shuddered as he woke from the nightmare. He lay blinking as his brain scrambled to restore his thoughts to the everyday. The voice, he realized, came from his communicator. Wearily, he reached to pull it from under his pillow and said, "Juke?"

Too loud! Guy felt the children stirring in the darkness of the attic. He knew better than to wake them, not when it was still dark. Had he missed his alarm? He cradled his communicator against his cheek as Jukona, a market trader and purveyor of London's finest strawberries, continued.

"I need you here, now. They have set up checkpoints on all the roads out of Domeside – the tailbacks are stretching right into the Dome; we need to get going. Grab your stuff and look lively. Mam will feed you when you get here."

The message cut out. Guy lay for a moment in the semi-darkness. It was morning. Well, almost. It was the Ascot Races. He had been due to meet Jukona at five.

What time was it now? 4:22. "Get over here," Jukona had said. Checkpoints, what was that about? Oh yes, the Prince. He had been kidnapped.

Last night, he had been dressed in black satin trousers and a red fashion shirt, serving drinks from a silver tray in the Cap of the Dome, the VIP suite at the top of London's famous Dodecahedron Dome. There had been cocktail tables designed to look like stylized palm trees, with flat tops and column bases. Someone had removed the tabletop from the tubular column. Inside, Guy had seen dirty feet wearing golden sandals, footwear of a fallen angel. No cocktails, no party hats, but Guy had seen Prince Teodor and done nothing. Chart Segat and Emperor Frederon had done nothing either.

Chart Segat was the administrator of the Dodecahedron Dome and leader of the Dome Militant space defenders, and Frederon was the emperor of the twelve planets of the Dodecahedral. Drinks in hand, they had peered down at their captive. Why would they kidnap and hold the future king? God help Prince Teodor.

Why did I do nothing? I should have – What? Shouted or pointed or something. What, with Chart Segat just standing there? Are you mad?

Squirming out from among the other children who slept in the attic, Guy went to where the night before he had stacked and folded his clothes. He picked them up, along with his boots and rucksack. He stripped off his night shorts and pegged them to a line along the wall, then headed into the bathroom. Three small toilets, including one which was permanently blocked, and three showerheads of which only the first had any real water pressure. He washed and dressed, all without switching on the one working light. He picked up his rucksack, paused, and looked inside; he hoped it might not be true, but no, he saw a pair of polished patent leather shoes.

Oh no, he groaned and reached inside the bag to remind himself. Yesterday, before the cocktail party, before the kidnap at the Cathedral, there had been the rehearsal with the Domeside choir. Prince Teodor had been there and so had Guy. They had dressed the prince as a golden angel, and Guy had stolen his shoes. He had thought no one was looking, but one person had seen. It was the prince. He had seen Guy take his shoes but had said nothing. His eyes had said: Take them if you want them.

I don't want them. I'm going to give them back, Guy told himself as he slung the bag on his back and headed down the stairs at a run.

"You hear me, Prince Teodor," he spoke aloud to the empty staircase. "I'm not a thief! I will give you your shoes back."

Chap 2. A Cold Awakening

"The glass floor was cold. The space was blindingly bright with morning sunlight.

"Where are you?" Teodor frowned. Was that his father? Why was he so impatient?

"What day is it?" Teodor replied. "On Sunday, I will be sixteen."

"Forget that! Where are you?" Teodor rolled his stiff and aching shoulders. They had shackled his wrists behind his back using the large lead handcuffs normally reserved for securing out-of-control Borgs, so twenty centimetres of skin - from his wrists and up his forearms - were chafed and bloody. He drew his arms up to examine the damage. He wished he had some antiseptic cream, some bandages, some warm water...

"Are you injured?" His father's voice again.

"It's not bad." He looked around and suddenly felt like he was falling. He sat on a transparent floor, and beneath him was the City of London. He did fall forward, and his hands hit the glass floor. Spreading his palms and fingers wide to steady himself, instinctively he spread his legs as well. Soon, he lay starfish-like on the floor – his eyes mapped out the districts beneath him: Blackfriars, St. Pauls, and the City.

"I am lying on top of the Dodecahedron," he thought. "The Dome you built, father."

"The alien Valvanchi built it, not I. You know that, Teodor."

"But Dad, I've never been on top before. This must be the top of the Dome, but the floor is transparent – as are the sides of the Dome, so it feels like I am falling, but I'm not."

"Where are you?"

Slowly, he drew himself up to kneel so he could look around. His elbows and knees were scuffed from where they had stuffed him in a circular tube; that was yesterday. At least he assumed it was yesterday. Later they had chained him to a heavy metal shelf alongside an out-of-date cleaning droid, some half-used tins of paint, and a jumbled pile of dirty dust sheets. As if someone had recently finished decorating. So, had he been asleep? They had used drugs, sleeping fluids onto rags then pressed to his face. Was this place new? The Cap of the Dome was new – the squat flat rooms Chart Segat had built for his own use on the roof of the Dome.

"I'm in a storage cupboard," he thought, looking down once more. "A storage cupboard in the Cap of the Dome."

"Chart Segat has you."

"But father, he's the man who killed you. You and baby Deodran!"

"I better go," his father replied.

"No, please don't!"

In an instant, Teodor was standing by the black coffin on a golden dais – the high Dome of St Paul's above and behind him, the choir sang.

"'In darkness, you are never alone, for I will always be in your heart."

He hadn't cried at his father's funeral. The Press had reported that he looked in shock. In truth, he remembered little except what he watched on repeat, and he hadn't remembered this hymn until this moment. Who had chosen it?

In darkness, you are never alone, for I will always be in your heart. Had they foreseen that he would arrive at this desperate plight?

But tomorrow is my birthday, Teodor stopped himself. If I survive until tomorrow. But, I will survive. I must believe it. I must.

"I will be King of Earth!" he said aloud.

Even to himself, he sounded ridiculous – why did an entire planet need a King? Of course, the planet didn't, but the United Races required a single representative for each race at its assembly; for this role, humankind had designated an Emperor. A single man to represent the entire race, only it was never intended that he would rule.

So much power should never rest with only one man. That's what his father said.

When I become Emperor, I will give the power back to the people, Teodor thought. That's what my father wants, Teodor hesitated. Wanted. That was what his father had wanted.

Who could imagine this? Teodor sighed and bent to lick the worst of the scratches on his wrists. The warmth and saliva were strangely comforting. He licked it again. Am I a wounded animal?

Oh well.

"As your King..." he spoke aloud to the shelves. "I find these conditions deplorable." His voice cracked with broken laughter, and he realized if he didn't do something, he would start to cry. And he didn't want to cry. To cry would mean they had beaten him, and he wasn't beaten yet, was he?

He froze. Footsteps. ***Who was coming?***

Appendix 1.

NAMES AND PLACES

A
AENGUS
One time bodyguard to King Serge, now a cyborg serving in the Royal Guard

B
BARONS
There are twelve barons, one for each of the twelve planets of the Dodecahedral empire. They head up the twelve families, each has a seat at the high council of empire, advisors to the emperor.
BATTLE BORG
The Battle Borgs of Dome were once fighting men who died on duty and were resuscitated as borgs to fight on.
BISTRO JEWEL
A large restaurant-bar in the atrium of the Dome, run as a concession of the fashion house Jewel and as a showcase of their products.
BLACK FRIARS

District of inner London, but also a medieval order of Monks who worked with the poorest in the city. They put together the first brotherhood of Dome Militant, fighters drawn from the poorest men and boys of the city who were then trained and armed and sent to liberate Jerusalem during the Crusades.

BLADES

The Fighting sport of choice of the young men of the Dodecahedral Empire. In duels, two young men face each other within a fighting ring, wearing running/spring blades on their feet and using two daggers – a blade in each hand. They fight three or five rounds. Importantly, if at any time a fighter steps outside of the fighting ring they are disqualified. The winner is the fighter who gets close enough to his opponent to wield a mortal blow. The tradition then is to shout: Do you yield?

BLUE BARBARINA

Two-meter-high racing snow cat originally from Sas Darona. At the time of this story, it is the Regent's best racer, and due to compete in the 3 o'clock race at Royal Ascot.

C

CHARTSIE / CHART SEGAT

Administrator of the Dodecahedron Dome, Mayor of Domeside, former political ally of King Serge.

COMMUNICATOR

Communication device which includes messages, voice and video.

CREAM CAROLINA

Giant racing cat.

CRYSTALLESCENCE

Last stage of Sas Darona plague when the victim is converted into crystal-like cocoons, hosts to the plague flies.

CYBORG

Cybernetic man. half-man, half-robot – normal lifespan about two years. Families will often gift the bodies of their adult children where they died prematurely to be resurrected as cyborgs. Appears to be 100% human.

CY-ROACHES

Cybernetic cockroach. half cockroach, half robot – used for surveillance.

CY-SECT

Cybernetic insect. Genetically enhanced Sas Darona plague fly – more deadly, faster to breed, quicker to evolve.

CY-WOLVES

Cybernetic wolves. half-robot, half-wolf.

D

DEODRAN

Younger brother of Teodor, Prince of Earth. Died two years before this story, killed by a terrorist bomb.

DES PARKS

Dome Militant soldier and champion blades fighter.

DODECAHEDRAL

Empire of 12 planets, asteroid mining, gas planets, outposts and colonies. Dodecahedral claims a 13th planet but is in disagreement with United Races as to ownership.

DODECAHEDRON DOME

The largest geodesic Dome in the Dodecahedral Empire. Made up of 12 vast pentagons. It houses entertainments, sports fields, casinos, hotels, an ancient village square and cathedral, a small port and a military training facility for 100,000 men and boys.

DOME DEBATE

Debate of whether Chart Segat should continue as the administrator of the Dome.

DOME MEDALLION

Identification tag worn by the Dome Militant. On one side is the name and ID, and the motto 'Loyal to Empire, Fear only God'. On the other side is set a crystal dodecahedron filled with poison, so that a Dome Militant soldier always has to the choice to take his own life rather than be taken captive or suffer through severe injuries.

DOME MILITANT

Military unit drawing on the men and boys of the inner-city wards of Domeside. Their uniform is black and gold.

DOMESIDE

Inner-city neighbourhood of London

DOMESIDE EVENING NEWS

Local newspaper of Domeside.

E

EDDIE / EREDERON

Only son of Frederon, emperor of Dodecahedral. Died before this story begins.

ERMA

In Domeside, Erma is given as a surname for boys of unknown paternity.

F

FIGHTING BLADES

Hand-held weapons used in blades fighting.

FIREWALL

Slim wall of dense, intense fire that is used to contain forest fires and Sas Darona plague flies.

FREDDIE / FREDERON

Emperor of the 12 planets of the Dodecahedral.

FREYNE

Imperial Planet, home to Emperor Frederon of the Dodecahedral.

G

GAUNTLETS

Leather arm protectors embedded with three curved blades, worn when fighting with blades.

GORAN

Giant racing cat.

GREAVES

Leather calf protectors embedded with three curved blades, worn when fighting with blades.

GOVE (& JON)

Twin brothers. Geneticists based at Mezzatorra, a centre of research into entomology on Sas Darona. Murdered in raid by SDLA.

GUY ERMA

A 16-year-old boy born in House Jewel, good at maths and blades, applicant to the Dome Militant, unregistered, no known father or mother.

H

HOUSE JEWEL

Fashion House, one of the eight houses at the heart of London's fashion and tailoring Industry.

I

IMPERIAL RINA

Giant racing tiger goran, raised by Emperor Frederon.

IMPERIAL GUARD

Bodyguards of Emperor Frederon. Wear the magenta and gold of the Imperial house.

J

JON (& GOVE)

Twin brothers. Geneticists based at Mezzatorra, a centre of research into entomology on Sas Darona. Murdered in raid by SDLA.

JUKE, JUKONA
Market Trader (Fruit & Veg) Domeside. Employs Guy Erma.

K

KARL VALVANCHI
Zaracan alien. Youngest son joined the Zaracan Space Rangers to escape his family's expectations. Commander on Sas Darona

KARL VALVANCHI II
Zaracan alien. Five-year-old son of Karl Valvanchi II, living on Zarac 1 in Valvanchi House.

KARL VALVANCHI CURSE
Though Karl Valvanchi the third is only five years old, there is an old prophecy that says Karl Valvanchi III will never survive to father a son of his own. Thus, giving rise to the Karl- Valvanchi Curse.

L

LOULOU
Model of Fashion House Jewel, probable age 29.

LUCY
Stable girl in the goran stables at Magnolia Palace. Tends to Prince Teodor's gorans.

M

MAGNOLIA PALACE

Emperor Frederon's Palace on Freyne, the capital of the Dodecahedral.

MARLINE

Newest Fashion Model of House Jewel, just had a birthday, age 14.

MEZZATORRA

Research base on Sas Darona.

MONAZITE-9

Precious metal used to create space magnets. Extracted from Samarium. At the time of this story, it was in short supply.

N

NIKKI VALVANCHI

Zaracan alien. Second eldest of four sons and Ambassador to the Freyne Empire

NIKATO VALVANCHI

Zaracan alien. Scholar and explorer first discovered that 13 disparate planets were the remnants of an ancient Empire.

NURIA VALVANCHI

Zaracan alien. Daughter of Syemon Valvanchi, age 15. heir to Zarac fortune.

O
OLD FLEET STREET
Avenue in Domeside where fashion houses Jewel and the Riffaut are located.

P
PATRICE MACEY
Prime Minister on Earth, head of Regent Sayginn's ten-year-old Democratic Government.
POISON PILL
Glass brick containing miniature eco-system where plague flies can live, until released by small explosive mounted on the outside and remotely detonated.

R
RIFFAUT / THE RIFFAUT / HOUSE RIFFAUT
Fashion House, one of the eight houses at the heart of the Freyne fashion and tailoring industry.
ROYAL ASCOT WEEKEND
Festival of Flowers and Fashion. Takes place each spring on Earth.
ROYAL GUARDS
Personal guard to Regent Sayginn. Wear red and silver

RUNNING BLADES

Curved metal extensions that are worn on the sole of shoes during blades combat, but also commonly worn by the soldiers and trainees of the Dome Militant. Running blades help the wearer run faster and further, leap higher and turn tighter. Boys of Domeside such as Guy Erma are rarely seen without them.

S

SARA

Girl in House Jewel, friend to Guy and Marline. Living in the attics of Old Fleet Street in Born of Empire

SAS DARONA

Planet on the outer rim of space, currently under licence for exploration to the Zaracan Democratic Union, also claimed by the Dodecahedral Empire.

SAS DARONA PLAGUE

Plague native to Sas Darona, spread by biting insects deadly to all animal and human species on Sas Darona.

SAS DARONA SAND LIZARDS

Large fat lizards of the Sas Darona savannah known for their fine white flesh.

SAYGINN / REGENT SAYGINN

Queen of Earth, Regent and ruler of six planets in the place of Prince Teodor who is only 13 years old. Probable age 32.

SDLA, SAS DARONA LIBERATION ARMY

A secret army drawing on the native tribes and dedicated to fighting the Zaracans on Sas Darona, supported by the Dome Militant

SEBASTIAN, SEB
Teenage model and impersonator of Prince Teodor, from the Riffaut fashion house, age 17.

SERGE / KING SERGE
King of Earth, husband to Sayginn, father of Teodor and Deodran. Established the Dodecahedral Dome as a place of education and training for the men and boys of Domeside, the poorest quarter of his capital city. Died two years before this story begins.

SNAKE DROID
Weapon in the shape of a snake, a long line of connected bullets ending in an explosive.

SONIA
Young researcher working in Mezzatorra, research base on Sas Darona. Killed by Sas Darona Plague.

ST PAUL'S
Name of ancient cathedral and modern clinic, both located at the heart of the Dome.

SYEMON VALVANCHI
Zaracan alien. Eldest of the four Valvanchi brothers, father of Nuria Valvanchi.

T

TEO / PRINCE TEODOR 15 -year-old son of King Serge and Queen Sayginn, and great nephew and only surviving male descendant of Emperor Frederon. King of Earth and heir to the Dodecahedral Empire, goran rider, blades fighter, trained in all necessary skills required for leadership.

TILSON Commander of the Dome Militant and senior instructor of the Dome blades programme.

U

UNITED RACES Government body of Known Space.

V

VALVANCHI Name of a great house of the Zaracan Democratic Union, specialists in diplomatic relations and great explorers.

VALVANCHI HOUSE Home of the Valvanchis on Zarac 1.

W

WALESBURY (LORD) Baron of Dodecahedral Empire, resident on Earth. Loyal to King Serge, Regent Sayginn and Prince Teodor.

WHITEFRIARS STREET Street in Domeside, off Old Fleet Street.

Z

ZARAC Capital planet of Zaracan Democratic Union.

ZARACAN DEMOCRATIC UNION Great power of the United Races. Rules / controls vast swathes of Known Space.

ZARACAN Ancient Alien species, shapeshifters and telepaths

About the Author

The best place to find out about me is **here:** www.sallyannmelia.com

And as I like writing, this is where you can **sign up to receive e-letters** about me, my writing, new books and promotions.

As the Dodecahedral series continued **I will also be releasing extras, add-ons and art-work, that you might also enjoy.**

You can also find me:

- on Facebook https://www.facebook.com/SallyAnnMelia/

- on Twitter https://twitter.com/Sally_Ann_Melia

Thank you for taking the time to read Born of Empire. I'm thrilled to know that you made it to the end!

If you enjoyed the story, **I would greatly appreciate it if you could leave a review on Amazon.** Your honest feedback will not only help other readers discover my book, but also encourage me to continue the series. Son of Empire is already available, Soldier of Empire is coming soon, Captain of Empire is coming in 2024.

Thank you for being a part of this journey with me, and for your support in spreading the word about my work. **I can't wait to share the next chapter of this adventure with you.**

Sally

UK:

https://www.amazon.co.uk/review/create-review/?asin=B0BY7QBQJF

US:

https://www.amazon.com/review/create-review/?asin=B0BY7QBQJF

My books:

Dodecahedral Series by S.A Melia

- Born of Empire

- Son of Empire

- Soldier of Empire

- Captain of Empire

Aliens Series by Sally Ann Melia

- Aliens in Paris
- Aliens in Windsor
- Aliens in Sequoia National Park
- Aliens On the International Space Station
- Alien In Mysuru Dasara
- Aliens on Kangaroo Island

Flash Fiction Series by Sally Dickson

- How to write Flash Fiction to Win Competitions
- How to use AI to improve your Flash Fiction
- How to write Genre Flash Fiction

Flash Fiction, Edited by Sally Dickson

- 2024 Farnham Flash Fiction Competition Winners
- 2023 Farnham Flash Fiction Competition Winners
- 2022 Farnham Flash Fiction Competition Winners

- 2021 Farnham Flash Fiction Competition Winners

- 2020 Farnham Flash Fiction Competition Winners

- 2019 Farnham Flash Fiction Competition Winners

- 2018 Farnham Flash Fiction Competition Winners

- 2017 Farnham Flash Fiction Competition Winners

See Amazon Page: Sally Ann Melia

Thanks

This series has been a long time in the making and there are many people to thank for their patience and support.

First and foremost, I have to thank my husband David for his endless supply of great meals, and my children Rose and Hazel who have been patient during all the time it takes to 'do the writing', and my parents, Peter and Elizabeth, who inspired and believed in me, and my sister Jane who was endlessly encouraging.

I also have to thank the Hogs Back Writers: Richard Fuller, Alan Findlay, Alison Moulden, Armando Halpern, Charles Burrows, Clare Golding, Debbie Roberts, Douglas Brownlaw, Gabriella Byrne, Hanne Larsson, Jack Laurence, Janine Yiannakis, Jenny Greenland, Joanna Barnard, Kat Guenioui, Kevin Puttick, Laura Bell, Mark Easton, Mary Ellen Foley, Peter Gillespie, Rosemary CassBeggs-Burstall, Sammy Stacey, Tim Ellis and Venetia Maltby. Plus any other past members I may have forgotten.

My writing friends from Hope Cove in Devon: Anne Rainbow, Linda Huckle; Sabrina Spencer; Elizabeth Seal; Sara Martin and Kerry Hadley.

My self-publishing digital tribe: Nick Stephenson, David Gaughran, Mark Dawson, James Blatch, David

Cheeson, Alex Newton and Bryan Cohen. Thanks to all you guys.

My editors, copy-editors and proof readers: at Cornerstones, Kathryn Price; on Reedsy, Tim Major, Martha Sprachland, Kankana Basu, Deborah Murrell; Anne Rainbow; and on Fiverr: Sachal Aqeel and Anne Brownlow.

The last and perhaps the most important thank you is to my artist Lazar who has been such an amazing support creating original art to illustrate my words. Thank you Lazar, there is much more to come. Lazar Kacarevic, planet.caravan@gmail.com, artstation.com/boink.

Finally, we got there. Thank You.

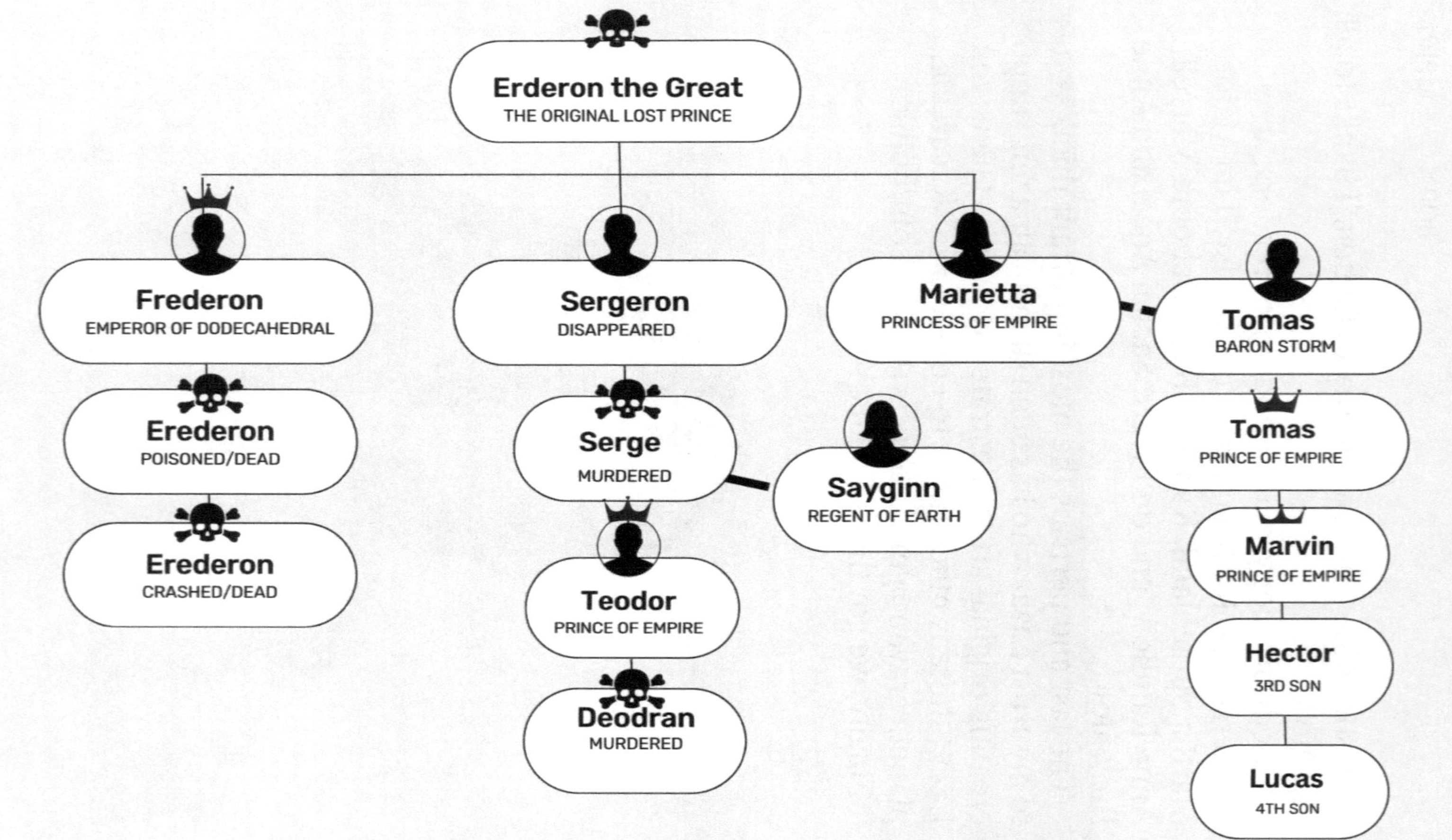

Erderon the Great
THE ORIGINAL LOST PRINCE
Frederon
EMPEROR OF DODECAHEDRAL
Sergeron
DISAPPEARED
Marietta
PRINCESS OF EMPIRE
Tomas
BARON STORM
Erederon
POISONED/DEAD
Serge
MURDERED
Sayginn
REGENT OF EARTH
Tomas
PRINCE OF EMPIRE
Erederon
CRASHED/DEAD
Teodor
PRINCE OF EMPIRE
Marvin
PRINCE OF EMPIRE
Deodran
MURDERED
Hector
3RD SON
Lucas
4TH SON

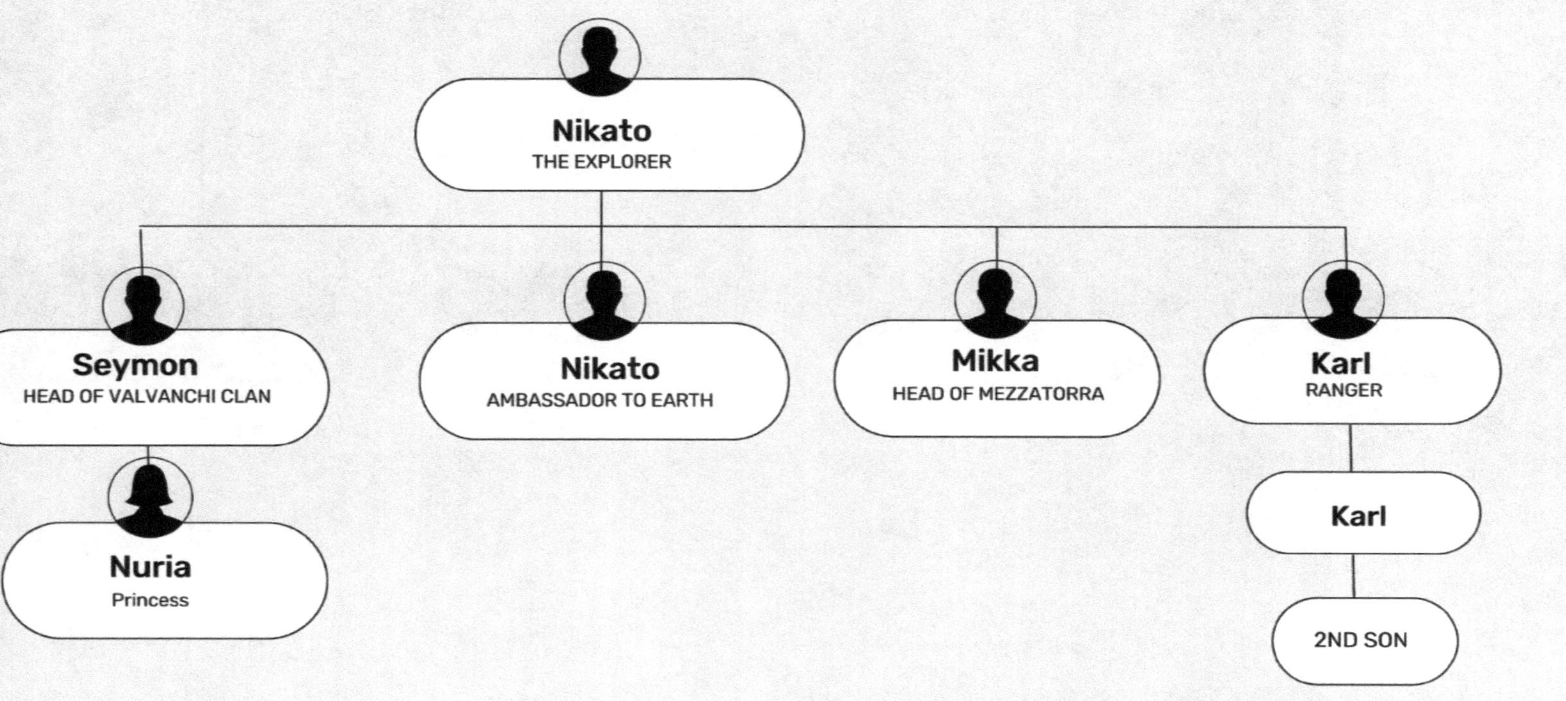

Nikato
THE EXPLORER
Seymon
HEAD OF VALVANCHI CLAN
Nuria
Princess
Nikato
AMBASSADOR TO EARTH
Mikka
HEAD OF MEZZATORRA
Karl
RANGER
Karl
2ND SON

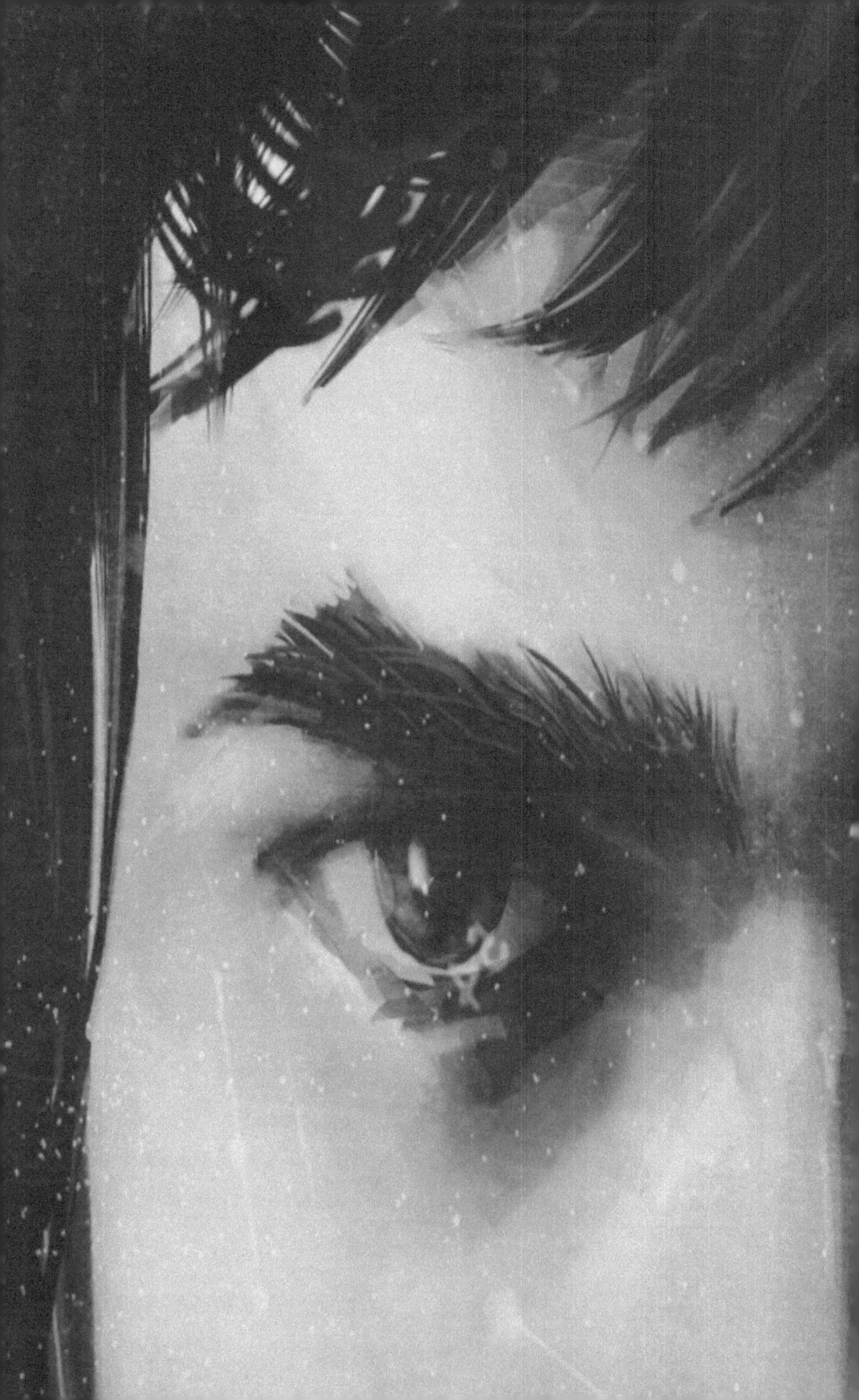